Wall Of Eyes

"A true, adult novel, with wit, satire, fine characterization—and a beautiful plot of crime and mystery."

Book Week

"Capital."

Saturday Review

"Mystery enough and to spare."

The New York Times

Wall Of Eyes
Margaret Millar

AVON
PUBLISHERS OF BARD, CAMELOT, DISCUS, EQUINOX AND FLARE BOOKS

AVON BOOKS
A division of
The Hearst Corporation
959 Eighth Avenue
New York, New York 10019

Copyright 1943 by Margaret Millar.
Published by arrangement with Random House, Inc.

ISBN: 0-380-00067-9

First Avon Printing, July, 1974

AVON TRADEMARK REG. U.S. PAT. OFF. AND
FOREIGN COUNTRIES, REGISTERED TRADEMARK—
MARCA REGISTRADA, HECHO EN CHICAGO, U.S.A.

Printed in the U.S.A.

To My Aunt

ALICE FERRIER GOULD

THEY moved briskly along the street, the girl carefully indifferent to the stares of the people who passed, the dog unaware of them. He padded along looking neither to the left nor right, his eyes careless and shifty. But when he came to a hole in the sidewalk he guided Alice around it and she felt the firm gentle tug of his harness and followed him.

I wonder if he knows I'm not blind, Alice thought.

He paused at the corner and ran his eye casually over the traffic. Then he stepped off the curb and Alice stepped off too, smiling a little. He's very conscientious, she thought, he's doing his duty but he doesn't have to like it.

When they were across the street she leaned over and put her free hand on his head for an instant.

"Good dog. Good Prince."

He was bored with the compliment. He turned his head away with a stern there's-a-place-for-everything movement and continued to walk, picking his way among the fallen leaves.

They were still on St. George Street, but the street itself was changing. They had passed the section of crumbling grandeur, of decayed castles with "Rooms for Rent" signs hammered on sagging pillars and listing porches. This part of the street alternated quaint tea rooms with filling stations and fraternity houses.

She slowed her step and began peering at the numbers of the houses. A young man in a gray topcoat was coming toward her. When he saw the dog he stopped and said, "Could I help?"

The dog didn't even look at him but sank onto the sidewalk with his head between his paws.

Alice turned and saw that the young man had a wet leaf

plastered to his hair. She tried to make her eyes blank, like Kelsey's, to avoid embarrassing him.

"Yes, thank you," she said. "I'm looking for Dr. Loring's house."

He looked at her curiously, shyly, as one looks at a cripple. Even though he thinks I'm blind, Alice thought, he is too polite to stare.

"Next house up," he said. "May I help you there?"

"No, thanks," Alice said. "Prince and I will find it."

Prince was already on his feet, sensing the call of duty, feeling the subtle movement of her hand on his harness. They walked on. Alice wanted to turn around to see if the young man was looking back but she kept her eyes on Prince, still smiling. The young man had delighted her, he was so earnest and so completely unaware of the wet leaf clinging rakishly to his hair.

But with the elation there was the old feeling of strangeness, loneliness, because it was such a silly, sly thing to find pleasure in.

The house was old but the lawn was freshly raked and the sign, "Dr. T. Loring," gleamed like a small brass sun. On the veranda there was another sign, "Ring and Walk In." She rang the bell and opened the door with the brisk precise movements of one who feels she is being watched from behind curtains and wants to impress the watcher.

There was no one else in the office. She had been afraid that there would be someone, but now that there wasn't she felt no relief. The fear was still there, but it had divided like an amoeba, and the two new parts were full-grown, self-sufficient, able to slide through her veins and divide again and again. Fear of Kelsey, of scandal, of the doctor, of her own security, fear of being wrong.

And perhaps he wasn't a good doctor—she refused to think of him yet as a psychiatrist, refused to let her mind or mouth form the word—or perhaps most of his patients were too bad to come to his office, like the cretin she had seen years ago, a gibbering, drooling, fat-tongued boy who had stroked her damp hand with his hot, dry one.

Prince was lying on the floor beside her feet, not in the easy relaxed manner of ordinary dogs, but watchfully, his eyes moving in their sockets.

Alice heard the door open. She did not look around immediately but waited until the doctor said, "Miss Heath?"

Then she put down the magazine carefully and picked up her gloves and turned to him.

He wasn't frightening, he didn't even wear a white coat to distinguish him from other young men, to mark him out as a man who dealt with things dark and ugly and never to be talked about. But the uneasiness swept over her again and she made a quick little movement which brought Prince to his feet, alert, ready to leave again, to visit strange places and strange houses, bored and despairing of making sense of any of it.

"I'm Dr. Loring." He looked at Prince, his eyes uncertain. "Is this your dog?"

She stood mute, shaking her head. She wanted to run out, shouting her explanations over her shoulder as she ran, "You're too young! I can't talk to you!"

She didn't run. She merely put on one glove as a symbol of running.

"It is my sister's dog," she said. "My sister Kelsey is blind."

"Ah," he said, as if that explained everything. "You've come about her, your sister?"

"Yes."

"All right. Come in here, please." His voice was professional, matter-of-fact. He stood back from the door and nodded his head slightly. "Do you want to bring the dog in with you?"

"No," she said quickly. "Oh, no."

He glanced at her and said, "Ah," again with the same undertone of smugness, as if his mind were saying, "Aha! All is now clear!"

It irritated her and, to cover up her irritation, she laughed softly, nervously. "He reminds me of a governess I had once. She never missed anything and she never got excited."

She walked to the door, peeling off her glove again. Her voice had faded into a whisper. Loring closed the door loudly behind them and began to bang things around, a chair for her, his own chair, a lamp that was in his way. When she sat down he continued to make noises; he walked up and down the length of the room; he thrust some papers into the filing cabinet and slammed the door shut again.

She stared at him, her nervousness falling under this barrage of noise and movement. When he saw that she had stopped twisting her gloves he sat down abruptly behind the desk.

9

She said, "That was very good."

"What was?" He sounded on guard, suspicious.

"Trying to make me feel at ease. You can't, of course. Perhaps if you were older . . ."

"No. You'd have the same difficulty," he said crisply. "It's because you've come on behalf of someone else. If you yourself were the patient you'd be eager to blurt things out."

He began to write rapidly on the pad in front of him, hardly bothering to keep his eye on the pen, looking up swiftly at Alice now and then.

"Kelsey. How old?"

"Twenty-six," Alice said. "Two years younger than I am."

"Brothers, sisters?"

"One brother, John. He's thirty."

"Parents?"

"My mother is dead. She died a year and a half ago of cancer, soon after Kelsey was blinded."

"Accident?"

"Yes." She saw his frown of impatience. "Do I tell you about the accident?"

"Is your father living?"

"Yes."

"All right. The accident."

"She was driving Johnny's car that night. They were on their way to a party and . . ."

"They?"

"Johnny and his girl and Kelsey and Philip James. The girl was killed."

"Oh." He looked up, interested. "The girl was killed and your sister blinded. And your sister was driving at the time. The girl was a friend of hers?"

"No." She was with Johnny. She was one of Johnny's girls. Kelsey had never seen her before."

"And Mr. James?"

She turned her head and looked out of the window. "Mr. James was—is—engaged to Kelsey."

"Was, is," Loring repeated. "Why the change in tense?"

"I made a mistake," Alice said hoarsely. "He is engaged to her. It was a slip of the tongue."

"All right." He stopped speaking, laid down his pen and rubbed his eyes, waiting.

"All right," Alice said finally. "He intends to marry her

but she doesn't intend to marry him. She's kept him waiting now for two years. He lives with us right at the house, waiting to marry her. They were engaged at the time of the accident."

She spoke slowly as if she had projected herself into the past and was feeling her way along among the ghosts.

"When Kelsey came home from the hospital she knew that she could never be cured, that she was going to be blind for the rest of her life. She didn't keep Philip waiting until she *knew*—she knew already. She never planned on or hoped for seeing again. There is none of that in Kelsey, no self-deception, no softening of blows for herself." She paused again, feeling her way back to the present. "So Philip is waiting. They never even talk about the marriage any more, she gives no reason, nothing is brought into the open. A few months ago she stopped wearing his ring. She said she lost it. Later on I had to hire a new maid. Her name is Ida. About two weeks after Ida came she was wearing the ring, on her little finger. Kelsey had given it to her."

"Strange," Loring said.

"No one else has noticed it and I haven't talked to Kelsey about it, but she's waiting for me to bring the subject up. I can tell it in the way she looks at me, half-sly, half-challenging." She drew in her breath. "She's through with Philip. She hates him, I think, but she won't let him go."

He was writing rapidly again, and the sight of him, the realization that he was writing down what she said shocked her.

She said stiffly, "I wish you wouldn't write this down."

"Why not?" He smiled dryly. "Isn't it true?"

"Of course it's true," she said harshly. "Why did you say that? Did you think I'd go to all this trouble, suffer this indignity, to tell you a pack of lies?"

He was young and inexperienced enough to resent her tone and the word "indignity," but he hung on to his smile. He recognized the natural antagonism between this girl and himself.

It's because, Loring thought, we're close in age and she's the kind of girl who girds herself for the battle of the sexes, automatically, instinctively, smelling the battle from miles away. He knew by just looking at her that she bathed and changed all her clothes once or twice a day,

11

that she applied her lipstick carefully and lightly so it wouldn't be noticed, that she would wrinkle her nose or even faint if she had to ride on a Harbord Street trolley on a rainy day. The smell and touch of human beings would be too much for her. He began to wonder about her parents and the kind of life they had lived.

He said abruptly, "How old is your father?"

"Fifty-three," she said. "Do you intend to keep on asking me questions or shall I just talk?"

"Go on and talk."

"It wasn't fair to tell you about Kelsey first, giving her to you without her context. We are—we are all of us queer, I suppose, except Johnny. You've known families where the unspoken word is stronger than the spoken word, where everything that happens is drawn out into tenuous wisps, half-thoughts, shadow feelings. . . . You know?"

"Inverted," Loring said. "Turned in."

She repeated the word. "Turned in, toward ourselves and toward each other." She smiled self-consciously. "There is always a great deal of atmosphere around us. If we have something for lunch that Kelsey doesn't like the dining room is charged with electricity. Sounds uncomfortable, doesn't it?"

He smiled at her. "It does."

"Only Johnny isn't like that. He feels the atmosphere but it merely puzzles him. He is very simple-minded."

"Simple-minded might mean anything."

"He's not a moron," she said sharply. "I meant, it's easy to figure out his reactions."

"Simple, then."

"Yes. I imagine my father was, too, a long time ago. He and my mother didn't like—*hated* each other."

He nodded, as if an idea of his had been confirmed. "The children of mismated marriages are often over-perceptive. They become accustomed to interpreting small signs of tension. Because they dread quarrels they are quick to see the signs."

"There were no *quarrels*."

Loring was interested in her quick denial. She didn't mind his knowing her family was queer, neurotic. Neuroses occurred in the best of families, quarrels were merely common.

The implication of anything as common as quarrels

12

changed her voice and her words. Her voice throbbed with culture and she chose her language more carefully, pausing to find the striking word, the telling phrase.

"No quarrels," she said, "simply atmosphere, black, fat clouds of it. They were in love with each other in the beginning. He did actually marry her for love, but she was rich, you see, she was never quite *sure*. Father rarely talks about it, but he told me years ago, before she died, that it was all right to marry a wealthy woman for her wealth but not for love. It gave her too much power over you, he said, you became doubly sensitive. Then, too, she was ill most of her life. She had a soft, sick voice, and her bones were small and brittle but threaded with iron. She hated living, but I think she hated dying even more. She couldn't bear to die leaving him alive. I am telling you about her so you will understand about Kelsey."

Her speech had a queer rhythm which Loring found disturbing. It was almost, he thought, as though the rhythm was a deliberate method of emphasizing and explaining her words, like an invisible footnote: *We are all queer, we even talk queerly, op. cit., ibid.*

"When she died we were sick with relief, sorry, too, but mostly relieved, thinking we were free of her. But we weren't because she's back again, in Kelsey. Nothing has changed, not even the money. She left it all for Kelsey, every cent of it. We live in Kelsey's house and eat Kelsey's food."

"Is that why you stay?"

"For free board and room?" she said. "No, it's not as simple as that. We're all capable of supporting ourselves. Johnny has a job, Philip is a pianist, and I—I could at least be a housekeeper. It's what I am now. No, we don't stay for economic reasons, we stay because we *can't* leave. She's blind, we *can't* walk out on her."

"Conscience?"

"If you must have a label," she said shortly, "call it conscience."

"Yet none of you had anything to do with the accident?"

"No. She was driving herself. It was her fault. She can't blame any of us."

"Does she?"

"No, not in words, but in attitude. She's bitter and hostile. She seems to like nobody but Ida."

13

"The maid who wears the ring?"

"Yes. She makes us feel that we are responsible for her blindness—guilty and ashamed. But none of us has done anything to be ashamed of."

She paused, waiting for his reassurance, "Of course not. Of course you haven't."

He said nothing and she lowered her eyes. "I have done nothing I'm ashamed of—until now, until I came here. I shouldn't have come. She's not insane, she's twisted. I thought you could help her and us too. I shouldn't have come here. Could I just pay you and walk out?"

"You could," Loring said. "Waste of money, though. Her money. I suppose you did come here about your sister and not about yourself?"

"Myself?"

"It occurred to me," he said dryly. "I get people—girls like you especially—who simply come here to talk to me. Ingrown, lonely women who don't need a psychiatrist, who only need someone who'll listen to them. Sometimes they come twice a year and tell me about their jobs and their lives and their families. Sometimes they're in love and are radiant or weepy, depending on the lover. But most of the time nothing at all has happened to them between visits and they go back into the past and repeat what they've told me before, how at the age of four Uncle Charley came for a visit from Montana and how many valentines they received in the fourth grade. . . . The lonely ladies. I can't do anything about them. That will be five dollars, please. I hope your sister got her money's worth."

She made no move to open her purse. She said, "I have no Uncle Charley and I didn't go to grade school."

"No? Well, other things."

"Nor did I talk about myself," she said quietly, "except to give you an idea of Kelsey."

"That's true," he said with a faint smile. "Sorry. My profession is one that breeds suspicions."

"Since you intend to be reasonable, I'll be just as reasonable and admit that I didn't come here strictly for Kelsey's sake, nor for my own. Whatever the others do I shall have to stay with Kelsey. I don't expect much from life and that is all right. But I want you to save Johnny and Philip."

"Save them?" he said ironically. "From what?"

14

"From Kelsey, from this feeling of guilt that keeps them there when they should both go away and live their own lives. She's only keeping Philip to make him suffer. She tells him to get out and when he tries to leave she won't let him."

"She's not a witch," Loring said. "And he's not a cripple."

"You're wrong. She's part witch, and I think he's part cripple. Philip isn't strong enough to stand up to her. And now it's worse than ever because about three months ago she began to imagine that there were eyes watching her, a wall of eyes."

He leaned forward across the desk. "Whose eyes?"

She didn't see him or hear him. "She has built a wall of eyes around her, the good eyes of the rest of us, the eyes of the people who hate her and watch her and wait for her to die. That's what she says, that the eyes are watching and waiting. Yesterday she was clawing the wall, the ordinary wall of her room, trying to . . ."

She stopped, sucking in her breath. "Letty found her on the floor, crying."

"Letty?"

"She was my mother's nurse. It is a terrible thing to see a blind person cry, eyes that can't see shouldn't cry, blind eyes should be tearless and unseen. But there she was, crying, on the floor. Her eyes look real, they haven't faded, they look as good as new."

"Don't *you* cry!"

She stared at him. "I'm not one of your lonely ladies—in love."

"They're not my ladies," he said irritably. "Don't get personal. I haven't done anything to you."

"You're cold, without sympathy, and you're too young. I don't trust you. I think I want to go home."

"Five bucks," Loring said wearily.

She half rose from her chair. He reached his hand across the desk and made a violent pushing motion toward her. The hand didn't touch her but the gesture was so savage she fell back in her chair, cold with fright.

"There," he said. "I've lost my temper. Every time I lose my temper I double my price. You'd better get out of here while you're still solvent. Try Graham at the Medical Arts. He's twice as old as I am and twice as

15

sympathetic and consequently twice as expensive and twice as rich. He'll suit you on all counts."

"You can't order me out of here. I don't want to go. I'm all mixed up. . . . "

"You're mixed up because you *talk* too much. You're even dragging me into the conversation." He saw that she was going to cry and his voice coaxed her. "Tell me about your sister. Good Lord!"

Her crying was as quietly intense as her voice. She cried for some time, holding the sleeve of her suit over her eyes to hide her face from him. When she had finished she put her arm down again and he saw with a shock the two dry deep lines from her nose to her mouth. She looked forty. Tears were not a balm to her as they were to the lonely ladies.

She probably never cries, Loring thought, so why in hell is she crying now?

"Please," he said. "Tell me about your sister. What do you want me to do about her?"

"See her," Alice said. "Talk to her. Make her realize her own motives for some of her actions, let her see that she's only ruining her own life."

"A tall order."

"Yes, but she's reasonable, she's more coldly reasonable really than any of the rest of us. And some of it—I'm sure that some of it is only pretense. Not the eyes, but some other things. She pretends that she's forgotten she used to smoke and she refuses to let us smoke in the house."

"Was she smoking when the accident occurred?"

"No. She had asked Philip to light her cigarette. The windows of the car were open and Philip bent down, cupping the match in his hands, when the car crashed. He tried to twist the wheel at the last minute."

"Will she see me voluntarily?"

"No! She doesn't even know I've come here. Could you—couldn't you come to the house? We could pretend that you were a friend of mine. You could come for tea. I know this is imposing on you."

"No." he said dryly. "I like tea. When?"

"Tomorrow?"

"All right," Loring said. "What about the dog?"

She stared at him. "What about him?"

"Why did you bring him along?"

16

"Oh." She hesitated. "I know what you're thinking, that perhaps I like to pretend I'm blind, identify myself with . . . "

"You're at it again."

"I brought him because he has to be kept in practice. Is that good enough?"

"Fine. Tomorrow at what time?"

"Four. You have my address. What—what is your first name?"

"Tom."

"Mine is Alice. I think you had better not be a doctor tomorrow. What will you be?"

"I have sold insurance," Loring said. "I could sell it again."

"I hope—I'm sure you'll be able to help."

"Don't hope anything," he said curtly. "The girl is blind and she's young and she was in love. What good can I do? I can't make her see again." He opened the door and saw Prince. "How would you like to be led around by a dog?"

She went past him. Without turning around she said, "Well, you can *try,* can't you?"

"Sure," he said cynically.

"Good day."

"Good day."

He watched her from the window, liking the way she walked, with smooth arrogance, as if she had paid for every inch of the sidewalk and her own personal engineers had constructed it, guaranteed without holes.

CHAPTER 2

SHE lay on her lounge beside the window, her neck twisted to one side so that a blue net ruffle of curtain softly touched her hair, coaxing her to wake up. But it wasn't time yet, she would wake when the sun came round the corner of her window and gradually warmed her hair, her forehead and finally her eyelids.

Even when the sun did come she didn't open her eyes but lay quietly, feeling the heat on her eyes like hot slivers of steel prying at her eyelids. She tasted her pain like an epicure, not moving her head out of the sun's way or putting up her hand to draw the blind. She had to know that the sun was there, the room light, and she had to find out by herself, without asking anyone, "Is the sun out today?"

Not one of them would say simply "Yes," or "No," without pity or impatience, without telling her that the leaves had turned and were beginning to fall and suggesting that she go for a walk. She had her ways, like this one, of outwitting them, giving them no opening. They were all in a conspiracy to get her out of the house, walking on the street where people would stare at her or hurry past to avoid staring. Out there on the street she'd be helpless, she'd have to cling to Alice's arm or lean on Prince's harness, utterly dependent.

No, she'd never go out, she'd never give them such an easy victory. *They* were the dependent ones, they couldn't get ahead of her.

She heard the door open and someone come into the room. She didn't move or ask, "Who's there?" She had a bitter pride in this independence. Later on, if she was patient, she would know who was there. It must be Letty or Alice or Ida, and pretty soon whoever it was would make some sound that singled her out from the rest. She lay still and listened.

But Letty knew she was not sleeping because her arms were too rigid, her body too stiff, as if it refused to yield to sleep, considering comfort a weakness or sleep a danger.

Once Letty opened her muth to say "Kelsey?" to let her know who had come in, but she didn't say it.

She's sulking again, Letty thought, for some trivial reason she's sulking, pretending to be asleep. No, it is subtler than that. She doesn't want me to think she is asleep, she wants me to *know* she is pretending to be asleep.

With a sigh Letty turned back to the closet and took down the rest of Kelsey's summer dresses. As she worked she hummed very softly so that Kelsey would know her. Her big bony hands looked out of place against Kelsey's fragile dresses, but Letty, once sensitive about her size, didn't notice the contrast.

The room was bare. There was Kelsey's bed along one wall, her lounge against the window, a bureau, a deep chair covered in blue chintz and a small table beside the bed. The rest of the furniture had been removed piece by piece: the bookshelf, the pictures, the mirrors, a vanity over which Kelsey had once stumbled.

A hanger clattered to the floor. Letty bent over it, knowing that Kelsey would come awake now.

"Letty!"

The voice did not come up, muffled, through clouds of sleep, but sprang sharp and sure across the room.

"What was that, Letty?"

"A hanger," Letty said. "I thought I'd put away your summer things."

"Now?" The head came up, the neck twisted, the eyes stared, cold and unseeing. "While I was sleeping?"

"Were you asleep?" Letty said. "I'm sorry, I thought I'd better do this today. Alice said she wanted to spray the closet."

Kelsey sat up and swung her legs to the floor. For just a moment her mind tricked her and she thought that her eyes were closed and if she opened them she would see herself in the mirror across the room, catch a glimpse of yellow tousled curls, slim arms stretching over her head, long lazy legs. She would open her eyes and walk across the rug toward the mirror, her image becoming clearer and prettier as she drew near, and at the very last she would look at her eyes, blue and dreamy from sleep but excited at waking.

"Have the mirrors been taken away?" she said. "All of them?"

"Last week," Letty said. "Remember, Alice helped . . ."

"I *don't* remember.'

"Well, they were taken away, even the one in the bathroom."

"The bathroom? You didn't poke around in any of my things?"

"No," Letty said. "No."

She picked up the dresses, piling them over her arm, but she didn't move toward the door. She knew that if she walked away the voice would spring at her again, pulling her back.

"You didn't take the clock away," Kelsey said. "I can hear it."

"No, that's my watch. The clock is gone."

"What are you standing there for? What time is it?"

"Nearly four," Letty said. "Today is Tuesday. Johnny will be here early. Hadn't you better dress?"

"Tuesday," Kelsey repeated. "Why do you say it in that special way? What's Tuesday?"

Letty walked to the door and closed it softly. "You remember. Johnny is bringing someone to meet you. A girl, a Miss Moore. What will you wear?"

She spoke briskly and walked back to the clothes closet, making bustling noises that were unnatural to her. "The black suit would be nice—or the blue wool."

"Wait! I told John I didn't care to meet Miss Moore!"

"But you said later you would, that you wanted . . ."

"I don't remember that," Kelsey said. "I'm not going down. I've seen enough of his women to know they're all alike anyway."

Her voice was rough as if the teeth of the past had gnawed at it and left sharp little splinters on the surface. No, Johnny's women weren't all alike, no, there was one who wasn't like the others, one girl who had detached herself from the mass and hung suspended in Kelsey's mind. The girl's face was like an animal squatting in the chair, sometimes it breathed and came alive, a sick breathing face. Then it died again and the dead face was better.

"What was her name?" Kelsey said.

"Her name?" Letty turned. "Miss Moore."

"No, the other one."

"Oh, her," Letty said. "I don't remember. Geraldine, I think. I think the blue wool would be nice. You could wear your sapphires."

She took the dress out of the closet, making the bustling noises again, pretending that Kelsey had not refused to go downstairs. They had played this game together for a long time and each of them knew the rules. Kelsey began to unbutton the neck of the yellow dress she was wearing. Then she held up her hands and waited for Letty to pull the dress over her head.

"It's hot," Kelsey said.

"I'll open the door again."

"Why did you close it in the first place?"

"Because," Letty said calmly, "I thought you might make a fuss. About meeting Miss Moore."

"Why should I make a fuss about meeting Miss Moore?" Kelsey asked in a reasonable voice. "She's nothing to me or to Johnny either. I don't suppose she has enough sense to know that Johnny will never marry her. Can you imagine Johnny getting married on thirty-five dollars a week?"

"He wouldn't be doing that," Letty said. "There's his allowance."

"Be careful of my hair. No, the other side."

"You wouldn't stop giving him that," Letty said.

"I'm getting thinner. Look, the belt is too loose. No, leave it like that today. There isn't time to take it in: we must hurry."

She leaned over and began to take off her shoes, very slowly, pointing up the irony. It was her way of putting Letty in her place, of closing the discussion of Johnny. In silence Letty handed her a comb and Kelsey began to comb out her hair, still moving with the planned deliberate slowness.

"Is the part straight?"

"Yes," Letty said.

Kelsey's hands dropped suddenly into her lap and the comb fell to the floor.

"How do I know you're telling the truth?" she whispered. "Even about a little thing like that."

"I am. Now you're not going to be silly."

"Silly? You think it's silly for me to want to see myself again? It's harder never to see yourself again than never to see other people."

For you, Letty said silently, for you it is. She dropped on her knees to put Kelsey's shoes on.

"Other people aren't real," Kelsey said.

"No, I guess not."

"You can't understand. You're thinking badly of me, I can feel it. You're frowning, aren't you?"

"There's a spot on your shoe," Letty said. "Maybe I was frowning. I'll get a brush."

Kelsey waited, knowing there was no spot on her shoe at all, but keeping her foot rigid against the floor while Letty solemnly brushed at it. Over the whisk-whisk of the brush Kelsey could hear voices from the first floor, murmurs and then a big bass laugh that belonged to Johnny, and Johnny's swift heavy step on the stairs. Six steps. That meant Johnny had come up three at a time. He must be excited (so the girl had really come), and happy (so the affair must be just starting).

She waited, rigid with distaste and dread, like a very small girl awaiting a visit from a frolicsome St. Bernard.

The door exploded, something rushed at her across the room, making the floor tremble. There was a confusion of sounds, his shoes striking the floor, "Hiya, Letty!" and then, "Hello, baby!" and Kelsey was lifted off the couch and swung into the air, round and round.

She screamed, "Johnny!" as her feet left the floor and she dangled in space, panic blowing in her face and taking her breath away.

"Johnny!" she screamed, and beat her feet up and down. "You fool! Let me down, you fool!"

She was set down on the couch, dizzy, frozen with fear. Even her voice had frozen and only a thin trickle melted out of her mouth, "Bull elephant!"

He didn't hear her, but Letty did and came forward and stepped into the circle of sounds.

"Now, now," Letty said. "Now, now, I guess you kind of scared her, John."

"He didn't scare me!" Kelsey said. "I'm not in the least . . . " She felt Johnny's hand on hers, squeezing hard, apologetically.

"Sorry, baby."

"I wasn't in the least frightened," Kelsey said sharply. "John, you're *crushing* me."

"Sorry again," he said quietly. He rarely spoke quietly and when he did he had no dignity, as Alice did; he was merely humble and beaten.

As if, Letty thought, watching him, someone had turned a valve inside of him and let out the air. People often tried to do that to Johnny, though no one had so much success as Kelsey. It was their attempt to bring him down to life size. He was an enormous man, like his father, and everything was drawn to scale, his voice, his big white teeth, his ears pink with health, his hair thicker and coarser than other men's, yellow and curly like Kelsey's but carefully darkened by brilliantine and clipped short so the curls wouldn't show.

But if the gods had constructed Johnny they had made some omissions under the surface.

He looked across at Letty, his eyes bewildered, demanding some answer to some question. Letty smiled at him and shrugged her shoulders.

Johnny returned the smile. It crowded the bewilderment out of his eyes. Johnny's emotions came one at a time, they chased each other in and out of his mind like scampering squirrels.

"Well, she's here," he said in his normal voice. "Marcie's downstairs waiting for you."

"Marcie?" Kelsey said.

"Marcella. She's little, like you, but she's dark. . . ."

"Marcella. Her *own* name?"

"Of course. Her mother read the name in a story."

"Yes, I can believe it," Kelsey said dryly. "Where did you leave her?"

"With Phil," Johnny said. "He's playing for her."

"Charming," Kelsey said.

Letty said quickly, "I guess you're all ready except for your makeup. Maybe John will go down and tell her we're coming."

Johnny got up from the lounge and the floor trembled again under his weight. Kelsey felt the vibrations run up her legs like baby mice.

"Damn it, John," she said. "Can't you be quieter? Do you have to lunge around like . . . "

"Now, now," Letty said, while she gestured to Johnny with her head. "We won't be longer than five minutes, John. Has Alice come in yet?"

Johnny paused at the door. "No. Phil said she took Prince for a walk."

When he went out one of his huge shoulders struck the door frame. He said, "Out of my way, door," and went down the steps. By the time he reached the bottom he was whistling.

Marcie was sitting on the piano bench beside Philip. She was dressed specially for the occasion in a black silk suit purchased from a clerk at Simpson's who had assured her that the best people always wore black. She looked pale and smaller than ever sitting at the very end of the bench as far away from Philip as she could get without falling off. Her arms were pressed tightly against her body so they wouldn't get in Philip's way.

When she saw Johnny standing in the doorway she threw him a small agonized smile and poised her body for flight. But she didn't get off the bench. From the moment she had entered the house and seen the butler, all her initiative and will power seemed to have drained out of her. She was helpless, she couldn't get off the piano bench because Johnny had told her to sit there and now she was waiting for him to tell her to get off.

She was a newcomer to a strange world. The black suit didn't help, and so far she had little opportunity to repeat the sentences she had planned with due regard for grammar. She knew that Johnny's sister wouldn't be able to see her or the black suit, that she would be judged by her voice and the English she used. She had gotten up at noon, earlier than usual, and planned a few careful remarks on the beauty of autumn, the pleasure of meeting Johnny's sister and the situation in India. She had already tried the situation in India on Mr. James, but Mr. James had merely regarded her sadly and said, "Yes, isn't it?"

Although she knew nothing whatever about India she was a little shocked to discover that people who lived in a house like this didn't know anything about it either. She felt a sudden surge of patriotism. After all, people who had to earn their own living were too busy to bother about such things, but there was no excuse at all for men like Mr. James who had nothing to do but fiddle around a piano.

She looked at him out of the corner of her eye and was impressed to discover that he was playing with his eyes closed. She was angry with herself for being impressed. After all, if you had nothing else to do . . .

Johnny came over and put one hand on her arm, the other hand on Philip's back.

"Hello, you two," he said.

"Philip's hands paused, came off the keys. When he turned, Marcie saw that he still wore the expression of sad surprise that he had assumed over India. Maybe that was his usual expression or maybe he really did know something about it and the sentence had struck him hard. What if, in planning polite conversation, she had hit upon a great political truth? She'd try it again later, on Kelsey.

He was looking at her and she turned her head away, clinging to the end of the bench.

"Well," he said softly. "You look as if you've lived through a terrible experience. Am I that bad?"

"He's wonderful," Johnny said. "Isn't he wonderful?"

They were both watching her now, waiting for her answer, Johnny anxiously, Philip with one eyebrow raised.

She felt the weight of the house pressing on her. She wanted to throw it off and say, "Maybe he is and maybe he isn't." But she didn't have the courage.

She laughed nervously. "Wonderful," she echoed. "The boy that plays the piano at the club, gosh, he's good. He plays without music or anything, just out of his head."

"Phil's marvelous," Johnny said. "Phil, tell her what Percy Grainger said when you played for him in New York."

Philip muttered, "Please."

"He said Phil was terrific," Johnny cried. "Hard and brilliant, and what else, Phil?"

"He used to play in a big orchestra, this boy, but he was kicked out on account of he drinks." Marcie said. "I think drinking is a terrible thing."

"Very terrible indeed," Philip said, flicking his eyes over her.

She didn't like that glance, as if he had her all figured out and didn't think she was worth bothering about. If there was any figuring to be done she had done it: Mr. James was a stuffed shirt; and worse, he had no more right to live in such a house than she had. Less right, he didn't even work for a living. She wanted to confront him with these facts but when she met his eyes again she saw that it wasn't necessary, he knew them already. He didn't feel any more at home or comfortable in this house than she did.

The realization did not move her to friendliness. She was merely annoyed at the injustice.

She turned her face away stubbornly. "I mean it," she said. "This boy was making a hundred and fifty a week once playing in a big orchestra."

Johnny squeezed her shoulder. "Hey. I'm jealous."

"No, but . . ."

"Why don't we go over to the chesterfield and get comfortable?" He tucked her hand inside his. "You're cold."

"No, I'm not!"

25

But she was cold. Her legs didn't move properly. She plodded across the rug as if it were deep sand.

Philip remained on the bench leaning forward with his arms folded against the music rack. From a distance he looked dark and romantic. It was only when you were close up that you saw he was getting too fat and losing his black wavy hair and that his eyes were strained. There was a careful set to his face that made him look years older than Johnny.

He better be careful, Marcie thought viciously. He's got a fat living out of this, music lessons and a special room to practice in downtown, and going to concerts and operas all over the country. On the Heaths' money. Why, with that money I could be famous!

Philip said to Johnny, "Did you see Kelsey?"

"She'll be down in a minute," Johnny said.

"Shall I go up and get her?"

"That would be fine. She's not—she's . . . "

"I get it," Philip said.

He went out and closed the door behind him. He stood at the bottom of the stairs, looking up, like a man about to defy gravity and leap up to his death.

The door of Kelsey's room opened and Kelsey came into the upper hall with her hands stretched out in front of her. The moment for leaping had arrived but he didn't move.

"Letty?" Kelsey said.

Letty's voice came from the room. "I'm coming. Just a minute."

"Letty, there's someone in the hall."

"I'm coming."

"Who is it?" Kelsey said shrilly. "Who is it?"

Philip drew in his breath to speak but someone spoke first from the second floor. "It's me, Kelsey."

"Oh. Father?"

"Yes."

"Are you coming downstairs?"

"Am I coming . . . ? Oh yes, yes, today I thought I'd—yes."

Mr. Heath walked toward her slowly. His feet shuffled along the floor as if they might find a hole in it and had to be careful. His legs seemed too weak to support his huge body, his voice came in dribbles from a strong mouth.

26

"John," he said, "my son John has a guest. So I thought I'd . . . "

"Don't bother coming, Letty," Kelsey said. "I'll go down with Father."

Letty came into the hall. The corners of her mouth sagged. "But I wanted to. I'd like to see her."

"No, don't bother. Father will take me down."

"Of course I . . ." Mr. Heath said. "Yes." He took her arm.

"You said you wanted me to see her," Letty said, "so I could tell you."

"No, thank you. I'll be quite all right," Kelsey said. When she walked away her step was firmer. She had more confidence in herself, she was pleased because she had won a subtle victory over Letty.

From the bottom of the stairs Philip said, "Oh, there you are, Kelsey. We were wondering . . . "

"Philip," Kelsey said, "would you tell Maurice he may bring in the tea? We won't wait for Alice."

"I'll tell him," Philip said. Whenever he spoke to Kelsey he sounded too anxious to oblige, his voice was falsely gay insisting that everything was all right between them. His feet lied too, and struck the floor brisk and cheerful.

"Couldn't he," Mr. Heath said, "why couldn't he ring for Maurice?"

"You think it's too much to ask him to walk the length of the hall," Kelsey said softly, "in return for what I've given him?"

"Ah," Mr. Heath said. "Aaaah. . . . "

He opened the door of the drawing room and Kelsey went inside.

The voices ceased. Kelsey stood for a moment waiting for them to begin again so she would know where the girl and Johnny were sitting. She knew the girl would be looking at her, but she couldn't see the girl, she had to wait here, powerless, on the threshold of the room, holding herself stiff so no one could guess her helplessness.

She never knew that these times her dignity was almost a tangible force. To someone who was seeing her for the first time, as Marcie was, Kelsey's dignity was a slap in the face, a challenge to pity her.

Johnny came across the room and caught her arm and pressed it. He had been affected by the sight of her, and

27

he made the introductions in a subdued voice, "Kelsey, this is Marcie Moore. My sister Kelsey. And my father. This is Marcie, Father."

His tongue wrapped them together, rolling them up in a blanket.

"Ah," Mr. Heath said. "Marcie." He drifted away, vanishing into a chair like a shadow, breathing sadly, "Aaaah. . . . "

"I'm very pleased to meet you, I'm sure," Marcie said. Her voice was too loud and too high, a cheap tin whistle of a voice with a squawk in it. Kelsey smiled at it.

She murmured, " . . . so much about you."

Marcie kept smiling brightly at her, unable to realize that the smile couldn't be seen. "Oh, Johnny's always telling about his sisters! I just couldn't wait to meet you. Johnny's always telling . . ."

Squawk, squawk.

"So nice," Kelsey purred. "You're quite comfortable?"

"Oh, yes, oh, my yes. I couldn't be more . . . "

"John has so *many* friends," Kelsey said. "He brings them all home to meet me. Isn't he sweet?"

Johnny coughed and said, "Alice should be here any minute. You'll be crazy about Alice, Marcie."

"I just know I will," Marcie said. "Johnny's always telling about Alice and K-Kelsey."

"Is he?" Kelsey said. "All *nice* things?"

"Oh, my yes! All about . . . "

"You don't find the conversation rather *limited?*"

"N-no. It's f-f-fine," Marcie said weakly.

Kelsey smiled and sat down beside her on the chesterfield. The bad moments were over. She had the girl catalogued and filed now; the rest would be easy.

Philip came back.

"Come on over here," Johnny cried. "There's room for all of us. No, over here."

Johnny was happy, he had them all now where he could reach out and touch each of them. They were within sight and hearing, he could even smell them. "Phil, you should see Marcie dance." "Phil was playing that Debussy thing you liked, Kelsey." "Marcie was telling us about a guy . . ." "I'd love to see Marcie dance." "Debussy is too frail." "And this boy used to make a hundred and fifty a week, no kidding."

Kelsey sat back and let Johnny manage by himself. She

even enjoyed the confusion today because she realized that it was making Marcie nervous. She could feel the girl's hands twitch, could hear the panic in her voice.

Maurice came in with the tea, a small, middle-aged man whose hands moved delicately over the silver.

"Alice should be here," Johnny said. "Alice always pours. Has she come in yet, Maurice?"

"No, sir."

"Marcie will pour," Kelsey said. "Won't you, my dear?"

"Oh, no!" Marcie said. "Oh, please! I never . . . "

"I'll pour," Philip said shortly.

Kelsey turned her head toward him. "I asked Marcie to pour, Philip. Didn't you hear me?"

Without replying he rose and sat down again in the high-backed chair where Alice sat at tea. There was a clatter of silver and china.

"I had no idea," Kelsey said, "that your ambitions lay in that direction, Philip."

"Oh, I have my secret yearnings," Philip said with a laugh. "Cream and sugar, Marcie?"

"Oh, anything," Marcie said. "Any way at all. I'm not particular."

"Kelsey?"

"Lemon and one clove," Kelsey said. "I am very particular."

Cold little waves of silence began to lap against the walls. Marcie looked desperate, and when Johnny put up his hand to touch her cheek she slapped his hand away, defending herself blindly and instinctively against something—some danger.

"What is this," Philip said, "about female hands fluttering among the teacups? Mine don't flutter."

"Not a bit," Marcie said shrilly.

"Perhaps I haven't the right approach. I think you've got to work yourself up to it, get into the spirit, like a vestal virgin."

Marcie let out a giggle. "Like a virgin . . . " The giggle crept into a corner, alone and ashamed. Marcie's face dropped into sullenness. She wanted to strike out at them all, claw them without reason like a cat.

She drank her tea rapidly. She could hear herself swallow. Even when the others were talking she could hear the shameful gulp of tea in her throat.

"Johnny," she said. "It's getting late. I'd better . . . "

29

"But it's early," Kelsey said lazily. "You haven't met Alice."

"You just got here," Johnny said.

"No, no," Marcie cried. "No, I've got to go really, please, I've got to go."

"Perhaps she has a dinner engagement," Kelsey said. "Have you?"

"Yes, yes, I got . . . "

"Do come again. Perhaps we could be alone and compare notes on Johnny."

"Yes, yes, sure." She thrust out toward freedom like a bird seeing the door of its cage open. "Pleased t'have met you. I had a very good time."

Johnny said, "I'm taking you home."

"I had a swell time. Good-bye, Mr. Heath, good-bye, Miss Heath, good-bye, Mr. James."

The door banged shut and the room slyly changed its face.

"Well?" Philip said.

"Ghastly," Kelsey said. *"Horrible.* What do you think of her, Father?"

"Eh?" He stirred under her voice. "Yes, a spot more, thank you, with a little less cream."

"The girl," Kelsey said sharply. "What did you think of the girl?"

"Ah," he said. "Nice little thing. Quiet. Nice little thing."

There was silence.

"How John does it," Kelsey said at last, "I don't know. Remember the waitress from Childs? And the one whose father was a Communist? And the singer?"

"That was Geraldine," Philip said.

"No, no, it wasn't!" No, the other one was Geraldine, the one whose face breathed and died and breathed again, a bloated face dangling in a dream.

She heard Philip twist in his chair and sigh.

"You're going to take Johnny's side against me," she said. "You, and Alice too."

"No," Philip said. "No, I'm not. But perhaps Johnny likes that kind of girl. He . . . "

"What difference does that make? Am I to cater to his cheap tastes and let him disgrace the family?"

"I believe I'll—" Mr. Heath said, "I think I'll—go up to my room."

"I have to fight you all," she cried. "Without eyes I have to fight you all!"

"Yes, I certainly—it would be better to go up to my room."

He shuffled across the rug.

CHAPTER 3

IT WAS six o'clock when Alice came home. The wind and the hill had tired her. A million years ago the hill had belonged to Lake Ontario, but the water had gradually receded leaving its long steep shore as booty to enterprising architects and real estate agents. Here, on the edge of the shore which was now St. Clair Avenue, Isobel Heath had built a house for her husband, and within its walls they had built together a life and a family, first John, then Alice, and last of all a small, delicate child, whom Isobel, without reference to anyone, had called Kelsey. It was Isobel's last concession to a physical world which repelled her. From that time on she began to recede like the lake, quietly and gradually drying at the edges, vanishing, but leaving a long deep shore behind her. On this shore she left her husband, cast up on the beach like a fish after a storm, gasping and feebly twisting his body.

Even Prince was tired and lay on the stone steps while Alice took out her key and fitted it into the door. The door opened, and here were the familiar sights and sounds and smells coming out at her, dragging her inside. The potted hyacinth on the hall table, the distant clink of dishes from the kitchen—the smell and sound of home that you always came back to.

But how much stronger were the sights—the red and blue Persian rug, the two bird prints one on each side of the hall facing each other. Alice could remember believing implicitly in those birds, as a child believes. For a time she had gone out every day staring up into the trees,

31

expecting to come upon birds as huge and bright, expecting so hard that her whole body was stiff and set against the fright she knew would come when the birds appeared. She could remember, too, the terrible sinking in her stomach when all she ever saw was a sparrow, small and drab, sitting ignominiously among the horse leavings on the road.

She closed the door quietly and bent over to take off Prince's harness. As she moved her eye caught a glimpse of white down the hall. She turned quickly.

In front of the closed door which led into the drawing room stood a small stout girl in a white and green uniform. Her ear was pressed tight against the door, her body bent sideways into an angle of eagerness.

Alice said, "Ida!"

The girl turned, gasping, and saw her. Her fat red mouth split open like a cherry wounded by a robin's beak.

"Awk," she said. "Awk."

"What are you doing there, Ida?"

"Nothing. Honest, I wasn't doing . . . "

"Don't listen at doors, Ida," Alice said. "It's not polite."

The wound healed gradually, puckering at the edges. "Yes, ma'am," she said, backing up as Alice walked toward her. "But I didn't *hear* nothing, ma'am."

"Go back to the kitchen," Alice said quietly. "It's time for Prince to be fed. Take him with you."

The girl stood still, breathing very heavily so that her body seemed ready to pop out of her uniform and splash against the wall.

"Maurice said to come and fetch the tea tray."

Ida turned and walked away. Kelsey's voice came through the door of the drawing room. "You're away half the time anyway. You might as well get out for good! I don't want you here!"

Without looking around Alice knew that Ida had heard, that Ida's head was swinging up in the gesture that said, *"I'm just as good as you are."*

Alice stood with her hand on the doorknob. What could you do with the Idas of this world, she thought. Put your fists over your eyes, as children do, to squeeze the evil in behind the eyes where it could lie in secret and gradually die, too well hidden to be found again.

She jiggled the doorknob to warn them she was coming,

and then quickly, before she could change her mind, she slipped through the door and closed it again.

Kelsey was standing behind the high-backed chair, wrenching at the wood. In the chair Philip sat, doubled over, with his hands clasping his stomach as if he had a cramp.

"Who's that?" Kelsey screamed. "Who came in?"

"Alice," Philip said dully.

Alice came toward them, tossing her gloves casually on the tea table, pretending the scene was too ordinary to notice.

"Hello," she said cheerfully. "What did I miss at tea? Cucumber sandwiches! Wait till I get Maurice!"

"Where have you been?" Kelsey said. "You should have been here. Leaving me to fight alone . . ."

Alice put her hands over Kelsey's to quiet them.

Philip remained doubled up in the chair with the two women behind him. He did not turn his head or listen to them, as if by shutting them out of his ears and eyes he could leave them there forever, behind him.

But what could you do about the touch of Alice's hand on your shoulder, coaxing you to recognize her, asking to come to life again?

"No, Alice," he said. "It's no use. No."

"Such *children*," Alice said, "both of you. And do you know who was listening with all ears to the row? Ida."

"Ida's on my side," Kelsey said. "I asked her to be on my side when she came."

"What did you say to her, Kelsey?" Alice said sharply. "You shouldn't confide in the servants, especially Ida. She's sly, you can't trust her."

"I can't trust anyone," Kelsey said. "Can I, Philip? Can I?"

Underneath the cold irony a plea fluttered like a baby bird, unfeathered, defenseless. Philip heard the plea and shut his ears.

"No, better not trust anyone," he said.

"Children," Alice said again, but Kelsey had slipped her hands away and was feeling her way to the door, stumbling once, regaining her balance with a little cry of rage. The door opened and closed. They could hear her going up the steps, the banister creaking under the weight of her hand.

"You're worse than she is," Alice said in a small cold voice.

For a long time he didn't answer, didn't move his eyes to follow her when she walked from behind his chair and sat down opposite him. She was so quiet that he raised his eyes finally and looked at her. *Quiet dead Alice. No emotion at all, like a corpse.*

"Don't look at me," he said, almost whining. "You're so still."

"I'm not looking at you," she said in a surprised voice. "Not at all."

"I know. I want you not to."

"Very well." She turned her head and looked out of the window. "Is that better?"

"Yes. I'm going away."

"Oh?" She didn't turn.

"Tomorrow."

"Why not tonight? Tomorrow Kelsey may change her mind."

"Kelsey has nothing to do with it," he said savagely. "I'm just going. It has nothing to do with what Kelsey said, or anyone, or anything."

"I see," Alice said dryly. "Entirely your own idea." She turned and glanced at him. "Well, good luck to you, Philip. Have you told Johnny?"

"No. He's out."

"Johnny will miss you. We all will."

"You don't believe I'm going?"

"I'd like to believe it," Alice said. "I want you to go."

"Well, I'm going. Tomorrow. Tomorrow night."

"Why not tomorrow morning?"

"Stop repeating that," he said hoarsely. "You don't have to be afraid I'll change my mind. You heard what she said. She doesn't *trust* me. She wants me to leave. After eight years she . . . "

"Don't waste your energy in words," Alice said grimly. "You've done that before. Save some for actually going away."

He stared at her bitterly. "Thank you for your sympathy."

"I think you've had your share of sympathy," she said, flushing. "All of you have had your share. Maybe I'm tired of being an unmarried mother!"

"You were never . . . ."

34

"I've known for some time that Kelsey would never marry you. She doesn't need a husband, only a good strong nurse like me whose feelings are not easily hurt. Go away for a while, Philip. Forget this house and these years for a time. Go back to where you were before."

Go back. He said the words silently to himself. *Forget these years. Roll them up and throw them over your shoulder and start hiking.*

"I haven't any place to go back to," he said, "no place, and nobody. You picked me out of a vacuum. My mother died when I was small and I ran away. . . . "

"I know," she said, impatient not that he should repeat himself but that he should be trying to change the subject. "Will you go by train?"

"Train? Oh. I hadn't thought of that."

"Where will you go?"

"I—New York, perhaps."

She got up and began to switch on the lamps.

"You despise me," Philip said.

"That's nonsense. I'm very fond of you."

"You've never been fond of anybody."

"Haven't I?" She walked over to the fireplace, smiling slightly. She was always flattered when people commented on her coldness. She liked to think that the coldness was of her own making, that she could step out from behind her self-constructed refrigerating coils any time she liked, or step back in if she found the warmth too much for her.

Maurice came in for the tea tray. He packed the dishes slowly. Alice saw that his lips were moving silently as they did when he was planning to say something to her. He stood straight with the tray held high across his chest and cleared his throat.

"I beg your pardon, Miss Alice."

"Yes?"

"Ida . . . "

"Oh, yes. She was eavesdropping again. You'd better confine her to upstairs work."

Maurice coughed again. "Yes, ma'am. But I thought of letting her go. She is unsatisfactory in every respect."

"Give her another chance, Maurice," Alice said. "It isn't easy to get help now."

He turned away uncertainly, a frown flickering through his eyes.

"Kelsey has taken a fancy to the girl," Alice added.

35

His face relaxed. "In that case, ma'am . . . "

"Yes," Alice said, unsmiling, "in that case, yes."

At the door he stepped aside to let Johnny come in. Johnny brushed past him and shouted directly at Philip, "I thought everything went all right! Didn't you? Did you think Kelsey snubbed her? She said Kelsey snubbed her. I no sooner got her outside than she began to bawl."

He hurled his hat across the room. "And bawl and bawl and bawl! Oh, hello, Alice. Goddamn women anyway!"

"Who bawled?" Alice said. "I missed the first instalment."

Johnny scowled at her. "Marcie. You know. I told you. You should have been here. Why weren't you?"

"Business. Sorry."

"I thought everything was fine and then she started bawling. I don't understand. I thought Kelsey was all right, better than usual."

"And that didn't make you suspicious?" Philip asked dryly.

"Then there was something—something I didn't catch?"

"Always," Philip said. "It's practically a rule of thumb that there should be something you don't . . . "

Alice said hastily, "Philip is leaving tomorrow, Johnny."

"Leaving?" Johnny stood in front of Philip's chair and looked down at him, grinning. *"Again?"*

Philip saw that there was no trace of uncertainty in the grin. It said, *Good old Phil, he'll never leave.*

"Oh, hell," Johnny said. "Cut the comedy, you two. I've got enough trouble."

"There's no comedy," Alice said. "Philip is leaving here tomorrow. It was his own suggestion and I approve."

"Approve being the mildest word for it," Philip said with a wry smile. "Alice thinks it's time I went out into the world and stood on my own two feet. And when I've made good and proven my worth, I have her permission to come back and recapture the Heaths. You'll all be here when I come back, just as you are. Nothing will be changed, least of all Alice, sane, sensible, know-it-all Alice. If in doubt, ask Alice."

"You're being unpleasant," Alice said coldly. "Sorry I can't stay to hear the rest."

Johnny stared at Philip, bewildered. "What in hell's got into you? I've never heard you talk like this."

"He wants me to coax him to stay," Alice said with an

36

ugly smile. "And I didn't. And I don't intend to. I've quit my job as wet-nurse to the artistic temperament."

She walked to the door, her legs weak and heavy with rage.

When she closed the door she could hear Philip's voice begin again, a smooth drone. She walked slowly up the stairs and the drone became fainter and fainter and died so gradually that there was no moment of death, only a vanishing.

She sat down on the top step, too feeble to go on. She covered her face with her hands, but a minute later she was on her feet again. *Someone might come along the hall and see you. Don't give yourself away to anyone. Keep yourself to yourself. Forever and ever. Amen.*

The control she had forced on her body spread to her mind. She repeated silently to herself the comforting formula she used in bad moments. "I am Alice. I am Alice Heath."

CHAPTER 4

SHE rapped on Kelsey's door and Kelsey's voice rang out sharply.

"Who's there?"

"Alice."

"Oh." There was a pause, then a grudging, "Well, come in."

Alice opened the door. The room was murky with twilight and Kelsey lay on the lounge melting into the darkness like a ghost.

Alice turned on the lamp beside the bed. Kelsey heard the click as it went on and turned her head slowly toward the light.

"Why did you put the light on?" she said.

"I wanted to talk to you."

"I don't need lights, Alice. The night is my time. In the night you're no better than I am."

Alice sat down at the end of the lounge. "Don't talk like that. You'll only get excited."

Kelsey's eyes brooded on the lamp, sullen and unblinking, eyes that were unfaded and looked as good as new.

"You're no better than I am in the dark, Alice. You have to listen too, sift out the sounds. You have only your ears like me."

"Kelsey . . ."

"Remember how I used to be afraid of the dark?" She put out her hand to Alice and clutched her. *Well, I still am*. I'm still afraid of the dark. I want to scream and scream and tear away this black curtain. I'm afraid of it. I can hear the night coming at me in waves. . . . What are your eyes like, Alice? I forget your eyes sometimes."

Alice drew in her breath. "Brown," she said gravely, "like a cow's."

"I see them in the wall, but they may have changed. Oh, yes, your eyes are in the wall, soft like a doe's."

The fingers clutched at Alice's arm, tight and hot. "If I wanted one of your doe eyes, you'd give it to me?"

"Please . . ."

"Why, you're crying!" Kelsey said. "Aren't you?"

"No."

"I believe you'd give me one of your eyes."

"Yes."

"Ah, but I can't take it, so you're safe. You're safe. Everybody's safe but me, closed in here in the darkness by myself, lonely."

"If you—if you wouldn't talk like this or think like this—Kelsey, please. If you'd learn to go out with Prince you could be—be more independent. You could go out for long walks by yourself if you liked."

"With a dog for my eyes?"

"Better than nothing," Alice said with bitterness.

"For you, perhaps, for you anything is better than nothing. But not for me. There's nothing for me, no miracle, no operation, no hope."

Alice got up and began to walk about the room, her arms folded across her breasts. She said silently, "I am Alice Heath," but the formula failed her. It always failed her in her relations with Kelsey, it couldn't fortify her against the love-pity-hate she felt for Kelsey, undo all those years when she had looked after her and been jealous of her and proud of her.

Kelsey's eyes followed the sound of her steps up and down the room.

"Don't prowl," she said after a time.

Alice swung around, her arms falling to her sides. "I have something to tell you."

"Oh?"

"About Philip."

Kelsey rolled her head impatiently. "Is it the usual? Am I to be nicer to him? Don't you ever get tired of being Philip's advocate?"

"He's going away."

"So?" Kelsey said mockingly. "Where is he going?"

"New York, I think."

"Why?"

"Because you don't intend to marry him," Alice said.

"Intelligent of him to find that out."

"I urged him to leave. I don't think the two of you could make a go of it. He can't stand up to you. He's too sensitive, on his own account and on yours."

"Poor weak Philip, eh?" Kelsey said, smiling.

"There's no reason why he should stay, Kelsey. You haven't been in love with him for a long time; perhaps never, I don't know. Don't ask him to stay this time."

"And you want him to go?" Kelsey said. "You really do, Alice?"

"Of course."

"You liar, Alice." She sat up and her eyes sought the sounds that were Alice to her. "You liar! You puling little lovesick . . ."

"No! Please!"

"Do you thing I'm deaf?" Kelsey screamed. "Can't I hear you gasp over his name like a breathless adolescent? Can't I hear you purring over him? 'That was lovely, Philiy.' 'Please explain this, Philip.' You say Philip as if it were a watchword, a prayer, little Jesus James!"

"I don't," Alice said, gasping. "You're wrong. I don't —think anything of him."

"All these months I've listened to your love-sounds and it's made me sick, do you hear? It makes me vomit to hear your soft sighs and the catch in your voice."

She got up from the couch and stumbled toward Alice with her hands out.

"Do you hear me? Are you still there? Thank God I can't see! Thank God I don't have to look at your face drooling with love, and your eyes sick and tender and stupid like a cow's."

"You can't," Alice said, "you can't say these things to me!" She put out her hand to touch Kelsey but Kelsey felt the movement and drew back.

"Get out of my room, Alice. Sneak back to my lover. You, Alice with your two good eyes, get out of my room."

She raised her hand and pointed. "Get out."

There was a silence, then the hiss of Alice's breathing, and Kelsey's voice, torn into shreds. "Alice?"

"Yes."

"I *am* pointing to the door?"

"Almost," Alice said quietly. "Pretty nearly. You have a good sense of direction."

"But I wasn't pointing right at the door?"

"No."

Kelsey threw out her arms wildly and her right hand struck Alice's shoulder. With a cry of pain Alice staggered back.

Almost instantly Kelsey was quiet again.

"Ah," she said in a pleased voice. "I hit you, didn't I? Not on purpose. It was an accident, but I'm not sorry for it. I had to do something to you, didn't I, for getting Philip away from me?"

"No," Alice said. "Philip doesn't know I'm alive."

"Oh, but I know that!" Kelsey cried. "I must punish you just for trying."

She leaned over and groped with her hands until she found the bed. "There. I am not lost any more. Go and bring Ida, Alice."

"I didn't try," Alice said. "I didn't do anything."

"Go and bring Ida. Ida is my friend. I can trust Ida." She sat on the bed and smiled craftily in Alice's direction. "You saw Ida's ring, Alice? Pretty, isn't it? How does it look on her? She's got fat hands, hasn't she? Fat red puffy hands?"

"You shouldn't," Alice said dully. "You shouldn't have given it to her."

"Does Philip know?"

"No."

"You'll bring it to his attention some time, won't you? Promise me."

"No. No, I won't."

"I want Ida," Kelsey said querulously. "Go and get Ida."

"I'll have Maurice tell her."

"No, you tell her, Alice."

"Maurice will," Alice said. "Will you be down for dinner?"

"No, I'm not coming down for dinner any more. I don't want to see anyone."

Alice closed the door behind her and leaned against it for a minute. Maurice hadn't turned on the lights yet and the hall was dark, a place to hide in. When she was a child she had crouched here waiting for the doctor to come out of her mother's room, waiting so she'd be the first to see his face and know if her mother had died. In this hall she had hidden, peering over the top of the banister, waiting for the arrival of her music teacher. Sometimes Maurice would pass close by her, calling, "Miss Alice! Mr. Harrington has arrived. Miss Alice, you're not hiding?"

There was a feeling of guilt connected with this hall—perhaps she had wanted her mother to die; certainly she hadn't wanted to see Mr. Harrington, ever—and it rose in her now, pressing on her eyes and ears, taut against her forehead like an iron hand.

I've done nothing, nothing to be ashamed of.

She heard a step on the stairs and turned her head. Maurice was coming up, looking faintly worried, just as he used to look when he was searching for her. She waited, hoping, almost expecting him to say, "Miss Alice, Mr. Harrington has arrived."

But he didn't even see her and it wasn't the same Maurice after all. This one was old and couldn't see very well, and Mr. Harrington had been dead for ten years.

Alice said, "Maurice, Kelsey wants Ida."

He peered at her without surprise. "Yes ma'am. I'll tell her."

What a dreary voice he had, Alice thought, a voice to match the house and this dark hall.

Had it always been like this? Hadn't there been laughter sometimes, and parties and dancing? Or had she only dreamed that people went through this hall to lay their wraps in the guest rooms, laughing and talking? And children, too, dressed in their Sunday best, drinking too much lemonade and eternally running to the bathroom?

No, the children were no dream. She could remember one of them well, a sober child with brown braids, who sneaked upstairs to listen outside her mother's door and then crept back to the party. *I am Alice Heath.*

"Will that be all, ma'am?"

The lights were on and the child with the brown braids had gone back to the party.

"Shall I take Prince down with me, ma'am?"

Alice swung round sharply. In front of the door of her own room Prince lay with his head between his paws. His eyes regarded her, bright with interest. He had been there all the time watching her, knowing all about her, perhaps. She had the feeling again that the dog was human, that he could spy on her and be aware of her thoughts, even criticize her.

She called to him with a self-conscious laugh. He rose quickly and silently and stood beside her. She put a reluctant hand on his neck, as if she hated him but must be nice to him. *Don't tell on me, Prince. There'll be something in it for you if you don't tell on me.*

There were only the three of them at dinner, Alice, Johnny and Philip, and they ate in the drawing room at a table drawn up in front of the fireplace. They spoke seldom at first, their voices polite and formal.

"More lamb, Alice?"

"No thank you, John."

"Phil?"

"No thank you."

"It's a bit overdone," Johnny said. "Reminds me of the time Phil gave the concert in that church on Bloor Street and the Ladies' Aid or something made a supper for him in the Sunday School. Remember, Phil?"

"No," Philip said.

His face was cold wax. Only the flicker of the flames gave it a vicarious life, moving across it like probing sculptors' fingers, pinching the wax into a smile, smoothing it out again.

"I don't remember anything," he said bleakly. "I can't afford to. I've got to start all over with my mind stripped as clean as a newborn baby's. As clean as Johnny's even."

"So you're still in a mood," Johnny said, grinning.

Philip didn't answer. His eyes were on Alice as she

poured the coffee. When she handed him his cup he took it out of her hand quickly, as if he were afraid to touch her and wanted to get the contact over with.

"Johnny?" Alice said. "Have some?"

"Thanks. Maurice forgot the cognac. I'll ring."

"I thought you'd be going teetotal," Philip said.

"Me?" Johnny stared. "Why?"

"The new girl disapproves, doesn't she?"

"Oh. By God, she does. But you wouldn't think she'd count a couple of drops of cognac in coffee."

"T.T.'s count everything."

"Well, by God," Johnny said again. "Is that right?"

Philip smiled thinly. "Perfectly right. Be prepared to give it up for love. I seem to recall giving up a number of things for the same frail reason."

"Philip," Alice said sharply.

He didn't look at her. "Smoking was my sacrifice. Not a very big one, perhaps, for such a holy cause, but a persistent, nagging one."

"That's different," Johnny said. "Marcie is more reasonable than Kelsey."

"Shouldn't be hard for her. Kelsey is surely the ideal of unreason."

"Well, don't talk about it!" Alice said. "You're going away. Leave it at that." She turned to Johnny and gave him the parent-to-child smile that all women, including his sisters, were prepared to give Johnny when he was being a good boy. "You're really serious about this girl, Johnny?"

Johnny leaned back in his chair. "She's fine. You'd like her. She's never had much of a chance . . . "

"So few of them do," Philip said.

"Dry up, Phil. She dances. She does an acrobatic number at Joey's. She can twist herself into the most fantastic shapes."

"Oh, God," said Philip.

"She's good," Johnny went on. "Joey's isn't much of a place of course."

"Don't apologize for her," Alice said, frowning.

"But it's a start. She works hard at it because she wants to be really good some day. She lives at home with her mother. . . . "

"A prolific woman," Philip said, "with a real talent for reproduction."

43

Johnny scowled at him. "What in hell's got into you?"

"Well, isn't she and hasn't she?"

"No," Johnny said shortly. "I'd like to know what's the matter with you tonight."

"The matter is your sister." He paused. "Yes, and I have a mouthful of sour grapes, grapes as big as oranges and stewed in quinine. I have to spit them out some place, and you're handy, see?"

"You couldn't," Alice said coldly, "be expected to chew and swallow them like a civilized person?"

"Like Alice, like a civilized person," Philip jeered, "No, never. I don't deserve what I've got. Nothing has been my fault. Even that night I didn't want Kelsey to drive. She was half-tight."

"She was not," Alice said.

"Ask Johnny if she wasn't! She was feeling high and she said she wanted to drive. Johnny was in the rumble-seat . . . "

"Why go into it?" Johnny said feebly.

" . . . with Geraldine. That was her name, Geraldine. So Kelsey drove, as she wanted to."

"This is all so unnecessary," Alice said.

Philip looked at her. "You think so? Well, don't listen. None of it was my fault but I've had to answer for it all. She couldn't get back at fate so she got back at me. *I* was the one who plucked out her eyes!"

"I'll go and get the cognac," Johnny said. He went out quickly, slamming the door behind him.

"We've all paid," Alice said after a time.

"But *for what?* Do we have to pay because she is blind? What have I done to Kelsey that she'd like to see me dead?"

"She wouldn't," Alice said, but the protest was faint, there was nothing behind it to hold it up.

"She'd like to see us all dead, even the dog! Then she could die too, without bitterness. But she won't die till then, till we're dead. You notice what extraordinarily good care she takes of herself. Biding her time, that's what she's doing."

His voice rang out loud and strangely false, as if he were giving a reading full of passion and could reproduce the strength of the passion only by raising his voice.

Second-hand emotion, Alice thought, and second-hand

words. He doesn't mean any of it, he's flaying himself so he'll have the courage to leave.

"You imagine too much," she said. "You're like Kelsey. Kelsey has a new idea."

Something in her tone made him look up.

"Now what?"

"She thinks I am in love with you."

She saw that he couldn't believe it at first. His face loosened with surprise. When it tightened up again it looked peevish, as if he were saying silently, Haven't I enough trouble without that?

"It's not true, of course," he said at last.

Here is my chance, Alice thought. It will never come again.

She laughed and said, "Of course not!"

His whole body relaxed. Her laugh and her denial were a poultice drawing out the tension.

"Well, thank God," he said with a sigh.

"Yes, aren't you lucky? A completely free agent now." She was trembling with loathing for herself and for this man who would have denied her and flung her gifts back in her face. "Nothing to keep you here, is there?"

"No."

"Don't tempt your fates by saying good-bye to anyone."

"Sneak out with my tail between my legs," Philip said. "This is the way the world ends. What if I come back?"

"The door will be locked!" she said savagely. "So don't try it!"

He stepped back as if to see her better. He was smiling.

"Why, you do hate me," he said softly. "I didn't think you had it in you. Perhaps you're more like Kelsey than you . . . "

His head jerked toward the door.

Ida was standing just inside the room, twisting her apron in her hands, breathing noisily through her mouth. Her face shone red in the light.

"Ida!" Alice said.

The girl moved closer, all shining, her teeth and the ring on her finger and her eyes and her nails.

"She's dead," Ida said, glowing with sweat.

Philip strode across the room and grasped one of her damp fat arms. "What? *What?*"

"She's dead," Ida said, and her voice was gentle and sly. "She just died. She just died right now."

45

KELSEY was lying on the bed. The lamp was on and turned full on her face as if Ida had moved it to make sure she was dead.

Alice touched Kelsey's forehead and her hand came away drenched with sweat.

"Kelsey," she whispered. "Kelsey."

The skin was warmed but there was no flutter of her eyelids, no movement of her breast.

She turned and saw Philip leaning against the door frame and behind him Ida, rolling her eyes.

"A mirror," Alice said. "Fetch a mirror."

"No!" Philip shouted. "Leave her alone. Leave Kelsey alone."

Ida darted past his clutching hand and went to the bureau. She picked up the mirror and polished it with her apron as she walked toward the bed. Then she folded her arms over her breasts, waiting.

Alice held the mirror close to Kelsey's face. A fine mist dulled the glass.

"What did I tell you?" Ida cried.

"She's not dead," Alice said quietly. "Tell Letty to . . ."

"This is Tuesday and Letty and Maurice went to the pictures."

"Ida, get hot-water bottles. Philip, you'll stay here? I must phone a doctor."

"She is too dead!" Ida said. "I guess I seen lots of . . ."

She reeled back, holding her mouth where Alice had struck her.

"I've had enough from you," Alice said. "Get downstairs."

She pushed the girl out in front of her into the hall. Ida was crying now and muttering to herself as she lurched down the steps.

Alice went into the sitting room at the end of the hall and picked up the phone. She seemed calm and controlled now, she might have been phoning an old friend. Her fingers did not falter finding the numbers on the dial, Kingsley 2124.

He answered the phone himself. She recognized his voice.

"Dr. Loring? This is Alice Heath."

"I remember," he said. "Anything wrong?"

"Can you come out here right away? My—my sister—I think my sister is dying."

"*Dying?* What happened?"

"Nothing. Nothing at all. She was all right two hours ago and now she's like this, in a coma."

"Coma," he said. "Any heart history?"

"No."

"Diabetes, catalepsy, anything like that in her history?"

"No."

"I'll be right out. Ten minutes."

She hung up and went back to Kelsey's room. Philip was kneeling on the floor beside the bed, his face pressed against one of Kelsey's hands.

"Get up!" Her voice rasped across the room. "Haven't you any sense? You might do her some harm."

He turned his head slowly and looked at her, his eyes dazed. "You, Alice?"

"Get out of here," she said harshly. "The doctor is coming in a minute."

He didn't move. She went over and pulled him to his feet. Her thin fingers dug into his shoulders. It gave her bitter pleasure to hurt him and see him wince.

"I'm tired of fools!" she said violently. "Go downstairs and tell John to let the doctor in when he comes. Maurice is out. And you—you'd better go out, too. Go and walk somewhere. Do you understand?"

He nodded wearily. "Walk somewhere. Yes."

"You'll feel better," she said, more softly.

When he had gone she pulled a chair over to the bed and sat down to wait. Her hands were folded quietly in her lap, her back was stiff and straight. She was so intent on holding the pose that she didn't hear Loring come into the room.

Seeing her, he thought, smiling, She's still at it. But

he was a little touched because he saw that she was smaller than he remembered her.

"Good evening."

"Oh." She started. "Good evening."

She got up and gave him the chair beside the bed. He sat down with his instrument bag across his knees and took Kelsey's wrist in his hand.

"Dr. Loring . . . "

Frowning, he reached over and raised one of Kelsey's eyelids.

"What's wrong with her, Dr. Loring?"

He didn't answer her directly. He said, "Go and phone the General Hospital and ask for Hale, the chief pathologist. Tell him to come out here prepared to give a caffeine intravenous and a stomach wash for morphine poisoning. Got that?"

She nodded but couldn't speak.

"Now I want blankets and hot-water bottles. Where are the servants?"

"I've sent for the hot-water bottles," she said in a whisper. "There are blankets in the closet."

"Good. Hale at the General. Tell him it's an overdose of morphine. Please hurry."

Alice stood in the hall for a long time. On the other side of the closed door she could hear noises, a gasp, a muffled groan, the clink of metal, a liquid gurgle, a sharp command. Then the door opened and Dr. Hale was in the hall, unruffled, cheerful.

"She'll be all right," he said.

Under his smile Alice could see the question flickering in his eyes. *How did she get the morphine?*

But he didn't say it. He walked briskly down the steps whistling under his breath.

Alice went slowly to the door. The nurse was cleaning up the room. Loring was standing beside the bed looking down at Kelsey.

"Pupils expanding," he said to Miss Keller.

"That's good," Miss Keller said. "Good night, doctor. Good night, Miss Heath."

She went out. Loring picked up his coat from the floor and began to put it on, awkwardly, as if his muscles were stiff.

Alice said, "Doctor . . . "

48

"We'll talk downstairs," he said wearily. "She's sleeping naturally and we may wake her."

He checked the contents of his bag, closed it and walked to the door. Downstairs they passed the open door of the drawing room and saw Johnny huddled in a chair in front of the fire.

Alice started to go in but Loring held her back.

"I'd prefer to talk to you alone," he said.

"Very well," Alice said. "Come in here."

She switched on a light and a small, book-lined room sprang out of the darkness. But Loring didn't look at the books, he was watching Alice. He saw the hostility in her eyes, as if the sudden glare of the lights hadn't given her time to hide it.

He had expected the hostility. It was the regular reaction of his patients' relatives to himself. Because he was a psychiatrist he was held responsible for the need of a psychiatrist. A case of supply creating demand, he thought grimly.

Yes, the hostility could be explained easily enough. It was Alice's fear that puzzled him, and the wariness in her voice.

"Do you think—she took it herself?"

He sat down without haste and glanced around the room. "Has she ever talked about killing herself?"

"Not—not seriously."

He raised his brows. "How can you be sure whether it was serious or not? A grain or more of morphine is in my opinion very serious indeed. I suppose you know this will have to be reported to the police?"

"Yes," she whispered, "I know. They couldn't arrest her?"

"They wouldn't send her to jail," Loring said. "They might have her committed to an institution."

"Oh, no! They wouldn't, they couldn't!"

"Unless someone else gave it to her," he said quietly.

"Nobody gave it to her. Please, you mustn't think that. Nobody could have given it to her."

He stared at her. "Why not? It's simple enough to give morphine by mouth in food or drink. Statistically I believe it's the doctor's favorite method of homicide. Was there a supply in the house?"

"Not recently."

"When?"

"When my mother was sick we had some for the nurse to give her."

"What happened to it?"

"I don't know. You don't think of small things like that when . . ."

"Nurses do, or are supposed to. What was the nurse's name?"

"Miss Alison. Letty used to help too, but Miss Alison was in charge."

"I want to talk to Letty," Loring said.

"She went out. She ought to be back soon."

"Through what doctor did you get Miss Alison?"

"Dr. Beringer in the Medical Arts."

Loring took out an envelope and wrote the names on it.

"This maid," he said, "this girl Ida. She was with your sister, you said?"

"Yes."

"Why?"

"Kelsey wanted her around. I think—I think Ida reads her teacup and tells her fortune. That's what started the friendship. No, not friendship, exactly."

"Collusion," Loring said.

"Yes, that's the word."

"May I see Ida?"

"No," she said sharply. "It wouldn't do any good. She's too stupid to have noticed anything."

"Besides, it might humiliate you, eh? You'd rather have the police question her?"

"Why do they have to?"

"Because," Loring said, "your sister is blind. Someone gave her the morphine. Even if she took it herself *someone helped her.*"

She was silent for a long time. Then she raised her head and looked at him listlessly. "All right. Ring the bell."

It was five minutes before Ida came in, blowsy and disheveled in her wrinkled uniform. When she saw Loring her mouth fell open and she stepped back into the hall.

"Come in here," Loring said, "and close the door."

She sidled in, twisting her apron, and stood against the wall.

"I don't know anything," she said sullenly. "It wasn't my fault. I just thought she died by the hand of God."

"You took her tray up?"

"Sure. Being she wasn't going down she ate early, about half-past six. Some gooey stuff made out of chicken and mushrooms. The cook makes it for her special. And tea, on account of I was to read her teacup."

"A sideline of yours?" Loring asked dryly.

She tossed her head at him. "A lot of smart people aren't so smart about some things! My mother taught me to read teacups. She never failed. She was a seventh daughter of a seventh daughter and if she was in the dark you could see the sparks fly out of her. She couldn't even go to school when she was a kid because spirits rapped on her desk and the teachers were scared. The *teachers* were scared and teachers are just about as smart as anybody."

"You've been drinking," Alice said.

"I got a toothache," Ida cried. "I guess I got a right to get rid of a toothache, especially since I didn't touch none of your stuff." She turned to Loring and winked. "They got it padlocked. Can you beat it?"

Loring smiled slightly. "What did you see in Miss Heath's teacup?"

Ida rolled her eyes. "Money. Money with a curse on it, evil money. And a trip, a long long trip, maybe the kind you never come back from. I thought of that since, it seemed to fit so good. And a man was there too, a dark man."

"Ida!" Alice said. "Don't lie to Dr. Loring."

"There was too a dark man! He was standing right beside the long trip and the money was there lying all around his feet."

"Do we have to listen to this raving?" Alice said coldly. "Stick to the facts."

"Facts," Ida said. "It was a fact, wasn't it, about the rapping of the desks so my mother had to stop school which is why she never had any education and me neither. That was a fact."

Loring said, "Did Miss Heath complain about the food or the tea?"

"Oh, sure, she always did. She said the tea tasted bitter. So I said, well naturally, what can you expect with that man Hitler sinking everything. I said, you're lucky to have any tea, which she is too, because the cook gives up her coupons to Miss Kelsey every week. So Miss Kelsey gets twenty-four cups every week instead of twelve and a half, which I read them all, no, twenty-five."

51

"Did you take the tray directly from the kitchen?"

"No," Ida said scornfully. "I always take it for a walk around the block first to give it some fresh air."

"Then no one had access to the tray except the cook and yourself and Miss Heath?"

"And God." Ida moved closer to Loring and he got a strong whiff of brandy. "Yeah, I know you people what they call smart don't believe in God. But if you could ever of seen them sparks!"

Alice turned to Loring. "She's drunk, you can see that. It's quite useless going on with this farce. Couldn't you come back tomorrow?"

"Drunk, am I," Ida lurched across the room and stuck her face into Alice's. "Well, why am I drunk, besides the toothache I mean? Because I got things inside me like my mother had, only not sparks. It's just a *knowing*. When she closed her eyes up there tonight I knew she was for it, I knew she was going to die. A long trip, a long long trip."

"That's enough," Loring said curtly. "If I can't get any information from you, the police can and will. She was poisoned."

"Poisoned!" Ida stretched out her hands to him. "I never did anything to her, mister! I never did it. She's my only friend in this house!"

"Sit down." He pushed her into a chair and towered over her. "Did she ask you to bring her anything, any pills that she'd hidden, perhaps?"

"No, no, I never did! No!"

"Did she ask you to?"

"No!"

"Did she tell you she was feeling ill?"

"Sleepy, she said. She said she was sleepy. And then she laid there like someone had turned out the lights in her and I knew she was dead."

"Don't let her talk like that!" Alice cried. "Kelsey isn't dead. She's all right, you said she was going to be all right!"

Loring went over and took her hand. "Go upstairs and stay with her if you're worried."

"Shouldn't ought to leave her alone anyway," Ida said aggressively. "My only friend in this house which the others in it look down their noses . . . "

Alice closed the door. She had to stand in the hall a

minute until her legs stopped shaking and her tears were forced back behind her eyes.

The police were going to come, as they had come the other time.

Mr. Heath, tell the court where you first met the deceased, Geraldine Smith.

Had there been any liquor consumed, Mr. Heath?

You and Miss Smith were riding in the rumbleseat, Mr. Heath. Go on.

Mr. James, you tell the court . . .

The court extends its sympathy . . .

She walked across the hall into the drawing room. Johnny was still huddled in the chair and when he looked up she knew by the glassiness of his eyes that he had been drinking steadily.

He's remembering too, Alice thought, he's thinking of Geraldine.

"Where's Father?" she asked.

"I went up to tell him," Johnny said. "He wasn't in his room. Is she all right?"

"She will be."

"How much did she take?"

"Over a grain."

"Where did she get it for God's sake? And why would she want to kill herself for God's sake?"

"Better stop drinking now, John," Alice said.

"Going to send me out for a walk, too?" he said in a hard voice.

"I sent Philip out because he was upset. I thought he would feel better if he had some fresh air. You could do with some too. Might sober you up."

"I'm not . . . "

"I'm going upstairs to sit with Kelsey. Don't come up."

In Kelsey's room she sat beside the bed for a long time, not thinking at all. Already her mind was closing over the fresh wounds, sewing the edges together, so that there was only a dull ache which spread over her whole body and seemed to have no source.

Kelsey was breathing naturally and evenly. Once she moved her hand on the covers and sighed and turned her head toward the light, as if to remind Alice: See me, how young, how pretty; see the curve of my shoulder, the firm breast, the flushed cheek. These are nothing to me, I want to die. . . .

The clock in the hall struck twelve. Kelsey stirred again. Alice bent over her. "Kelsey?"

"Aaah," Kelsey sighed, the sound of her father, the infinitely tired sound that was almost a groan. "Aaah. . . ."

"It's me, it's Alice."

"Alice." Her voice was soft and tattered like torn chiffon. It brushed against Alice and she felt it but didn't hear it.

"How do you feel, Kelsey?"

"Philip . . ."

"Oh, Philip's all right," Alice said eagerly. "He won't be leaving. He's going to stay. Is that why you did it?"

"No—no."

"What? I didn't hear you, Kelsey."

"Dead."

"But you're not dead, darling! You're going to be all right again!"

"Came back."

"Of course, of course you came back! Mustn't talk now. You're tired."

Kelsey's hands plucked at the covers. Alice caught them in her own. "Please. Be quiet. Try and rest."

"I know—what to do."

A voice, a thin thread like a spider's web spun from a long way off, broken by a breeze. "Aaaah. . . ."

CHAPTER 6

BY THE time the last show came on at one o'clock Stevie Jordan was always a little tight. But by one o'clock those patrons who intended to get tight had already done so and those who didn't had gone home, so Stevie's lapses went unnoticed. Discrimination dissolves in alcohol and the last show was the best. Everything looked fine under the dim lights, the drinks, the chorus girls, the orchestra and Stevie.

Stevie himself made no concessions to glamor, did not attempt to conceal what he was. He hadn't, as some people thought, fallen out of the top drawer into Joey's. He had climbed up as far as Joey's from one of the bottom drawers. It was the best job he had ever had or ever would have. He was at the top, but because it wasn't a very high top he didn't try hard to stay there. He was always in trouble of some kind and always falling in love with the wrong woman.

"Marcie Moore. You all remember Marcie. You know what we call her round the back of this dive? Pretzel, we call her, and you'll see on account of why. Are you ready, Marcie?"

The lights were still dimmer. A baby spot fumbled over the floor, found the entrance and the girl standing there looking as if she were afraid to come out.

"Her real name is Marcella but you'll want to call her Marcie. Say hello to the suckers, Marcie."

Then Marcie's voice, shy, barely audible, "Hello. Hello, suckers."

She came out onto the floor, reluctantly, as if the baby spot were a tangible force which pushed her along. She wore skin-tight black satin shorts and bra, but she didn't look as naked as some of the patrons. She was too scrawny, like a young bird only half feathered.

She wasn't scared of the crowd at all, despising them as a bunch of drunks, but Joey liked her to pretend. He kept up his part of the pretense by dismissing gentlemen who asked for her phone number with the statement that she lived at home with her mother.

"—lives with her mother," Stevie bawled. "No kidding. Now how many of *youse* guys out there live with *your* mothers?"

A drunk at one of the floor tables said his mother was dead and began to wail softly to himself because his mother was dead, died when he was a baby, poor old mother, worked hard all her life. . . .

The orchestra drowned him out with a tango. Marcie jerked, dipped and spun around the floor. The routine was vigorous and she had no energy to waste smiling at the gentlemen.

Half of the orchestra laid down their instruments and purred and whistled when Marcie did the splits or a backbend. At the end of the dance she bowed briefly and unsmilingly and disappeared behind the curtain, followed by the thunder of tablepounding and stamping feet and cries of "More! More!"

Then Stevie came on the floor again, still clapping and looking toward the curtain as if he expected Marcie to come back for an encore. It was just a gag to work up more applause for her. He knew she never did an encore for the last show.

"Swell, eh? Glad you liked it."

The drunk was still crying. Stevie went over and touched his shoulder.

"What goes on? A big boy like you crying about your mother!"

"Worked hard all her life," the drunk sobbed.

"Oh, dry up, George!" said his lady. "Oh, dry up! Somebody dry him up!"

"We'll have to cheer this gentleman," Stevie said gravely. "It is our God-given duty to cheer this gentleman. Any ideas? Anyone?"

"Sweet Sue," yelled a lady.

"Sweet Sue. Hear it, boys? Make it Sweet Sue."

Sweet Sue didn't cheer the drunk and he had to be removed. It was Stevie who did the job. He put his arm around the drunk's shoulders and guided him off the floor with the lady weaving along behind, half crying herself:

"It's a shame. That's what. What did you have to go talking about mothers for in front of him for?"

Stevie got their hats and coats from the checkroom and helped the man with his coat. He told the doorman to get a taxi and then he stood with the couple until the taxi came. The drunk clung to him and told him he was a real gentleman, a gentleman with real feeling, a good guy, a real pal, the kind of guy there should be more of in this world.

"Sure," Stevie said, grinning. "Sure. Happy landing."

He opened the door of the taxi. When it was gone he stood on the sidewalk for a time, with the wind ruffling his hair.

"Troublemaker," said the doorman. "Busy night, eh?"

"Yeah."

When he went inside he smoothed his hair with both hands and straightened his tie. The drunk had made him think of his own mother. She lived down in the Village. She made pottery and she hadn't been sober for ten years.

He stopped at the checkroom, grinning automatically at the girl attendant.

"Busy night," she said.

"Yeah." He paused. "Marcie's gorilla shown up yet?"

She giggled and said, "Nope. Not tonight. Anyhow, that was no gorilla . . ."

"Yeah, I know. Maybe he's staying home tonight because he's only got one suit and he wouldn't be seen dead in the same suit two nights in a row."

"Oh, *go on,* Mr. Jordan!"

"Bloated plutocrat. I hate plutocrats when they're bloated around the shoulders."

She giggled some more and he pinched her cheek politely, because after all it was something to make somebody giggle. He never got a rise out of Marcie at all. She would stare at him coldly and say, "I'm sorry, Mr. Jordan. I guess I got no sense of humor." Or, worse still, "You sound like you've been drinking, Mr. Jordan." Whenever she talked to him her voice and face were full of disapproval or reproach. He didn't like her very much but he was pretty sure he was falling in love with her.

The chorus were on again, thumping their feet, and Mamie Rosen was braying to the moo-hoon. Stevie knew from the way she sang that her boy friend, a wop called Murillo, had walked out on her again. He threaded his way among the tables and went backstage. He found Marcie behind the entrance curtain, looking out at the girls dancing. She was keeping time to the music with one foot, and her eyes were intense because she was short-sighted.

But the whole pose was false. Stevie knew she didn't give a damn about the music or the show, and the girls gave her a pain. She was looking for someone.

"Stood up?" Stevie said.

She jumped, as if he had poked her, then resumed the pose again, tapping her foot and humming.

"Never trust a gentleman," Stevie said, "not from where you sit. Any time, any place, he might meet a lady and then where'd you be?"

"You're drunk," Marcie said, without turning around.

"Naturally. Gentlemen get funny ideas, about homes and gardens and kids and all that."

She turned around this time and stared at him angrily.

"Well, what about it? I'm crazy about kids. I could have kids as well as anyone."

"*And* gardens," Stevie said. "Sure. Hoe me for a turnip. But . . . "

But the chorus was stamping in through the curtain. Professional smiles faded and gum parked in tooth cavities was deftly removed.

Mamie Rosen burst into effortless tears and came over to Stevie, wiping her tears away with the back of her hand.

"Stevie. That louse . . . "

"Yeah, sure." He patted her shoulder. Drops of sweat had wormed their way through the pink greasepaint. Stevie's hand was wet, so he patted her head this time to dry his hand.

"He'll come back," Stevie said. "Doesn't he always?"

"But if I could be *sure*, Stevie! Maybe this time . . ."

"You're safe. He can't support himself." He gave her a little push towards the dressing room.

When he turned back he saw that Marcie was looking out through the curtain again. She forgot to tap her foot and her eyes looked frantic, the way short-sighted people's eyes look when they can't see something they know should be there.

"What's his name?" Stevie said.

"None of your business."

"You think so?" He walked up and stood behind her, touching her only with his breath. "Everything's my business. I'm Joey's ears and eyes and feet, bouncer de luxe."

She shrugged her thin shoulders. "Johnny could bounce you like a ball. And don't *breathe* on me."

"My way of making love," Stevie said. "I breathe on 'em."

"Mr. Jordan—Stevie."

Stevie saw that she was going to ask a favor. She wasn't used to asking favors and she couldn't be gracious about it. The best she could do was call him by his first name.

"Stevie, do you see him anywhere?"

"Who?"

"You know. Johnny. Everything's sort of blurred this far away."

He made a pretense of looking out on the floor. He frowned to make it more realistic.

58

"Over on the left," Marcie said. "Over there on the left where he usually sits."

"No."

"Over by the band."

"No." Stevie let the curtain drop. "Unless he's a drunken bum like me and slid under a table, my verdict is he's not here. I'm here, though. I haven't slid under a table since New Year's Eve and you know how it is on New Year's Eve."

She didn't hear him. She was hugging her bare shoulders and staring straight in front of her. Her features had sharpened and she looked almost vicious, like a small untamed animal caught in a trap.

A ferret, Stevie thought. He didn't like her at all and he was even a little frightened of her. But he said again, "I'm here."

She moved her head to one side and said, "Oh, *you.*"

He almost gave up then and told her that he'd seen Johnny Heath sitting over on the left beside the band and that he was still there waiting for her. But he didn't tell her.

"Why that tone?" he said. "I'm clean and sweet like I just stepped out of the tub."

"Go away."

"You go and get dressed and I'll drive you home to momma."

"No. No thanks."

"Sure you will. I got a rumbleseat full of etchings but I won't even open it. Go and get dressed."

She hesitated, her thin fingers pulling at the flesh of her shoulders. "I wouldn't want you to think it means anything if I let you drive me home."

"I won't think a thing," Stevie said cheerfully.

He watched her until she disappeared into the dressing room, then he went to get his coat, whistling under his breath. He felt so good that he leaned over the checking counter and gave the girl a playful whack on the rear. She let out a squeal and scurried between the rows of coats. She was easily excited so it took her some time to find Stevie's coat. When she finally came back Stevie wasn't feeling playful any more. He was talking to a big man with a bass voice and muscle-swollen shoulders.

"You did, eh?" Steve was saying. "You got here late, eh? So what?"

The big man was very polite. He looked down at Stevie and said, "I was wondering if . . . " Then he saw the girl behind the counter and turned to her with a smile. "I'm waiting for Miss Moore. She hasn't gone yet, has she?"

The girl winked slyly at Stevie. "I'm sure I don't know. Do you know, Mr. Jordan?"

"Sure she's gone," Stevie said. "She checked out early with a case of double pneumonia. It's the clothes she doesn't wear."

The man smiled again, absently. "You're Mr. Jordan, aren't you?"

"Yes sir, Mr. Jordan, the wit."

"Marcella talks about you. She thinks you are very funny."

Stevie stared at him. "Yeah? She does, eh? Well, I'm glad to hear it."

"If she's still here, will you tell her I'm waiting? My name's Heath."

"O.K., Mr. Heath," Stevie said. "I'll do that."

He told her. He went back and told her in a flat, bored voice because suddenly it didn't matter much one way or the other.

After that he went outside by the back door. Some of the girls were there waiting in the alley for their dates to show up. Mamie Rosen was waiting with them, just for company. She was a Polish Jewess with very blonde brittle hair and sad dark eyes. She had been living with Murillo for years, ever since Stevie first knew her, but she was still intense about him and frequently cried when he was away, which was most of the time.

When she saw Stevie she followed him out to his car and got in beside him. She was still sniveling.

"Tie a rag around it," Stevie said.

"Yeah, but you don't know, Stevie. He didn't even say good-bye, just walked off and maybe I won't see him again for months."

"That should save trouble," Stevie said, "and money."

"You get kinda used to waking up in the morning and having somebody there next to you."

"Sure. I guess you can get used to sleeping with anything, even a cobra, especially if you're another cobra."

"He's not . . . "

"You know the one about the skunk? A skunk sat on a

60

stump. The skunk thunk the stump stunk and the stump thunk the skunk stunk. Now you say it."

"Oh, gee, I can't!"

"Go on. Say it."

"A skunk sat on a stump. The skunk thunk the skunk . . . God, that's a scream, Stevie."

"Yeah, isn't it," Stevie said.

Neither of them smiled.

Stevie swung the car through the broad alley and came out on Bloor Street. He saw a long yellow roadster just pulling away from the curb in front of the club. Without turning his head he knew Mamie was looking at the roadster too because it was the kind of car people like Mamie and himself and their friends always looked at and thought, "What's he done to deserve a car like that?" or "Some day . . . "

Mamie let out a sigh that was soft but spiked with envy.

"Same guy," Stevie said, "but a different car."

"What?"

"The other car was wrecked, the one I remember him driving."

"What other car?" She frowned at him. "Say, are you plastered?"

"It was blue," Stevie said. "I went to see it at the garage where they were trying to fix it up. A lot of people went to see it. There was no admission charge but you had to tip the garage man a quarter. So I went. To see the blood, I guess. I guess I'm a morbid guy. When I got there I saw the blood but it wasn't hers, it wasn't where she'd been sitting."

"I don't know what . . . "

"Geraldine."

"Geraldine?" She frowned again, pretending she was trying to remember, but Stevie knew she knew.

"You took her place as singer," Stevie said. "Now you remember?"

"Now Stevie, you quit, you stop that. I got enough on my mind. I don't want to think about things like that."

"So Joey took you out of the line and let you sing, the night she didn't show up because she was dead."

"I don't want to talk about it!" Mamie said shrilly.

"Hell," Stevie said, "neither do I, come to think of it."

So they drove off in silence for a time. Mamie huddled in the corner as far away as she could get, stroking the collar of her coat for comfort. It was a fine collar, real genuine silver fox. Tony had bought it for her a couple of years ago with the proceeds of a fantan game in Elizabeth Street. Later on a Chinaman came to the club and demanded the coat, but she'd hung on to it. Tony had left town for a couple of months after that and when he came back he had some scars over his chest which seemed to indicate that the Chinaman had caught up with him.

"But I still think it's funny," Stevie said at last.

She stirred impatiently and tweaked out a silver fox hair. "Yeah, what's funny?"

"Heath."

"Heath." She repeated the name, thoughtfully, as if she recognized it and it meant something to her.

"That's the name of this guy," Stevie said, "the one who calls for Marcie, the one who called for Geraldine two years ago."

"Well, what's so funny?" Mamie said. "A lot of these big bugs go for that kind of girl."

"What kind?"

She twisted her hands in her lap. They were nice strong-looking hands but they never seemed quite clean.

"My kind," she said. "You know. Easy, I guess you call it."

He looked at her deliberately. "Marcie is no slut."

"Well, all right, who cares? We all gotta live our lives and if one girl likes it and another one don't, well, so what!"

"Where do you live?"

"You know damn well where I live. You make me sick, Stevie."

"Me too," Stevie said. "I thought maybe you'd moved."

He didn't say any more about Geraldine until he stopped in front of Mamie's boardinghouse on Charles Street. He leaned across her to open the door and said, "There were some others in the car too, but Geraldine was the only one who got killed."

She tried to get out but he held her back with his hands.

"There was a girl," Stevie said. "A long time afterward some guy tried to cheer me up about Geraldine by telling me the other girl got blind. Worse than being killed, being blind."

"Let me go," Mamie said. "The other girl was his sister.

62

I remember reading about it in the papers. Thanks for the ride."

"Listen," Stevie said, holding her arm hard. "Don't tell any of this to Marcie."

She glanced at him and away again. "Well, I wouldn't. Hell, I'm no blabber." She was already planning how she'd tell Marcie but her face didn't change expression. "Why not, though?"

"She thinks I don't even know his name. Can you beat it? Me not know his name when all I see in the middle of the night is his face, so I got to get up for a drink."

"Hell." She pushed him away. "You're plastered. Forget it."

"No," Stevie said. "And every time I walk around a corner I think, maybe this is the corner he'll be behind and I can hit him. Only I wouldn't hit him. I'd run."

"You *might* hit him," Mamie said cheerfully. "Sure you might. Though why in hell—well, good night, Stevie."

He didn't answer so she slammed the door behind her and went up the steps of her boardinghouse.

"Listen, Mamie," Stevie said. "I didn't hit him." But the car windows were closed and his voice wasn't loud enough.

He sat there behind the wheel and closed his eyes. Whenever he closed his eyes lately something came up at him, something black like a velvet curtain distended by a wind. He opened his eyes quickly and reached for the gears.

"Gotta get glasses," he said aloud.

He talked to himself because it comforted him. This was the time of night he didn't like, when the city was dead or else living silently behind closed doors. This was the time you looked over your shoulder, you looked back to reassure yourself.

When he turned north on Avenue Road he heard the clock on the Soldiers' Tower strike three. Bong bong bong. One for Geraldine. One for Marcie.

"One for me," he said. There were only three but he kept imagining there was more. "One for Joey. One for Murillo. One for Johnny Heath."

He stepped on the gas to get away from the clock. The car climbed the hill, past the boardinghouses and small

63

shops, then the apartments getting swankier as the hill grew, then more shops, a better kind now.

And then St. Clair. It wasn't until he was actually at the top of the hill that he realized he should have turned off three blocks down. He didn't feel right up here on the top of the hill where Johnny Heath lived. Johnny Heath lived up here to the left, with his yellow roadster and his blind sister. Stevie had driven past the house once just for the hell of it.

He turned left, driving very slowly, not intending to stop but just to go past the house. The car stopped itself, so Stevie turned off the ignition and parked along the curb. He couldn't see the Heaths' house very well from the curb. He could only see a faint glow behind the trees.

He sat there for some time looking at the glow. There were no cars moving along the road that he could wave at. After three o'clock he always waved at cars because the very lateness of the hour and the darkness were bonds between him and the people in the cars.

Someone was walking, though. The steps were behind him, slow steps and heavy, like an old man's.

Stevie opened the car window nearest to the curb, and when the old man was abreast of the car Stevie said, "Could I trouble you for a match?"

On the seat beside him he had a whole box of paper matches advertising the Club Joey, Toronto's Smartest Nightclub, Cover Charge One-Fifty. But he had to talk to someone, someone who was awake in the sleeping city.

The steps paused.

"A match," Stevie said.

"Ah?"

"A match. Could I trouble you . . . ?"

"A match?" The man leaned down and looked inside the car window at Stevie. "Do you want a match?"

"No," Stevie said hoarsely. "No, thanks."

This was the corner Johnny Heath was behind, this was how he looked when you came upon him unawares, the skin sagging over his face, and this was how he sounded, like an old man with a thin cracked voice.

"I have a great many matches," the man said. "It's no trouble."

"Guess I don't need any," Stevie said. "Look. I found a whole boxful."

He held up the box and they both stared at it solemnly.

"So you have," Mr. Heath said. "Goodnight."

"Goodnight, Mr. Heath."

The face vanished, came back again.

"You know me? I'm sorry, I . . . One of my girls' young men, are you? Sorry I don't . . . Goodnight."

"Goodnight," Stevie said again.

After a time the glow from behind the trees disappeared.

CHAPTER 7

FIVE minutes later Mr. Heath had already forgotten the young man in the car. Remembering was difficult for him and he was too tired to make the effort.

He turned off the hall light downstairs. Maurice had left it on for him. Maurice was the only one who knew that he went out like this at night when he couldn't sleep and prowled through the dark city, heavy limbed and dull eyed like an aged lion.

When he reached the second floor he saw the light shining underneath Kelsey's door but he noticed it only for a second, a moment of puzzlement, and then he passed on. Going from the second floor to the third he always used the back stairs that the servants used. He had never stopped to reason this out, only realizing vaguely that it had something to do with Isobel. Isobel had sent him up to the third floor. They had shared the front bedroom which was Kelsey's now, but Isobel had always hated this convention of happy marriages. When she became ill she sent him up to the third floor where, properly, he belonged since he was no longer of any use to anyone. He could not help her pain or comfort her or support his children or give orders to the servants or even say anything that he had not already said a hundred times.

When Isobel died he hadn't moved down to the second floor again. It was too much trouble and you couldn't be

65

sure that Isobel was really gone from the room, or if gone that she wouldn't come back and shatter your sleep with her groans.

At the top of the stairs he turned and looked down, cupping his ear in his hand to catch a noise he thought he'd heard for an instant between the creakings of the stair treads. A padding noise like swift silent feet running over a carpet. It was gone now. It was not Isobel; perhaps it was the dog.

He went into his own room and undressed in the dark.

"Dark," Kelsey said. "It's dark, Alice. Come and help me, Alice!"

"I'm coming. Don't be frightened. I'm coming."

They were in a dark wood and the bleak and hungry trees stretched out their branches, quivering at the tips like the tentacles of an octopus, sucking out at Alice as she ran.

But Kelsey was running too, away from her, fleetly, as if she knew this dark wood well.

"I'm coming! Wait for me, Kelsey!"

She heard the soft laughing of birds from the branches, and a cry that throbbed into an echo. She came upon Kelsey lying on her face in the moss, and lifted her up. But it was too late. This face was dead.

It was Kelsey who had died, not the other girl. The other girl lived, blind, but this was Kelsey here dead, cuddled in the bruised and bloody moss.

She fingered the dead face, and the hungry tentacles of trees swooped down. . . .

She woke groaning and fighting for her breath. The dark wood and the dead girl rolled off the stage. Only the soft derisive laughing of the birds remained, the clock saying, "Tut *tut!* Tut *tut!*"

Bong bong bong bong. One for Geraldine. One for Marcie. One for Stevie. And one for the pot.

Victoria College, the Soldiers' Tower, the Parliament Buildings and Queen's Park.

He hadn't walked through Queen's Park for over two years. The last time something had happened to him. He'd been walking with a girl, and the girl had talked in a low voice with her head bent down and half turned away as if she were ashamed of her words. But he could see that her eyes were shining and that she was happy, and he hadn't said anything at all.

"Listen, Stevie. I thought I could tell you this better if we took a walk, you know, with people around so you won't do anything like lose your temper. I mean, sometimes I'm kinda scared of you. . . . "

He had never lost his temper with her, struck her or sworn at her, but he had been too shocked to reply. Maybe she saw through him and there were things in him to be afraid of. "Well, anyway, Stevie. I guess you know what it is. I'm not coming back to your place tonight. Margy is going up this afternoon to get my things. No, he hasn't said anything about you-know-what. Only I saw his sisters on the street yesterday, Margy pointed them out. And I guess I just want to move out, Stevie. You know how it is. I guess I felt kinda funny when I saw his sisters, me sleeping with you all this time. . . . "

"I hope Margy don't forget my toothbrush."

Charles Street. Maybe he'd go back to Mamie Rosen's and get a drink. Mamie's landlady wasn't fussy. His own landlady was a terror. She was always tacking up signs, especially in the bathroom:

"Kindly refrain from baths after eleven o'clock. Ethel G. McGillicuddy."

"Consider the other tenants and please do not use the toilet for serious purposes after twelve o'clock as the noise is disturbing. By order. Ethel G. McGillicuddy."

You hardly ever saw her. She did all her communicating by signs and small notes left pinned to the pillows. "Mr. Jordan. What do you want done with the pile of socks in the closet? And oblige. Ethel G. McGillicuddy."

Stevie always saved the notes and read them to his friends for a laugh. Once he had borrowed the "for serious purposes" sign and taken it to the club because no one would believe it. He forgot to take it back, but that night there was a second sign in the same place with the same wording.

She had always called Geraldine "Mrs. Jordan," though she knew different. Her only way of putting Geraldine in her place was to ignore her, that is, write all the notes to Stevie. Like, "Please ask Mrs. Jordan to refrain from washing her hair under the showers. And oblige. E.G.M. It clogs the drains."

Stevie didn't go to Geraldine's funeral, but Mrs. Mc-

Gillicuddy did. She carried a bouquet of chrysanthemums and she was heavily draped in black. When she came back her eyes were red with weeping. She flung herself into her work and new signs sprang up all over the house, dealing with the morals of her tenants.

Steve parked in front of Mamie's house. Mamie's shade was down but a light shone through the cracks.

"Come on out!" Stevie shouted. "Oh, MAmie! MamEE!"

A window was flung up on the second floor.

"Go drown yourself," a man's voice yelled.

"MamEE!"

"I'll call the police on you!"

Stevie waved up at him. "Sure, and is it a crime to be seekin' me own sister Mamie Rosen?"

The window closed with a bang. A couple of minutes later Mamie's window opened and Mamie stuck her head out.

"Oh, for Gawd's sake, Stevie," she said. "You again."

" 'Tis your own brother Stevie come home, Mamie. Tell me mither and me——"

"Oh, shut up. What do you want?"

"A drink."

"I haven't got a thing."

"One drink and I'll tell you a secret."

"What about?"

"Hush." He came closer to the window, brushing aside a lice-eaten rosebush, and whispered, "Tony."

"What about him?" Her voice was excited. "You saw him? Where is he?"

"I have a theory," Stevie said. "If you'll hand me your key I shall step inside a moment. . . ."

"You didn't see him," she said dully, but she left the window and a minute later the front door opened. Stevie went through the gloomy hall into Mamie's room. She hadn't been to bed. She still wore her stage makeup and the red velvet evening dress, and there was a glass and a half-empty bottle of rye on the table.

Stevie sat down on the edge of the bed and poured some rye into the glass.

"To Tony," he said. "May his dismembered torso find its way into a trunk."

She watched him while he drained the glass. "All right. You've had your drink. Now beat it."

"I thought I'd stay and see the sun rise over Charles Street," Stevie said. "Be kind of a gruesome sight."

"Go on, beat it. I'm going to bed."

"I could sleep on the couch."

"Why?"

He poured out the rest of the bottle. "Well, I just had a bad shock. When I got home there was Mrs. McGillicuddy on the front steps with an axe. So I thought I'd come and stay with you."

"Well, you can't." She reached for the glass. "That's my last bottle. Give it here."

She sat down beside him and they shared the rye.

"Cut the gags," she said. Why'd you come back?"

"Oh, I don't know. Maybe I'm going for you."

"The hell." She stared at him.

"All right, the hell." He swished the rye around the glass. "What ever happened to Margy?"

"Margy?"

"Geraldine's cousin."

"Oh, her. She got married. Married an electrician. She's even got a kid."

"Yeah?"

"I saw her in Eaton's last week and she had the kid with her."

"Be kind of funny to have a kid," Stevie said.

"For Christ's sake what's the matter with you tonight? First Geraldine and now kids. Next you'll be getting the D.T.'s." She got up and yawned. "I'm going to bed. I can't kick you out so I guess you can sleep on the couch."

"Thanks."

He sounded so grateful that she turned to look at him, suspicious. But she couldn't tell anything from his face, and his eyes were closed.

With her eyes still tightly closed Ida reached over and turned off her alarm, switched on the light and fumbled with her bare feet for her slippers.

The sounds of morning began to seep through the house, the plop-plop-plop of Ida's slippers along the hall, the swish of a tap, and the gurgling of drains, the faint tinkle of another alarm, the thud of a dropped shoe.

Descending the back stairs Ida began to hum loudly to herself. She didn't feel like humming this morning—the toothache had gone, giving place to a headache—but she

69

hummed in the hope that Maurice and Letty would hear her and know she was up and doing her duty.

She paused on the second-floor landing and ran her eye along the hall. Kelsey's light still shone underneath the door. Ida stopped humming and walked on tiptoe down the hall. In spite of her size she was as stealthy as a cat when she was stalking a closed door.

Was it possible that Kelsey and Mr. James . . .?

She crept to the door and listened but heard no sound. Then she rapped softly, blinking her eyes in concentration. Suppose she walked in and found Mr. James there in his pyjamas—or *not* in his pyjamas.

She shivered with dread and delight and began to turn the knob slowly, giving herself time to think of something to say, just in case . . .

But there was no need to say anything.

She stepped back into the hall. She tucked in a stray piece of hair and smoothed her apron carefully. Then she opened her mouth and screamed.

"Stop that screaming!" Mamie hissed. "Stevie! Wake up!"

Stevie rolled over on his back and groaned, "What? What?"

"You were yelling in your sleep. How do you expect me to get . . . "

"Yeah?" He was awake now. "What was I talking about?"

"Her again," Mamie said, "and that Heath guy. I thought it was just crazy people who talked in their sleep."

"Maybe it is." He yawned. "What time is it?"

"I don't know. I just been lying here."

"Want to turn the light on?"

There was a creak of bedsprings as Mamie rolled off the bed and lurched over to the switch. She blinked her eyes and said, "Gawd!" when the glare struck her.

"Quarter to seven," Stevie said. "Maybe we can catch that sunrise after all."

"Oh, dry up about the sunrise. Charles Street is just as good as a lot of other streets. I'm out of cigarettes. You got any?"

Stevie reached into his pocket and brought out a package. He had been lying on it and the cigarettes were flat but they weren't broken.

"Tony and I often did this," Mamie said.

"Did what?"

"When we couldn't sleep we'd get up and turn on the light and smoke."

"I think that's real touching," Stevie said. "Though I may say that Tony's special brand of cigarettes stinks up the room."

"He's off reefers," Mamie said. "And if you don't like the stink why don't you go home? Why'd you come for in the first place?"

"Company. Same reason you let me stay."

"Well, I wouldn't of if I'd known you were going to talk all night in your sleep. Maybe you're going crazy."

Stevie flicked ashes on the rug. "Maybe."

"Raking up all that old stuff about Geraldine. A lot of other people die all the time."

"Too true," Stevie said.

"I got nothing on my conscience, about taking her place, I mean. I sent her a wreath, didn't I? And it wasn't anything anybody could help, like a murder. It was just an accident."

"Sure, and now there's going to be another."

"What?"

"He called for Geraldine and took her out and she died. He came tonight for Marcie . . ."

"Oh, you're nuts, Stevie!"

"I went and looked at his house tonight, before I came here. It was the middle of the night and the lights were on and the old man was out walking."

"Well, who cares?" Mamie flung herself across the bed. "Who in hell cares?"

"At first I thought it was him—Johnny—Johnny Heath. Listen, Mamie. You say that name to yourself, say it, go on."

"Johnny Heath," Mamie said in a bored voice. "So what?"

"Doesn't it give you a funny feeling? Because it sounds like he is. It sounds like the name of a guy who's got everything, money and looks and everything, including two of my girls. Say it again."

"Oh, for Christ's sake!"

"Johnny Heath. There, you get it? It sounds like he's got plate glass around him to separate him off as something special. He can do anything and nobody can touch him. He can get away with murder. Tonight when I saw his father I thought it was Johnny and that he'd just come from killing Marcie and the strain had aged him . . . Mamie."

"Yeah."

"Is there a phone around?"

"What for?"

"I thought I'd phone Marcie, see if she's all right."

"For the love of the Lord who made little green apples," Mamie said.

"I've got to phone."

"Haven't you done enough to get me kicked out of this place? You can't phone from here this time of morning. There's an all-night drugstore a couple of blocks up."

Stevie got off the couch and began brushing off his clothes.

"Leave me the cigarettes," Mamie said. "And buy a bottle of rye if you can."

"Sure, sure," Stevie said, but he hadn't heard her.

She waited up for the bottle of rye but Stevie didn't come back.

"She wasn't meant to come back," Ida said. "That's what I told you."

Alice walked toward her slowly. "What are you saying, Ida?"

"I'm saying she's dead," Ida said. She stood in the open door of Kelsey's room and the light streamed around her. She posed in it like a blowsy sibyl in a spotlight, her breasts jiggling. In the dark hall Alice was only a gray blur.

"Dead," Ida said. "Soaking in her own blood." She did not move aside to let Alice go into the room. Even when other doors opened and other gray blurs came into the hall Ida did not move. It was her moment, her corpse, her friend who had died, she had predicted it, she had found it, she was guarding it.

"Someone screamed?" Letty said uncertainly. "Alice, what is it?"

"What in hell?" Johnny said, and Ida's moment was over. He thrust her aside and strode into the room. When he came out he closed the door behind him and they were left in utter darkness. For a time no one spoke or moved.

"She killed herself," Johnny said into the darkness. "With a knife."

"The lights," Alice said. "Maurice."

"Yes, ma'am."

The lights sprang up and caught them stupid with sleep and shock.

"Dead?" Philip said as if he didn't know the word. He took a step toward the door.

"Don't go in," Johnny said sharply. "Don't any of you go in!" He caught Philip's arm and swung him around. "I'm telling you."

"That's right," Ida said softly. "She looks real bad. So much blood. All over the carpet."

Letty whirled savagely toward her. "Get back to your room and stay there!"

"I don't take no orders from you!"

"John." Alice's voice seemed to come from a distance. "Will you make everyone go away, John?"

She did not hear or see them go. She felt a hand on her shoulder and turned slowly.

"I thought I'd better stay," Letty said quietly. "Don't go in."

"Let me go in, Letty."

"No. She wanted to die. She had no peace in this world. Leave her alone, Alice."

"Like I told you," Ida said from the back of the hall, "she wasn't meant to come back."

"Get upstairs, you slut," Letty said.

Ida retreated slowly, lingering on each step, lolling against the banister. "Think you can shut me up . . . Another think coming . . ." Her voice faded into a mumble.

"I'd better phone," Letty said.

Alice repeated, "Phone?"

"We—I have to phone—somebody."

"The police."

"A doctor," Letty said, "A doctor first, anyway."

"Yes. What time is it?"

"Early. Not seven."

"Early," Alice said. "She wouldn't wake up and kill herself so early."

Letty looked down at her gaunt hands. "She wouldn't have known what time it was."

"No."

"And she always felt bad when she woke up. You remember how bad she felt, waking up and opening her eyes and not seeing anything. She said it was like waking up in a coffin with the lid nailed down. That's what she used to dream before she woke up, and I'd go in and find her beating her hands in the air to get the lid off. . . ."

"Don't, Letty."

"No."

"I have to see her, Letty."

"Yes, I guess you do," Letty said. She walked away, clutching her bathrobe together at the front. The belt was half off and trailed behind her along the rug. Alice watched the belt and when it had disappeared she went into Kelsey's room and closed the door.

Kelsey stared at the ceiling in eternal surprise. The ivory hilt of the knife lay between her breasts like a lover's finger and her mouth was open for a kiss. The blood had bubbled out like a fountain and splashed the bed and the rug and grown cold and dark and sluggish. Alice touched it with her finger.

CHAPTER 8

THOUGH it was not yet eight o'clock and Sands had been up most of the night he caught the phone on its third ring. He lifted the receiver and said softly, "Sands?" as if he wasn't quite sure whether he was Sands or not, or whether it mattered if he was or not.

He had no strong sense of identity. He lived alone with no wife or child or friend to call attention to himself or to look up or down at him. Because he lived in a vacuum he was able to understand and tolerate and sometimes to like the strange people he hunted. As insidiously as a worm burrows into an apple he burrowed into the lives of criminals and lay at the core, almost a part of it, yet remaining secretly and subtly himself.

"Sands?" he said.

"Sergeant D'Arcy speaking, sir. Sorry to bother you, sir."

"Go on." The apartment was cold and D'Arcy's zealous stupidity irritated him.

"A Dr. Loring just called in. He said he was at 1020 St. Clair. A girl committed suicide with a knife."

"Send McPhail up."

"Yes, sir, but I thought I'd better tell you first. The doctor doesn't think it was suicide. There's no blood on the girl's hands and the blow seemed too violent for a suicide. I thought you'd like to know."

"I like it very much," Sands said dryly. "I'll get there as soon as I can. Round up Joe and the rest of them and tell them to come up. Got that?"

"Oh, yes, sir."

Sands hung up. Shivering slightly he turned on the light and took off his pajamas. He dressed quickly, avoiding the sight of his own body because its frailty annoyed him. There were no mirrors in his apartment except the small shaving mirror in the bathroom, and even when he shaved he did not look at his face, only the patch of it he happened to be shaving. He would have preferred to be without face or body, if other people would conform. Since this was impossible he did the next best thing and ignored his possession of both to such an extent that he could not have described himself accurately on a police bulletin. He knew roughly that he was middle-sized and middle-aged but appeared taller because he was thin, and older, because he was constantly tired.

The tiredness was a nuisance in several ways. The wives of the other policemen thought Sands should have someone to look after him. They invited him frequently for meals and gave him ties for Christmas. Sands always wore the ties and in return got more ties.

He picked one at random off the rack, remembering instantly that it had been given to him last Christmas by Mrs. Lasky, wrapped in blue tissue paper with silver stars and fat angels of peace and good will pasted over the surface. Mauve was Mrs. Lasky's favorite color, and freely striped with deep red she found it irresistible. Inspector Lasky had died last spring, not from Mrs. Lasky's taste in ties, but from a bullet in his chest. Lasky had always handled the big robbery cases in the city and no one had been found to take his place. So now even Sands, who preferred more intellectual crimes, was sometimes called in to take charge of a robbery. He had just spent half the night at a small tavern in West Toronto.

The tavern-keeper himself had not been anxious to call the police, since the attempted robbery had taken place long after the legal closing hour. But one of the customers had called, and eventually Sands had gone to bed thinking of the fingerprints on the glasses that matched the fingerprints of an ex-convict who had been honest, or discreet, for ten years. Though Murillo had been young when convicted of peddling marihuana and his sentence had been light, he was listed as potentially dangerous because he was an addict and carried a knife.

Hardly dangerous any longer, Sands thought knotting his tie. Stupid enough to sit around drinking and scattering his fingerprints all over the place. The last entry on Murillo's card had been made five years ago and stated that he was living with a singer, Mamie Rosen, and had no visible means of support.

Sands went into the kitchen and plugged in the coffee percolator. While he was waiting he wrote some memos in the small book he always carried in his vest pocket: "Get Higgins to pick up Tony Murillo. See Mamie Rosen. *Insist* D'Arcy's adenoids."

He drank his coffee, looking at the last note, and then stroked it out reluctantly. It was surprising how many large irritations a man could tolerate, yet find himself overwhelmed by a pair of whistling adenoids.

He rinsed out the coffee cup and began to wonder about the girl who had committed suicide at 1020 St. Clair.

"Detective-Inspector Sands," he told the butler. His voice was a little surer when he used his official title, as if the mere placing of himself within a group had strengthened his own identity.

"Yes, sir," Maurice said. "Will you come in, sir?"

"I believe I will," Sands said. He had a trick of sounding slightly surprised which made his listeners think uneasily that they had said something very obvious or stupid.

Flushing slightly, Maurice stepped back from the door and Sands came inside.

"Doctor still here?"

"Yes, sir."

"Where's a telephone?"

Maurice fixed his eyes on the red and mauve tie and said after a pause, "In the kitchen. This way, sir."

Sands laid his hat and coat carefully on the table reserved for calling cards and followed Maurice down the hall, smiling faintly at Maurice's back.

Though the lights were all turned on the house seemed to be deserted, the kitchen shining and spotless as if the cook had cleaned up and vanished without leaving even a footprint on the floor.

"Nice floor," he said. "What is it?"

"Red concrete," Maurice said coldly.

"Oh. Hello, Sylvia. Tom up yet? Rout him out, will you, and tell him to read my report at headquarters and pick up Tony Murillo. Murillo will have to be identified so Tom had better prepare a line-up. Thanks."

He hung up, dialed another number. "D'Arcy? Sands. I'm at St. Clair. Send the usual right away. No, very quiet."

Maurice said, "The—the body is upstairs."

"What's the name?"

"Heath, Miss Kelsey Heath."

"Heath?" Sands frowned. "Wasn't there something a few years ago?"

"An accident, sir. Miss Kelsey was in an accident. She was blinded."

"All right. Let's go up. What's your name?"

"Maurice King."

"All right."

The second floor was deserted like the first, and all the doors were shut. Behind one of them a man was talking in a low nervous rumble, but there were no sounds of excitement or grief.

"This is the room," Maurice said.

"Thanks. Anyone touch the knob?"

"Yes, sir."

"You don't have to wait."

Maurice muttered something under his breath and walked unsteadily away from the door. Sands went in alone. His movements were brisk as if he were eager to get started. But the briskness was forced. This was the moment he dreaded, this first sight of a body, the staring eyes, the sagging mouth, the stiffening limbs.

There was a trail of blood on the blue carpet widening at the bed. Sands stepped across it and touched Kelsey's forehead lightly. It was very cold. He brushed his hand on his coat and moved back from the bed.

The hole in the girl's breast was wide and deep, the skin jagged as if the person who thrust the knife there could not thrust deeply enough to satisfy his violence and had to rip the skin. A powerful hand had held the knife, a hand driven by hate or rage.

No suicide certainly. It was the wrong weapon and the wrong place. Knives weren't used for suicide by women, and even men used them to cut their wrists or throats and did not attempt to thrust a knife past the heavy bone that protected the heart. And this girl's hands were thin and weak-looking and bore no bloodstains. Besides, her very blindness would have made her hand uncertain, and the hand that held the knife had not been uncertain.

Sands walked back to the door, looked around the room again. After a time he moved toward the bureau looking intently at a small silver box which lay on its top. There were several short scratches around the lock. Covering his hand with a handkerchief Sands lifted the lid. The lock had been forced but the box was still crammed carelessly with jewels. A forced lock but the jewels still there. For an instant he had been reminded of something, something recent and puzzling. But it slipped his mind. A new fact was jabbing at his consciousness. It was the smell in the room.

A sick, sweet, cloying smell, more pungent than the odor of fresh blood. A drug, perhaps. Had the girl been sick? If she had, perhaps the lights had been left on in the room. The sureness of the blow argued for that. An easy time the murderer had had—the lights on, and the girl sleeping and blind, without even the frail defense of eyes and ears.

He opened the door into the hall and as he stepped out he caught a glimpse of a woman disappearing around the bend at the back of the hall. Her footsteps were inaudible but he heard the creak of a board in the stairs.

He tensed himself to run after her, had already taken a step forward before he caught himself up. Then he stood quietly, smiling to himself. I'm like a damn dog, he thought, I can't see anything running away without wanting to run after it.

The smile lingered but he was uneasy. He did not expect to be spied on in this house with its rows of closed doors and its atmosphere of genteel whispers and unobtrusive wealth.

He became aware that something else was watching him. There was a soft thump from the other end of the hall. He turned his head quickly and saw two eyes staring at him carefully but without personal interest. A huge German shepherd dog lay around the bend of the banister with only his head sticking out.

"Hello," Sands said. Conscious of the inadequacy of this address he added, "Hello, dog."

The dog blinked slowly.

"All right," Sands said. "Be nasty then. Where's Maurice? Go and get Maurice."

There was no movement at all this time.

Sands smiled cautiously. "So you just don't give a damn." He raised his voice.

A door beside him opened abruptly and a girl came into the hall.

"Maurice!"

"I'm sorry," she said. "I didn't know you were here. I was waiting for you. I'm Alice Heath."

"Inspector Sands," he told her.

"Come in here, please. Dr. Loring is in here."

She stood aside and the light fell full on her face for just an instant. Not a pretty face, Sands thought, too bloodless and tight, but its bones were small and beautiful, and it wore an expression of gentleness which might have been real gentleness or the kind that came from rigid control.

He went through the door, noticing her hand on the knob. A firm grip but not too firm. Again the word control came to his mind. He felt then that he was going to admire Alice Heath but never to like her, that she was the kind of woman a man recommended as a wife for his friends but not for himself.

"This is Dr. Loring, Inspector Sands," she said.

A tall young man rose from a corner of the small sitting room. His face looks as if he had slept in it, Sands thought.

"Glad to know you," Sands said. He held out his hand but Loring didn't see it.

He said in a cracked voice, "I—I have been guilty of criminal . . . "

"Please sit down," Alice said calmly.

"Criminal negligence," Loring said. "I expect to be

struck off the register when the story gets out. I have no excuse."

"You're the family doctor?" Sands said.

"No. No, I'm a psychiatrist. I have no excuse at all except that I was tired and I thought the report could wait until today."

"What report?"

"The girl was poisoned last night," Loring said.

"I'm quite sure Dr. Loring is mistaken." Alice said in a clear cold voice. "Naturally he is upset."

"Morphine," Loring said. "A grain or more of morphine. She had talked of killing herself but she was blind. How could she have gotten the stuff? And then this morning—she couldn't have driven that knife in herself."

"There are some men in the hall," Alice said.

Sands said, "Thanks," and went out.

Three of the men were already in Kelsey's room. The fourth, carrying a medical bag, was in the hall talking to the dog.

"Hello, Sutton," Sands said.

"Hello," Sutton said. "Nice dog."

"Yes. Nice day, too."

"I've always wanted a dog."

"Get one in your spare time," Sands said dryly.

Sutton grimaced and disappeared into Kelsey's room. Sands stood in the doorway watching the men work. They were well-trained, he had trained them himself, and it was his boast that they could collect more useless information than any group their size in Canada.

Sands went back to the small sitting room. Alice Heath had gone, but Loring was pacing up and down the room smoking. The delay in telling his story had unnerved him completely as Sands had hoped.

"You've got to *listen* to me!" Loring cried.

"Why, of course," Sands said quietly. "Go ahead."

"I—I didn't know whether the girl had taken the stuff herself or not. I intended to hold off my report until I got in touch with Miss Alison. She's the nurse who was attending Mrs. Heath when she died a year and a half ago. There was some morphine left over, I understand, and that could have been the stuff the girl used."

"There are other ways of getting morphine."

Loring shook his head. "This morphine came from a prescription. You know yourself that since the war started

80

bootleg morphine is so doctored with sugar of milk that hundreds of addicts are almost cured and don't know it. The stuff could hardly injure a cat. Aside from her blindness, Kelsey Heath was in good health and morphine had never been prescribed for her. Or for the rest of the household."

Sands said, "The rest of the household being . . . ?"

"Alice Heath, her father, her brother John, and Kelsey's fiancé, Philip James; and the servants, the butler, a nurse Letty, a maid Ida and the cook and another maid who is on holiday. I haven't seen the cook."

"I see," Sands said. "You seem to know the family well."

"I don't know any of them!" Loring shouted. "I never even saw any of them until yesterday afternoon! What I know of the family Alice Heath told me. She came to my office yesterday afternoon. She had made an appointment in the morning by phone. She said she wanted to consult me about her sister."

"Why?"

"She thought her sister was—was becoming unreasonable."

"Unreasonable," Sands said, "meaning crazy?"

"Not exactly."

"But exactly enough. Did you see the sister?"

"When I did she was unconscious from the morphine."

"You have only Alice Heath's word for the mental symptoms, then?"

Loring glanced up sharply. "Yes."

"Nice build-up."

"What do you mean?"

"Doubt is cast on Kelsey Heath's sanity and Kelsey Heath conveniently commits suicide as insane people often do. Also conveniently, she dies before a psychiatrist has a talk with her. Verdict: suicide while of unsound mind."

"But why?" Loring said. "Why?"

"I just gave you one reason, a build-up for suicide. There might be a second reason, connected with Kelsey Heath's will." He smiled briefly. "Loring, you've been used."

"For the love of God," Loring whispered. He stumbled into a chair.

"It is a cruel world, yes," Sands said. "Still, you're a

pretty big boy now and a psychiatrist as well as a big boy."

"I hadn't any idea, any remotest idea. . . . "

Sands said dryly, "You were told that Kelsey Heath talked of killing herself, I suppose?"

"Yes. But I thought that was natural enough. She was young and pretty and engaged to be married, and then suddenly she was blinded. It would produce a terrible emotional conflict, especially in a girl of her type, who was used to having everything. It would be more than enough to cause suicide in her case though perhaps not in a normal girl brought up in normal surroundings by well-adjusted parents."

Sands let him talk about emotional conflicts and the Heath family. After a time he interrupted. "What did Alice Heath want you to do about her sister?"

"Just talk to her," Loring said. "Reason with her."

"And eventually put her away some place?"

"Nothing was said of that," Loring replied stiffly. "Miss Heath was aware that the atmosphere in the house was unhealthy for both her brother and Mr. James and she wanted me to arrange it so they would leave."

He tugged at his collar. "I know it sounds fantastic today but I'm used to things that sound fantastic. I had no suspicions. If you only wouldn't make comments in that voice . . . "

"What voice?"

"Cold reason. You can't explain everything if you use cold reason."

"Have you ever tried?" Sands asked grimly.

Loring flushed. "I realize I'm not appearing at my best in this affair. But you can't think straight when your career is due to blow up any minute."

"Any other doctor involved?"

"Hale of the General helped me but I consulted him and it was my duty to report the poisoning, not his."

"And why didn't you? You said you were too tired, you thought it would wait until morning. Were you too tired to pick up a phone?"

"No."

"Do you have to be coaxed?" Sands said coldly.

"I—I intended to wait and come back this morning to question the girl. If I found that she had taken the morphine herself with the help of Ida I wouldn't have reported it at all. I don't like the laws governing attempted suicides and I was prepared to try and help the girl myself without reference to the police and without having her committed to an institution."

"You sound as if you thought that one up all by yourself. But you didn't. It's been done before and will be done again. Who's Ida?"

"A maid."

"Why should she help the girl kill herself? Love or money?"

"A dash of both," Loring said grimly. "Ida has spiritual contacts with tea leaves and the tea leaves revealed that Kelsey Heath was going to die. To a person of Ida's class the teacup is as omniscient as the newspaper is to the class above Ida's. If the death was inevitable, why not help it along and preserve your contacts?"

"Is Ida fat?" Sands said.

Loring frowned at him. "Why? Yes, she is."

"I think I've met her, at a distance."

He took out his notebook and wrote a concise report of the poisoning and Loring's part in it. He did not ask Loring to sign a formal statement of the facts. Loring noticed the omission.

"What do you intend to do about me?" he asked.

"Not a thing," Sands said, closing the book and replacing it in his pocket. Yet."

"You have to report me."

"Do I?"

"I'd rather you did it right away."

"You seem anxious," Sands said. "Don't you like being a psychiatrist?"

"I don't know what . . . "

"Watch those emotional conflicts," Sands said and closed the door behind him. From Kelsey's room came the busy sounds of men at work. Waste of time to go in, he thought. The men knew more than he did about what to do. He hesitated, not wanting to go downstairs and listen to Alice Heath and her brother and her father and Philip James. They would all claim to be in bed and asleep when the girl was killed in the middle of the night.

"Hssst!"

Sands turned his head quickly.

"Hssst!"

The whistle came from the back of the hall. Sands

could see nothing but a whitish shape. He walked toward it.

"Yes?" he said.

"Hush."

When he came to the end of the hall the white shape emerged as a fat girl in a uniform. She was leaning against the banister of the back stairs sucking her finger. She took her finger out of her mouth and wiped it on her apron. Then she looked up again and smiled slyly at Sands.

"Hello," she said softly.

"Hello."

"I'm Ida."

"Well, hello, Ida," Sands said.

"I found her."

"Well?"

"Sure."

"How nice," Sands said, thinking that monosyllables were a pleasant change but they didn't get you anywhere. "Do you want to tell me about it?"

"Why, sure," Ida said.

CHAPTER 9

WHEN Mr. Heath woke up in the morning the sun was pushing in at his window like a big bold blonde.

He opened his eyes and lay suspended between the two worlds of sleeping and waking, a man floating in air with nothing to clutch at. There was no returning to the safe world of sleep. It had been shattered by the sun, it had exploded like a bomb, and he was going up, up, up. . . . A scream formed inside his throat—"No! No! No!"—the protest of a corpse thrust into life again.

But it was only a little scream after all, barely a whisper, the plea of a man who recognized the uselessness of his pleading. His ears and eyes denied this new world but his mind crept toward it, painfully, gradually, and he began to be aware of himself, almost as if he were watching the birth of a grown man and the screams were screams of pain as he squeezed out of the womb. Yet when the birth was over he was complete. He had a body and a name, he had a house to live in and two daughters and a son, and once he had had a wife.

His hands fumbled out of the blankets and he reached over to touch her.

"Isobel?"

She was not there. He wasn't surprised that she wasn't there, but he wouldn't have been surprised if she had been. Anything was possible in this strange world. There was no harm in saying, "Isobel?" to make sure, because there was no one else there to make time relative for him. His mind knew no years or hours, only Isobels and Kelseys and Maurices.

"No! No!" The scream was nearly gone from his throat, it had fled before its own futility.

Because here he was, awake and living, here was the body, the house, the sun, the curtains blowing in and out as if they were breathing. Like an oxygen tent—in and out, in and out. That was how they made Isobel breathe in the end, they had pumped oxygen in and out of her all night, and in the morning Alice had come into his room and said, "She just died, Father."

"Father . . . "

Here was Alice, standing beside his bed. She had come to tell him all over again. That was a little surprising if you knew Alice, but not very surprising. Perhaps Alice had lost her place in time, as he had, or had come to realize that it wasn't very important after all.

"Father, are you awake?"

"Yes," he said. "Yes, I'm awake. I know. You don't have to tell me again. You've just lost your place, Alice."

"Wake up, Father," she said. "I have something to tell you."

"I know what it is."

"You—you heard the noise?"

"No. No noise," he said. "It was very quiet."

"Kelsey is dead."

She sat down on the bed as if she were going to try and comfort him with her touch. But her hands remained motionless in her lap. "I'm sorry I had to wake you, Father, but she didn't die—naturally."

"Kelsey?" He blinked at her, trying to blink away the mist in front of his eyes. Alice looked funny through the mist, as if she had grown fur which blurred her outlines. "You're sure?"

He knew what a silly question that was. Alice was always sure of everything. You could depend on Alice for facts, but for nothing else, nothing else at all.

"She was killed," Alice said. "The police are here and they say she was killed. They want to talk to you."

"Now? Before breakfast?"

"I've asked Maurice to bring you your coffee up here."

Ah, that was better. Once you had your coffee you knew where you were. You became adjusted to this world of waking, you were prepared for anything. Kelsey was dead. After coffee he would think about that, he would get used to the idea. You simply had to subtract one daughter and familiarize yourself with the remaining sum. Merely a problem in arithmettic.

"Thank you, Alice," he said.

She recognized her dismissal and rose from the bed. "Is there anything I could get you?"

"No, thank you."

"Father," she said, but the moment for weeping, for mingling tears, for the touch of hands in love and understanding and sorrow—that moment was gone. She turned to the door, her head drooping a little to one side in a gesture of hopelessness and submission. The moment had gone, no use trying to bring it back. There was only the faintest echo in her mind of the questions she had asked as a child: "Why are we like this? Why must we be? Why can't we change?"

To a child's questions there could only be a child's answer, "Because." The answer had walked across her mind so often that the track was worn deep, the "Because," was there without even the "Why?"

These things are, have been, will be, must be. Let yourself be acted upon by the fates, keep your face blank, don't squirm, if you move, the finger will move after you.

She closed the door of her father's room and walked away. She made no conscious attempt to forget that moment of uncertainty when she had almost reached over to comfort her father and demand comfort in return. But she did forget. The skin of her heart was loose like a lion's skin, and when the lion is wounded, the skin moves to cover the wound and stop the bleeding.

At the bottom of the stairs she met Maurice carrying a silver tray with a pot of coffee and a little pitcher of cream and a silver fingerbowl, floating two yellow rosebuds. He saw her staring at the rosebuds.

"I—I hope you don't mind, ma'am."

"No, of course not," Alice said. Yet she did mind. The rosebuds were a symbol to her of all the futile gestures that had been made in the house.

"How did he take the news, Miss Alice?"

"Very well," Alice said automatically. "You must stay with him until he has his coffee and then help him dress. The policeman is waiting to talk to him."

Maurice made clucking noises of sympathy. "It's a shame, Miss Alice, for the police to come bothering him at his age."

Alice looked at him, smiling slightly. "At his age, Maurice? Father is your age, fifty-three, isn't it?"

"Yes, ma'am." Maurice returned her smile, but he looked shocked and he unconsciously straightened his shoulders. "Yes, ma'am, I'll help him dress."

He went up the steps, trying to sound very brisk and youthful. The springy patter of his steps said, *I may be fifty-three but how am I doing?*

But when he reached the third floor he was panting and some of the cream had spilled out of the pitcher and the rosebuds had dived and come up gleaming with water. He stopped a minute to catch his breath and wipe away the cream with his handkerchief. There was a damp stain on the napkin but Mr. Heath wouldn't notice, he was too old.

Mr. Heath didn't notice the stain or the rosebuds or even Maurice until Maurice cleared his throat loudly and said, "Your coffee, sir."

"Ah?"

"Your coffee, sir."

"Coffee?"

"Yes, sir."

"Ah."

Maurice set the tray on the small table beside the bed. He moved calmly, but there was a panic bubbling up inside him. *I'm not that old, I'm not that old.*

"Cream, sir?"

"Yes, sir," Mr. Heath said. "Thank you, sir."

Maurice's hands were shaking. Some more cream jumped out of the pitcher.

"Miss Alice asked me to stay and help you dress," Maurice said. "If you prefer I'll wait out in the hall until you finish your coffee."

Mr. Heath looked at him over the rim of the coffee cup. His eyes were pleasantly puzzled like the eyes of a man who has just heard a joke he doesn't understand but is willing to laugh anyway.

"Why?" he said.

"Well, I thought you might like to be alone, sir," Maurice said weakly, "in view of—in view of your grief."

Mr. Heath bent his head and Maurice saw that he was chuckling silently to himself. He turned his back, flushing with vicarious shame. There was no grief here, there was nothing.

He stood stiffly at the window while Mr. Heath finished his coffee. Then he brought out the clothes from the closet, laying them carefully across a chair, while Mr. Heath watched him with an expression of wary interest. He looked more alive than he had for a long time and he refused to let Maurice help him remove his pajamas.

"Do you think I can't even dress myself?"

In the end Maurice had to help him with his tie. They went downstairs together, Maurice staying a little way behind. During the whole two flights of stairs Maurice kept his hand out in front of him like a watchful mother ready to rescue a tottering infant. The gesture was partly protective but it was defensive too, another denial: *I'm as old as he is but compare the two of us.*

Inspector Sands was waiting for them in the drawing room. Alice was with him and Mr. Heath knew when he walked in, shaking off Maurice's hand, that Alice had been talking about him.

She said, "My father. Inspector Sands." There was a faint note of apology in her voice, and a half-smug, half-embarrassed expression in her eyes when she looked at Sands. She might have been saying: *Here he is, what did I tell you? You're wasting your time.*

"Do you want me to stay with you, Father?"

"No, I don't." He glanced at her with distaste and motioned toward the door. When the door had opened and closed again he turned to Sands and smiled.

"Alice talks too much," he said in a surprisingly strong voice. "Don't you think so? However. You may smoke if you like. We have all had to give up smoking in this house because of Kelsey, but now that Kelsey is dead, go right ahead."

It was the longest speech he had made in years. It exhilarated him and whipped the blood into his cheeks. Whatever Alice had told this policeman about him was canceled out now by the *urbanity* of this speech. Very urbane. Even the policeman was impressed by it, almost awed, in fact.

"Thanks," Sands said. He did not reach for his cigarettes. "I noticed there were no ashtrays. Your daughter objected to smoking?"

Mr. Heath leaned forward eagerly in his chair. "Yes, and I know why. Nobody else does. But perhaps you're not interested. It's difficult to talk when nobody listens to you."

"I'll listen."

"Well, you see my wife didn't like smoking. It all goes back to Isobel; you will find that nearly everything goes back to Isobel. She was an amazing woman. Kelsey is— was—like her. Isobel objected to smoking but Kelsey objected to Isobel's objection and smoked anyway. Then when Isobel died Kelsey objected again." He smiled anxiously at Sands. "You see? Kelsey was carrying on for her mother. There was some nonsense talked about Kelsey objecting to smoking because Philip was lighting a cigarette at the time of the accident. But it really goes back to Isobel, as everything does."

"Even the murder?" Sands said.

"Murder?" Mr. Heath repeated. "Kelsey was murdered?"

"She was killed with the fruit knife that lay on the table beside her bed."

"Murdered *in this house?*"

"She was in bed," Sands said. "It was the middle of the night."

Mr. Heath leaned his head back against the chair. His color was gone and his voice was faint and querulous. "I'm tired. I'm too tired to talk."

"Your wife left her money all to Kelsey, I understand."

"Yes. All of it."

"Outright?"

"No," Mr. Heath said wearily. "That was not Isobel's way. She left the money to Kelsey and when Kelsey died the money was to go to all of us."

"Including Philip James?"

"Philip was to get a little of it, a monthly allowance, as long as he continued with his music. Isobel liked to think of herself as a patroness of the arts."

"The servants?"

"Bequests for all, except the new girl Ida."

Sands opened his notebook. There was no evidence of disappointment in his expression, but he thought, Kelsey Heath had no will and couldn't have made one, so Loring couldn't have been used for the purpose of overthrowing a will.

A sentence from the notebook struck his eyes: "He went out because I heard him, and he wasn't in when I went to bed because I looked and he wasn't."

He said, "You were out last night?"

"Yes."

"What time did you leave?"

"I don't know—early."

"You weren't here when Kelsey became ill and the doctor was called about nine or so?"

"Ill? Doctor? No, no, I wasn't here."

"You left before nine, Sands said, "and returned when?"

"I'm sorry," Mr. Heath said in a low voice. "I can't remember."

"Late?"

"Late, yes. There was something about matches. Out there." He gestured out the windows to the front of the house.

"Someone was there?"

"Yes."

"On the driveway?"

"Yes—no, not on the driveway. Driving. Someone was in a car out there."

"He lit a match and you saw him?"

"No. No, he hadn't any matches."

"You talked to him?"

Mr. Heath pressed his hands against his eyes. "He hadn't any matches. No, he did have some. I remember he had some matches. But I remember the other, too, that he didn't have any."

"Don't try," Sands said easily. "It will come back. Ever smoke yourself?"

Mr. Heath looked around guiltily. "Well, yes. Sometimes, in my room. I've got a room on the third floor."

"Have one," Sands said. He held out his cigarette case and Mr. Heath reached out his hand to take one.

"He wanted some matches," he said suddenly. "Then he discovered that he had some, a whole boxful. He showed it to me."

"A big box of big wooden matches?"

"No, in paper packets. The kind with advertisements on the cover."

"Advertisements like dog food, coal, restaurants . . ."

"Joey's!" Mr. Heath shouted. "Something about Joey's!" He was shaking with excitement and could barely hold his cigarette to the match Sands offered.

"Joey's Nightclub," Sands said.

"That was it!" Whatever Alice had said about him she'd have to take back now. He had remembered the matches and the young man sitting behind the wheel of the car looking pale and scared.

"He was frightened about something," Mr. Heath said. "I put my head down and looked in the window because I wasn't sure what he had asked for. When he saw me he seemed startled as if he'd seen a ghost. *And he knew me. The man knew me. He called me by name.*"

"He was a stranger to you?" Sands asked quietly.

"Yes, yes, I thought he was a stranger, but if he knew me . . ." He turned his head away. "Perhaps he wasn't a stranger. Nobody knows me except the people who come to the house."

"Your son is well known."

"Johnny. Yes, everyone knows Johnny. He was captain of the rugby team at McGill for two years."

"He looks like you."

"He does? You think he looks like me?"

"Very much."

"Ah, no. He was Isobel's son. She wouldn't have allowed him to look like me."

"But he does. You don't know where there's an ashtray?"

They both looked solemnly around the room but there was no ashtray.

"I usually use my pants cuffs in moments like this," Sands said. "But I haven't any cuffs."

"I haven't either," Mr. Heath said. He looked pleased and self-conscious like a schoolboy conspiring with his hero. "There's that vase over there."

A Greek black-figured vase stood on the mantel, alone and important. Sands lifted it off the mantel and passed it to Mr. Heath. They both flicked their ashes into it, then Sands placed the vase on the floor between their chairs.

"Isobel," Mr. Heath said.

"Pardon?"

"I said, that's Isobel."

"Oh. Where?"

"In the vase."

"Is it?"

"Yes, that's Isobel."

Sands looked inside the vase and there, sure enough, was Isobel, pulverized beyond recognition. He replaced the vase carefully on the mantel and brushed his hands on his trousers.

"Well," he said, "if it'd been me I wouldn't have minded."

"Ashes to ashes."

"Exactly."

Their voices were grave, but when Sands turned he saw that Mr. Heath was shaking with silent laughter. His whole huge body was convulsed and when the waves of laughter had subsided he had to wipe the moisture out of his eyes with a handkerchief.

His voice was choked. "I—haven't had—so much fun —in years!"

"Well," Sands said, smiling. "That's fine." He waited for a minute until Mr. Heath was sober again. Then he said, "I'm interested in your stranger with the box of matches. Do you remember his face?"

"I remember that it was young and frightened."

"Good, bad or indifferent?"

"Good, I think," Mr. Heath said slowly. "But he had his hat pulled down and I can't be sure."

"How did he discover that he had some matches after all? Did he look for some?"

"No. They were there on the seat beside him all the time. That was how I saw the name Joey's. It was printed across the top of the box. Funny how you've made me remember all this."

"Mnemonic midwifery," Sands said. "Part of my job. What kind of car was he driving?"

"There was nothing unusual about it that I can recall. Neither new nor old. I don't notice cars much. I never had a car. I used Isobel's."

"I hope I'm not tiring you."

"No, you're not! That's what they're always saying and never giving me a chance to talk!"

"Do you remember anything else about the young man?"

"His voice. I don't know much about anything else but I do like to listen to voices," he said with pride. "I used to be a musician in a small way and I have perfect pitch. I don't mean that as a boast because actually perfect pitch isn't much help in the long run. But I use it to amuse myself. Isobel used to talk on middle C. She was a monotone, so much that when she was angry her voice simply rose a whole octave to the next C. It was very interesting."

"A gift like yours would come in very handy in my profession."

"Would it?" Mr. Heath flushed with pleasure. "Well, most people talk on just three or four notes normally. Have you heard Philip talk?"

"Yes," Sands said. "Nice voice."

"He has a very expressive voice. It changes from second to second and without sounding affected he can use a whole octave to express one idea. If you stand far enough away so you can't hear his actual words his talking sounds like music played on a bad instrument."

"And the stranger's voice?"

"Like Philip's, but coarser than Philip's. It was almost a professional voice, strong and husky like a sideshow barker's." He glanced up apologetically. "Of course I'm merely guessing. He might have had a cold or he might drink too much."

Sands' pen paused over his notebook. His mind went back to the matches. Not long ago he had had a packet of matches, with Joey's Nightclub printed on the cover. The hat-check girl had given it to him when he was leaving the club. She had taken it out of a box.

What kind of customer received a whole box of them?

93

A friend of the hat-check girl's? Or a friend of Joey's? Or a customer who spent very freely?

The young man in the ordinary car wouldn't belong to the last group. It was odd, if you knew Joey, that anyone at all had been given a whole box. Joey respected the cent and he was still in business while other and better night-clubs had had the life span of a fruit fly.

A young man with a husky voice and an ordinary car and a box of matches . . .

"Did he drive away after you left?"

Mr. Heath hesitated. "No, I don't think so. I didn't hear the sound of a motor."

"Ignition was turned off, then?"

"Yes."

"And it was very late?"

"Yes."

"But he couldn't have been waiting for you because no one knew you were going out."

"No one at all. He could have been told, of course, but he'd have no reason to wait for me. I didn't know him."

"But he knew you."

"Yes."

"You have no way of estimating the time?"

"No—I—but Kelsey's light was on. Perhaps she hadn't gone to sleep yet."

"I think she was already dead then," Sands said. "Alice had turned the light off at twelve when she went to bed. You heard nothing, no noise, from Kelsey's room when you went through the hall?"

"No noise—then."

"Later?"

"Later, yes, when I was on the third floor. I thought I heard—Isobel. She was running along the hall."

But the fog was coming over him again. Sands could tell that from the uncertainty in his voice, the vagueness in his eyes.

Sands left him sitting in front of the fireplace. He wasn't comfortable about leaving him alone in the room with Isobel sitting on the mantel. Ashes or no ashes. Isobel wasn't quite dead.

CHAPTER 10

BEFORE the first show went on at nine o'clock Joey himself came backstage. He didn't go back very often, he left it to Stevie to see that the girls were ready on time, their squabbles settled without scratching and their costumes fit to be viewed by the pure in heart.

But tonight he went back himself and stood for a minute inside the door. The girls were ready, clustered in small groups, twittering and chirping. They became quiet gradually when they saw him; they were a little afraid of this soft-voiced, hard-eyed man who signed their checks every second Monday.

"Break it up," Joey said.

They broke it up but they didn't come any closer to him. Marcie emerged from the dressing room wrapped in a long black cape. Stevie appeared too, quite suddenly, as if he'd dropped from the ceiling.

"My master's voice," he said.

Joey didn't look at him. "There's a special guest out front. He didn't bring his ten-year-old son but act like he did. Keep everything clean."

"The cleanest show in town," Stevie said, but he couldn't be heard above the girls: "What do you mean?" "Who's out there?" "Why my own mother says it's a swell show!"

"That's all," Joey said. "Except—Mamie."

Mamie looked at him sulkily. "Yeah?"

"It's your job to make the customers sad, pleasantly sad, not to make them commit suicide. Get it?"

The girls giggled. Mamie took a step forward, her dark eyes already brimming with tears.

"Yeah, but Joey, you don't know—it's Tony. . . . "

"Dry up," Stevie said to her. "O.K., girls, go and lock

95

yourselves in the dressing room. We'll be a little late tonight."

"We will, will we?" Joey said softly.

Stevie waited until they had disappeared. "Who's out there?"

"A cop."

"A cop. Well, what of it? Don't cops relax?"

"Not this one," Joey said, "and not here."

"Which one is it?"

"He didn't introduce himself and he didn't tell me he was a cop. I just happen to know."

"Oh."

"What difference does it make to you?" Joey said dryly. "You're wearing enough clothes and you don't shake your rear. He was here a couple of weeks ago, too."

"He was?" Stevie drew in his breath. "That's swell."

"You haven't been doing anything, Jordan?"

"Not a thing."

"Well, neither have I," Joey said. "But it gives me the same kind of feeling I get when I cross the border. I never have a damn thing on me but I always feel I have."

"Guilty conscience."

"Yeah. Ready now?"

"Sure."

"Stay away from the booze tonight, Jordan. The boys will bring you cold tea. On my orders."

Stevie went with him to the door. "Which one is he?"

"Left. Second table from the floor. Alone."

Stevie looked out. After Joey had gone he kept the door open a little and looked out again, for a long time.

There was nothing to show that the man was a cop. He was quite small and even from a distance Stevie could see his little black moustache. Just an ordinary man in a dinner jacket. Maybe Joey was wrong. . . .

But he knew Joey wasn't wrong. Once you knew the man was a cop you found all sorts of reasons for believing it. The way he sat, motionless, almost rigid, as if his very muscles were determined not to relax or to have a good time. Some of the wives sat like that, the wives who didn't drink and came along just to keep an eye on their husbands.

Stevie closed the door. There was sweat on the palms of his hands and he was trembling, but he couldn't resist reading it once more. He took the clipping out of his pocket.

"The death occurred suddenly last night of Kelsey Heath in her twenty-eighth year, at the home of her father, Thomas Heath, 1020 St. Clair Avenue. Miss Heath had been in ill health for some time. Funeral arrangements have not been completed. She is survived by her father, a sister, Alice, and a brother, John. Please omit flowers."

The orchestra faded, there was a pause, a roll of drums.

That was for him. He replaced the clipping and smoothed back his hair and lifted the curtain. He walked briskly on to the floor and there was a smattering of applause, a dying down of many voices and finally a hush.

"Hel-*lo!*" Stevie said. "So some of you came back and even brought your friends. . . . "

He talked for five minutes, fast, not even giving them a chance to laugh. They didn't laugh much anyway at the first show. Then he walked around the floor, still talking, pausing at some of the tables, asking a question or two, getting blushes and giggles and soft embarrassed answers.

"And what did *you* do to deserve this lovely lady?"

A laugh, a whisper from the man, "I guess I'm just lucky," a blush from the lady, a yell from the crowd.

The spotlight swerved, rested for an instant on the solitary figure in the dinner jacket. The man looked across at Stevie. He didn't even blink at the spotlight, he just stared without moving.

It seemed to Stevie that the whole crowd was aware of it, there was a deadly quiet as if they had all withdrawn and left him alone to face this man.

"Break it up," somebody shouted.

"Sorry, folks, I just had a hot flash. Must have been something I et, or maybe something I drenk."

The spotlight moved with him and the man with the staring eyes dissolved into darkness.

Stevie walked off the floor five minutes before he should have, and the girls came on. He usually sat at one of the tables and ordered a drink while the girls were dancing, but tonight he went right out through the curtain.

The door of the dressing room was open but he rapped anyway, and said, "Marcie?"

She came out, with the long black cape clutched around her. She looked ill and her eyes were red-rimmed and slightly swollen.

"What's the matter?" Stevie said.

"Nothing." She leaned against the wall, a tired little bat with folded wings and the face of a girl. "Flu, maybe!"

"I've got something to show you."

"What?"

"From a newspaper."

"I saw it."

"Tough on you," Stevie said.

"Why me?" She opened her eyes wide.

"Tough on him, then, on Johnny Heath. So I guess it's tough on you, if you love him."

Her black wings stirred a little. "Don't tell anybody."

"About what?"

"Johnny and me."

"Why not?"

"I don't want to get into this at all. I don't see why I should have to." She came closer to him and spoke in a whisper. "One of them came to the house this afternoon. He said he was an insurance agent. He said Johnny had taken out a policy in favor of me and that he had to come around to check up. He asked me if Johnny and I were going to be married. I got suspicious because I'd never heard of insurance agents doing that, and Johnny never said anything about an insurance agent, so I made an excuse and went out into the hall and phoned Johnny. . . ."

"Yeah," Stevie said. "Yeah."

"So Johnny told me, he said somebody had killed her and I was to keep quiet if anybody asked me questions about us. And then"—she gulped—"somebody else was on the phone, because a man said, 'That's enough, Heath.'"

"Yeah."

"So I hung up. I went back and told the insurance agent that he was mistaken and that Johnny was just an old friend and wouldn't have taken out a policy in my favor. He knew I knew, then, but he went away without saying anything else." She put her hand on his arm. "Stevie. Joey said there was a cop here tonight."

"There is."

"What's he like? Is he—is he big, with a red face and gray hair?"

"He's small. No red face."

"Oh." She smiled shakily. "Just a coincidence. It's not *my* cop."

"Mine, maybe," Stevie said.

"What? What did you do?"

"We'll see," Stevie said. "We'll soon see."

It came sooner than he expected. It came while Marcie was on and Stevie was standing behind the curtain watching her. He was standing behind the curtain and somebody was standing behind him, close behind him so that the voice sounded right in his ear.

"Mr. Jordan?"

Stevie turned around, slowly, casually. "Yeah."

"Have you a match?"

"A match?" Stevie patted his pockets, one after another. "No, sorry."

"Well, I guess I don't need any after all. Look," the man said.

Stevie kept his eyes rigidly ahead of him.

"Look, Mr. Jordan. I have a whole boxful."

"Yeah?"

"I got them out of your car a few minutes ago. My name is Higgins."

Stevie smiled sardonically. "Now you know my name and I know yours, so that's a dead end."

"In my profession nothing is a dead end."

"In the insurance business? Well, tell me about it some time. I've got to go on now."

He raised the curtain and went out. Marcie had sunk into a small exhausted heap, which was her bow.

Stevie led the clapping and told the audience how good Marcie was and how good they were. When he came back, the man in the dinner coat hadn't moved. He was still holding the box of matches under his arm, casually, as if it was part of his costume.

"You still here?" Stevie said. "Maybe you'd like a cigarette to go with all those matches."

He hadn't intended to mention the matches again but the man was staring at him, he had to say something to break the stare.

"You're the one," Higgins said. "You were up there last night in your car."

"Up where?" Stevie said. "What car?"

If the man didn't have that box from the car he wouldn't have any evidence at all. Mr. Heath couldn't identify him. There had been only the light from the dashboard and he'd had his hat pulled down. If it weren't for the matches . . .

"Your car," Higgins said. "A Chevrolet coupé, 1940."

Stevie edged closer. "So I was up where?"

"On St. Clair Avenue."

"Doing what?"

Higgins smiled. "That's my question, Mr. Jordan. I have the answers to what goes before. I know you were there."

"I left work and went home," Stevie said. "I can't prove it because I live in a boardinghouse and by the time I get in at night the rest of the house is asleep."

"Except Mrs. McGillicuddy. Mrs. McGillicuddy reported your absence to the police early this morning. She was afraid you'd had an accident. You were gone all night."

"I was with a dame," Stevie said. If he could get the matches . . .

The girls would be coming out in a minute. If he was going to do anything he'd have to do it now. *Now.*

Higgins didn't see the fist coming. It caught him on the chin and he fell easily and gracefully like a woman fainting. The box of matches flew from under his arm. The lid fell off and half the paper packets were scattered on the floor.

With a little cry of rage Stevie got down on his knees and began stuffing the packets back into the box. *Hurry —the girls—any minute—hurry!* He had to jam the rest of them into his pockets, there wasn't room in the box.

Hurry. He had them all now and Higgins was still unconscious and the girls hadn't come out yet. He moved quickly towards the alley door. He heard footsteps behind him, the tap of high heels, the scream of a woman, but he was outside now and the door was closed behind him and he had the matches.

He ran down the alley, effortlessly, as if his fear and his ecstasy of triumph had combusted and given his body an engine that drove him along.

He reached his car, parked in the widening of the alley. The car was just the same except that Higgins hadn't relocked the door, and the engine wouldn't turn over.

The engine was dead.

"Oh, God,' Stevie said, and the engine inside him died too because the triumph was gone. He hadn't won after all. Higgins had done something to his car. Maybe Higgins had *wanted* this to happen, had been waiting for Stevie to give himself away.

He sat there for a minute staring dully in front of him. Then he heard the shrill blast of a police whistle from the Bloor Street end of the alley. He slid from behind the wheel, and the running began again.

The alley was a whole block long. He didn't look back until he got to the end of it, and had to stop running anyway because of the people walking along Davenport. He looked back only for an instant, and saw nothing but the alley itself unwinding like a gray ribbon, getting thinner and darker until it dissolved into the night.

Nothing else. He had won. *Except that he had left the matches in the car he had won.*

"Oh, God," Stevie whispered.

He had to lean against the show window of a store to keep from falling. A grocery store, he always remembered that. He heard someone walk past, stop and come back again. He didn't look up until a man's voice said, "Could I trouble you for a match?"

"No," Stevie said hoarsely. "No. No, you couldn't! I haven't got any matches!"

"Well, you don't need to get tough about it."

The man walked away. He was wearing a gray suit and his shoulder blades stuck out under it like wings.

A streetcar roared past and stopped at the next corner fifty yards up. Stevie began to run. The conductor saw him running and held the car for him.

Stevie swung aboard.

"How much?"

"A dime. Four tickets for a quarter."

Stevie brought out the dime. He became aware then that he was in evening clothes and that people were staring at him. The car was not jammed, it was just crowded enough so that he'd have to stand and people would get a good look at him.

He put his hand on the overhead rail and began to read the ads. They would see how engrossed he was in the ads and stop staring at him. They did stop, most of them, but only when the car had paused again to let on somebody newer than Stevie. Six or seven more blocks made Stevie a veteran. He was one of them now, he even had a seat.

All kinds of people were getting seats. An old lady scrambled past a fat girl, and the fat girl moved over and a middle-aged man sat down beside her. Then the fat girl got out and the man was left by himself. You could almost see the man expand with relief when the girl left, he seemed to grow suddenly and fill more of the seat, even though he was a very thin man. His bones stuck out, his shoulders were sharp underneath the gray coat. It was when the car jerked suddenly and the man leaned forward in his seat that Stevie saw the shoulder blades sticking out like wings. . . .

Stevie sat frozen, while the car lurched on and the man with the shoulder blades settled back in his seat. So far the man hadn't looked around at all, though every time someone walked down the aisle he turned his head a little, anxiously, as if he was afraid someone was going to deprive him of the luxury of a whole seat to himself.

An ordinary guy. An ordinary guy going home, Stevie thought, not following me.

But a couple of blocks later when someone rang the bell Stevie edged out of his seat. When the door opened he slipped out and began walking briskly eastward while the car moved on west.

He remembered that the car had passed a couple of small taverns, the kind that rented out a few rooms so they could get a hotel beer and wine license. A room was what he wanted, and a phone. He'd have to phone Joey, tell him that he needed money to get out of town.

Here it was. "The Palace Hotel" in small letters and "B E E R" and "W I N E" in big bright neons.

When he went inside and stood at the desk he had to wait while one of the bartenders twitched off his apron, smoothed his hair, and appeared behind the desk, looking as much like a desk clerk as he had like a bartender. He even said sir.

"Yes, sir?"

"A room," Stevie said.

"Single, sir?"

"Yes."

"We have one left with bath."

Actually they only had one with bath but it wasn't good business to admit it. Especially to a guy like this in evening clothes. Probably had a quarrel with his wife, the bartender-clerk decided, and he's going to show her what's what by staying out all night.

"How much?" Stevie asked.

"Two-fifty."

"O.K." He paid in advance.

"Sign here, please."

Stevie took the pen and wrote Steven—then he changed his mind and added an "s" to Steven and put two initials in front of it, M. R. Stevens, Hamilton.

"Hundred and three," the clerk said. "Here's your key, sir. I'll show you up."

"No," Stevie said, "No!"

He was staring at the door of the hotel. A man was coming in. When he saw Stevie he stood for a moment, frowning, and then he came toward him. He had a thin face and his lips were drawn back from his teeth in a silent snarl.

He said, in a low voice, "That's what I thought."

"What?" Stevie said.

"I said I thought you were following me. Just because I asked you for a match. You must be crazy. You got a complex."

"Your key, sir," the clerk said. He wanted to lean across the desk to hear what the two men were saying to each other. But that wouldn't be good business, and besides someone wanted another beer. He pulled out his apron from behind the desk and fastened it on again.

"I saw you run after the car when I got on," the man said. "You took the seat behind me. What's the game?"

"I never saw you before," Stevie said dully.

"You must be crazy. You ran after the car. Now you're here. I went past my stop on purpose to put you off. Now you're here anyway."

"Coincidence."

"Hell. I heard of guys like you before. You're per—persecuted, that's the word."

"Sorry," Stevie said, "I didn't mean a thing. I thought *you* were following *me*."

The man looked at him and the snarl gradually disappeared. "Yeah? Now that's funny."

"Certainly is."

"Wait'll I tell the wife." He was really smiling now. "I guess I'm too suspicious."

"Not at all," Stevie said politely.

"I owe you a beer for flying off like that."

He hadn't had a drink all night. Maybe that was why he'd acted so crazy all for nothing. Hitting a policeman . . .

"Thanks," he said. "A beer would be swell."

When they sat down the man looked across the table at Stevie and smiled rather sheepishly. "Well, what'll it be?"

"Molson's."

"Two Molson's."

While they were waiting Stevie kept looking around for a telephone and planning what he'd say to Joey: "Joey, I'm in a jam. Could you send fifty to my cousin in New-market and I'll pick it up?" Joey could spare fifty and he was a good guy in some ways.

"Something on your mind?" the man said.

Stevie gave a quick smile. "Girl trouble. I guess I'll phone her."

"Right over there's the phone."

Stevie got up and shut himself inside the booth. He had to wait until his hands stopped shaking before he could dial the number of Joey's office.

Joey answered it the way he always did, with a sharp alert "Yes?"

"Joey?" Stevie said.

Joey recognized his voice because he changed his tone and he said, "Yeah," instead of "Yes."

"Joey, listen. I'm in a jam. Could you—I need some money. Could you send—?"

Joey spaced his words evenly, and he spoke slowly: "You —God—damn—fool."

"Listen, Joey . . ."

But it was no use because Joey had hung up. Stevie hung up too, so hard that a nickel clanged out of the box. Stevie took the nickel out and held it in the palm of his hand. For a long time he stood there with the nickel. Then he said, "Thanks, Joey," but the words didn't come out as he intended.

He went back to his table. The beer was there and the man was already drinking his and munching popcorn from the bowl in the center of the table.

"Trouble?" he said. "Well, sit down and forget it."

"She hung up so fast I got the nickel back."

"You're lucky she's that way and not the other way. You know—blah, blah, blah."

"I sure am," Stevie said. "I sure am a lucky guy."

The beer hit him hard because he was hungry and tired and wanted to be hit hard. There was no reason to stay sober, there was no more shows for him tonight and he didn't even have to drive home. He had a room right here, he could just go upstairs and sleep it off. And in the morning he'd send out for a suit, a cheap suit so he'd have enough money left for train fare to some place.

"What's a good place?"

"A good place?" the man echoed. "What do you mean?"

"To go to, when you don't want to go home. I thought I'd go to another town."

"Just on account of a dame?" the man said, admiringly. "Well, personally, I'd like to live in the States, some place like Buffalo or Detroit."

"I have no passport."

"My wife's over there now. She's got a cousin in Buffalo. I'm on my own for a while. I've got a pile of dirty dishes in the sink and the apartment's so dirty I'm scared to start cleaning it for fear I'll get typhoid or something. If she doesn't come back soon I'll have to move out."

Stevie beckoned to the waiter. "Two more of the same."

"Not for me," the man said. "Three bottles is my limit. I'll be taking a taxi home at that. But you go ahead."

"I've got a room here."

"Well, that's too bad. I was going to say, if you didn't mind the dirt you could come home with me. The place is kind of lonesome and I thought—until your girl got over it . . . "

"Thanks," Stevie said. "I couldn't do that. I don't even know your name."

The man laughed, slapping his thighs. "By God, you don't! No more than I know yours. You might even be a crook for all I know."

"I might," Stevie said.

"I'm a great one for judging people by their faces. I *like* your face."

"I like yours."

"Anyway, I'm a sucker for people in trouble. That's how you look, like a nice fellow who's in trouble. It's none of my business what the trouble is, of course. Maybe it's a girl and maybe it isn't, but the offer still goes."

"Offer?"

"You can come home with me."

The kindness and the beer went to Stevie's head. He wanted to cry. He decided that he *would* cry and put his head down on the table. But one of the bartenders came over and tapped his shoulder and said, "Closing time, mister."

Stevie raised his head. "Yeah. What time?"

"*Closing* time." He turned to the man. "Is this a friend of yours?"

"You bet he is," the man said. "We're just leaving. Can you call a cab?"

"I can call a cab, sure," the bartender said, "if you got a nickel."

The man took hold of Stevie's arm and led him out. They waited on the sidewalk for the cab, with Stevie leaning against the man, saying, "Thanks, Joey. Thanks, Joey."

When they were inside the cab Stevie slid into a corner and closed his eyes. The man didn't bother him until the cab stopped. Then he said, "We're here," and Stevie opened his eyes and got out, not caring where he was. It was nice to have things decided for him, it was nice to have a friend who liked his face.

The cool air had sobered him a little and he could walk by himself, follow the man through the lobby and up a flight of stairs and through a door.

"Here we are."

The man turned on a lamp, and another lamp. The room sprang up at Stevie. There was something wrong about it, something wrong, something missing.

He rubbed his hands over his eyes to wipe away the blur. But there was no blur, there was nothing the matter with his eyes, it was the room, the room itself. . . .

"Sit down," the man said. "Make yourself at home."

"I'd like some water," Stevie said.

"Sure. I'll get you some."

The man went out. Stevie followed him, through a dining room into a kitchen. The tap roared for a minute. There was something wrong in this room too. If he could think, if he could remember . . .

It hit him when he was holding the glass of water to his lips. The shock was so sudden that his throat was constricted and the water couldn't get past. It dribbled down his chin.

There were no dirty dishes in the sink. There was no dirt anywhere in the apartment. There was no wife, no cousin in Buffalo.

He raised his head and saw that the man was watching him, quietly, the man was waiting for something.

"You've got it now, Mr. Jordan?" he said finally.

The glass fell out of Stevie's hand and splintered on the floor. His mouth moved stiffly. "Who are you?"

The man said, "My name is Sands."

CHAPTER 11

THE woman opened her mouth to scream again. Higgins said, "Shut up!" and crawled to his feet. The woman's mouth stayed open but no sound emerged.

"I fell," Higgins said, brushing off his trousers. When he talked his jaw hurt but he didn't mind, it had worked out all right.

"The floor's too slippery," he said. "It's a wonder you girls don't break your necks."

"What—what are you doing back here? Joey's got rules about that." She had a deep coarse voice.

"I wanted to talk to one of the girls," Higgins said easily.

"Which one?"

"You."

"Me?" She took a step back. "I don't know you. You better get out before I call Joey."

"I don't think you'll want to call Joey. This is just between you and me."

"I've got to go now. That's my music."

"Go ahead."

He stepped back and she went past him through the curtain walking with fast nervous steps. There was a smattering of applause, the orchestra was muted, the woman began to sing, "Oh, there's a lull in my life." She sang it badly, keeping a little ahead of the orchestra as if she were trying to hurry it along.

She came back in five minutes. She looked more sure of herself than she had before. She had been thinking during the lull in her life.

"I want to talk to you about a friend of yours," Higgins said. "You know what friend I mean?"

"No idea. Cop, are you?"

"Inspector Higgins, Miss Rosen. I'm looking for Tony Murillo."

"So am I," Mamie said. "And for his own good I hope you get there first."

So it's going to be like that, Higgins thought. He said, "We haven't seen Murillo for some time, nearly ten years. Thought we'd look him up. You didn't know him ten years ago?"

"No."

"He'd just got two years for peddling reefers. I want to see him."

"What for?"

"Questioning. Where is he?"

"I don't know."

"Living with him, aren't you?"

"Now and then," Mamie said coolly. "Off and on."

Joey came in through the side door. "You stank," he said to Mamie. "What in hell's the matter with you?"

"Nothing," Mamie said.

Joey turned to Higgins. "Policeman, eh? What have we done now? Where's Stevie?"

"Mr. Jordan took a walk to cool off," Higgins said. "He probably won't be back tonight."

"What's going on here?" Joey demanded. "What right have the cops got to come in and bust up my show?"

"Don't get excited," Higgins said. "We wanted to talk to Mr. Jordan, that's all. Now I want to talk to Miss Rosen. Alone."

"Well, by Jesus, couldn't you pick some other time? You frighten her half to death so she can only squawk when she should be singing, and you take Jordan . . . "

"Jordan went under his own steam," Higgins said, "and I'd still like to talk to Miss Rosen alone."

"What about?"

"Her boy friend."

Joey whirled savagely toward Mamie. "For Christ's sake didn't I tell you if you didn't keep away from that wop I was going to fire you? Every couple of months you show up all messed up with a black eye and a split lip and I should pay you for it! I'm in business. I'm not running a convalescent home for . . . " He took another step toward her. "Tell this cop where Murillo is. I want to see him in jail where he belongs. *Tell him.*"

"I don't know where he is," Mamie whispered. "I don't know."

Joey stared at her for a minute, then he turned back to Higgins and said calmly, "Murillo's probably hiding out in her room. She lives on Charles Street. Tell him the number, Mamie."

"A hundred and ten," Mamie said. "But he's not there."

"Not now he isn't," Joey said grimly. "But he'll be back. Once a guy like Murillo finds a sucker like Mamie he don't let go easy. He'll be back."

"He didn't come back last night," Mamie said. "I think he's out of town on business."

"Business!" Joey shouted.

"I'll handle this," Higgins said, waving Joey away. "Relax."

"I'll relax when you tell me where Jordan is and when he's coming back."

"I don't know," Higgins said. "Wait and see."

"Wait and see, hell! What did he do?"

"Possibly he did a murder," Higgins said thoughtfully. "We'd like to know."

Joey walked stiffly to the door. He was cursing under his breath. He cursed them all, Mamie and Higgins and Jordan and Murillo. They were trying to ruin him, send him to the poorhouse. He slammed the door and put his hand in his pocket to jingle the loose change he always kept there so he could listen to the sweet clink of nickels.

"So he was out of town," Higgins said. "You didn't see him last night."

"Someone else was with me," Mamie said. "I can prove it. When I woke up yesterday noon Tony was gone. He never told me where he was going or what he did. He said it was none of my business." She dabbed at her eyes. "What did he do? Tell me what he did."

"Who *was* with you?"

"Stevie."

"Jordan?"

"Yes."

"All night?"

Mamie blew her nose delicately. Her eyes above the handkerchief were wary.

"Not in the way you mean," she said.

109

"I don't care what he *did* there! I want to know if he was there."

"Why do you want to know?" He just kept looking at her and she knew stalling wasn't going to get her anywhere. She said, "He drove me home."

"And stayed?"

"Not then. He went away and came back."

"When did he come back?"

"I don't know. Late, I guess."

"How late?"

"I don't know. I had a bottle of rye and I wasn't paying much attention to the time. I was just sitting there and . . ."

"Why did Jordan come back?"

"For a drink."

"We found a full quart of scotch in his car."

Her eyes hardened. "You did, did you?"

"Maybe he likes to drink up other people's liquor first, eh?"

She didn't answer.

"I guess he figured if Murillo could use you so could he, eh?"

"Use me," she echoed in a tight voice. He let that sink in and he could see it was sinking in from the way her body seemed to grow rigid and taller.

"For a sucker," Higgins said.

"Who was murdered?" she said at last.

"A girl, a blind girl."

"Blind? Not . . ." She gulped. "Who was she?"

"Kelsey Heath."

"Kelsey Heath," Mamie said. "Heath."

"She was killed about three or three-thirty in the morning."

"How?"

"With a knife."

She rubbed the damp spot under her breasts.

"We know Jordan was up there," Higgins said, "about that time. No law against that, of course. But we have to check up on him because we found that the front door of the Heaths' house had been left unlocked. An outsider could have killed her. So we tried Jordan out."

"And he ran away," Mamie said.

"He might just have been nervous," Higgins said. "He didn't have any motive for killing the girl."

110

"Oh, didn't he?" Mamie said in a hard voice.

"We don't know of any."

"Well, you should of been around last night when he was talking in his sleep. *Kelsey Heath. Do you know who Kelsey Heath is? She's the girl who killed Geraldine.*" She paused to look slyly over at Higgins. "Well, you want to know about it? Kelsey Heath was driving the car. There were four of them in it but Geraldine was the one who was killed. Stevie went to see the car when it was in the garage, he went to see the blood on it, that's how crazy it made him. You got a cigarette?"

Higgins gave her one and lit it. She inhaled, letting the smoke curl out through her nose. "Well, that would of been all right, he would of gotten over Geraldine dying. But it's happened again. Johnny Heath has taken another girl away from him. You saw her in the show, a thin little thing who does handsprings and gives herself airs. Thinks she's Jesus Christ's first cousin. Well anyway, Stevie likes her, and he's just begginning to get some place when Johnny Heath starts coming in and sees Marcie."

Higgins said, "Geraldine was Jordan's girl?"

"She slept with him. When Johnny Heath started to take her out she left Stevie flat, moved right out on him."

Higgins smiled at the shock and reproof in her voice. Mamie would never walk out on her man. One hundred and ten Charles Street had better be watched very carefully. Murillo, like any other criminal big or small, would try to get to his girl after a crime.

"Well, a man don't like that," Mamie was saying. "If he does the walking out himself, well that's different, he's still got his self-respect. Women don't need that kind of self-respect, we get it from other things like nice clothes and hair-dos. Maybe if men could dress different, fix themselves up like, they wouldn't be so touchy."

Higgins agreed with her. "Jordan was touchy, was he?"

"Not more than most, I guess, but when you lose two girls to the same man it throws you. He acted funny when he drove me home, he kept bringing up Geraldine all the time. She's been dead for two years now and I think when someone's been dead for two years you ought to let her stay dead. But Stevie said it would happen again. He said Johnny Heath would come some night and take Marcie out and there'd be another accident—a lot of crazy talk like that."

"Threatening talk?"

"Yeah, but not against the girl, Kelsey Heath. It was all against Johnny Heath himself. Well, he drove me home and I got out and went in the house. About an hour later . . ."

"What time?"

"Maybe four. He came back again and said he wanted to come in and have a drink. Him with all that scotch in the car, the damn cheapskate. So I let him in because— well, I was just sitting there anyway, might as well have company. He came in and we finished the rye and he went to sleep on the couch. That was when he talked in his sleep. He kept talking about Johnny Heath. I had to wake him up."

She stopped and fished around inside her dress for her handkerchief. As soon as she found the handkerchief the tears came to her eyes. Perfect synchronization, Higgins thought, and a talent for tears. He watched her big soft eyes and then his gaze traveled down to her mouth. It was pulled tight and thin.

"I hate to rat on Stevie like this," she said through the handkerchief. "But he said Johnny Heath had killed Geraldine, murdered her. When I woke him up he said he had to phone Marcie, that's the one who does handsprings, and see if she was all right. I told him he couldn't phone from the house at that time of morning because that's my landlady's rule. He went out to phone from a drugstore and never came back. That's all."

She replaced the handkerchief, smiled brightly at Higgins and turned to walk away.

"No, it isn't all," Higgins said grimly. "Come back here."

"I have to go and change."

"I want Murillo."

"I swear to God I don't know where he is," Mamie cried. "I swear it. He never told me anything like that! There'd be weeks when I never heard from him at all."

"He lived with you, didn't he?"

"Sometimes. I told you, sometimes. But I guessed he had another place."

"A hideout."

"I guess."

"And you never tried to find out where it was?"

She looked at him defiantly. "I tried, all right! What do

112

you think I'm made of? I thought he might—might have another woman. So I asked him. And you know what that got me? A sock on the jaw. So I quit trying."

"Murillo still smoke?"

"Smoke?"

"Jujus."

"I don't know."

"You don't know anything at all about marihuana, I suppose?"

"Not a thing."

They were still trying to stare each other down when Joey strode through the door again.

"Still here?" he said to Higgins. "Go and get dressed, Mamie. Tell Marcie Moore she's wanted on the phone."

Mamie disappeared, and a minute later Marcie came out of the dressing room. She wore the same costume and she had the black cape clutched tight around her body.

She looked uncertainly from Joey to Higgins.

"Phone," Joey said.

"Who?" Marcie asked.

"Do I usually ask *who?*" Joey barked. "And you can tell the girls for me that this is the last time any of you are getting calls up front. Use the *pay* telephone. That's what it's *for.*"

"Yes." Marcie slid past him.

She looked out of place in the club, Higgins decided. Not too innocent, exactly, or too young. Just earnest and humorless and proud. A one-track mind and that track a career. Her eyes were harder than Mamie's.

She gave Higgins another fleeting glance and walked swiftly through the door. There was a small passageway and then the main room itself. She stayed close to the wall. The tables this far from the floor were not full and no one noticed her.

Joey's office was a dingy cubbyhole beside the check-room, furnished with a secondhand desk, a swivel chair, a paint-peeled filing cabinet and a small safe. Joey never spent money where it didn't show.

Marcie closed the door behind her and picked up the phone, leaning against the desk. For an instant she couldn't speak, then she drew in her breath and said softly, "Hello."

"Hello. Marcie?"

"Yes."

"It's Johnny."

"Yes."

A pause.

"You don't sound very happy about it," Johnny said. "Anything the matter?"

"Matter?" The phone trembled in her hand. "Oh, no, nothing's the matter! Except that you had to drag *me* into this mess!"

"Marcie, for God's sake!"

"And don't you swear at me," she said shrilly. "This is going to *ruin* me, do you understand? If I get mixed up in this I'll never get another chance. Can't you leave me alone?"

"Of course," Johnny said. "Of course."

He hung up quietly. For a minute he stood smiling dryly at the mouthpiece as if it were Marcie herself. *Well anyway, thank God there were no policemen listening in to that one.*

He walked out of the kitchen, not damning her or saying to hell with her, simply turning a page in his mind. *She wants me to let her alone. So I'll let her alone.*

He went back to Alice and Philip in the drawing room. The three of them had been there all evening. They had been asked not to leave the house, so they had sat talking, discussing, plunging into the uneasy silences, gnawing at each other's nerves. They had gone over everything Sands had asked and everything they had answered.

"Well?" Alice said.

"I phoned her," Johnny said slowly, "and she made it clear that I wasn't to phone again. I think I'd like a drink."

"You'll have to make it yourself," Alice said. "Maurice is in bed."

"I can ring for Ida."

She said sharply, "Make it yourself. I don't want Ida around any more tonight. I've given her notice. She'll be leaving sometime tomorrow."

"Then she might as well make herself useful tonight." Johnny rang the bell. "Phil, relax for once and join me."

"No, thanks." Philip didn't raise his head. He was sitting stiffly in a high-backed chair, his hands grasping the arms of the chair, his feet planted firmly on the floor. Only his neck seemed to have weakened and could not support his head.

He looks ridiculous, Alice thought, so comically dignified. Even though there was no one there to laugh at him

114

she couldn't let him stay like that. She must sting him into moving.

"Have a drink," she said. "You won't sleep well tonight, will you, Philip?" He didn't move or speak. "Philip, will you hand me . . .?" She couldn't think of anything for him to hand her. She put her hand up to her mouth.

Johnny stared at her. "What's the matter with you tonight?"

Her anger at Philip for looking foolish and at herself for not being able to stop him, instantly transferred itself to Johnny.

"Nothing," she said gratingly. "Nothing's the matter with me. I didn't know anyone considered me human enough to have something the matter!"

"You talk like a damned spinster."

"That's what I am! Exactly. A damned spinster. On behalf of my class, Johnny, I thank you, because you've done a lot for spinsters. More, I think, than your share, and perhaps not in the approved fashion . . ."

"Keep quiet," Johnny said harshly. "If anyone needs a drink you do. I don't know what's got into you."

Alice threw back her head and laughed. She stopped as abruptly as she had begun and when she turned to Johnny the tears were wriggling down her cheeks like bright worms.

"Sex," she said. "I guess that's what's got into me. Go ahead and look pained, Johnny. It's a word I'm not supposed to know, isn't it? Everybody else can know it but not Alice. It might interfere with my duties as housekeeper and nursemaid. Well, I've had a lot of experience in this house. I could go out now and manage a hotel, an orphanage, an insane asylum or a home for wayward girls! Come in."

Ida bumped the door open with her rear and bounced across the room. The tray tinkled, the glasses skated, Ida's breasts rode her in cross-rhythm like twin riders on a galloping horse.

She set the tray down on the small table beside Alice.

"Here's the drinks," she said, "ma'am."

"Thank you," Alice said. "That will be all."

Ida had intended to go directly and peacefully to bed, but she felt the crack of the whip in Alice's voice and it stung her into defiance. She was just as good as Alice was. Alice had no power over her; she, Ida could say whatever

115

she wanted to, and if they tried force to get her out she'd simply go and tell the police. She'd have the law on them.

Though Ida's alliance with the law was new, having begun that morning when a policeman smiled at her, it was as strong as her allegiance to God. It made her swell with power. She had God and the law on her side, she was strong enough now to stand up to Alice.

But she was too cautious to attack directly. She said, "A terrible tragedy. That's what the policemen said and that's what I say, a terrible tragedy."

She looked expectantly around the room. Neither of the men paid any attention to her.

Alice said curtly, "Have you packed your bags?"

Her voice slapped the blood into Ida's face. "Well, and if that's all the thanks I get for my sympathy . . . "

"You may go to your room. We won't be needing you any longer."

"And don't think I didn't hear what you said about me being a wayward girl! I could have the law on you! Nobody can ever say anything about my morals."

"I'm sure of it," Alice said.

Johnny said gravely, "Morels. An edible fungus found on the twenty-fourth of May."

Philip smiled slightly. Ida watched them, speechless with rage. They were laughing at her. These people, for all they were on the wrong side of God and the law, were laughing at her.

"You'll laugh on the other side of your faces," she said at last. But her voice wasn't as loud as she meant it to be. To make up for it she swung round with an exaggerated gesture of defiance, a toss of her head, a lift of one shoulder and a little wag of her buttocks.

Alice called her back sharply.

"Ida!"

Ida stopped but didn't turn her head.

"I don't want any more threats or hints from you, Ida," Alice said quietly. "It might help you to keep your mouth shut if I tell you that one of the policemen found traces of morphine on Kelsey's hands. You know what that means, Ida. It means that she tried to kill herself. *And where did she get the morphine, Ida?*"

Ida turned and ran down the hall. Alice followed her as far as the door, shouting, *"From you! She got it from you! You helped her!"*

116

There was no answer, but the diminishing sound of running feet. Alice shut the door and leaned against it, suddenly weary and without hope.

The two men were staring at her.

"What did you mean?" Philip said hoarsely. "Where did you find that out?"

Alice walked slowly back into the room. She looked deliberately at Philip. "I eavesdropped."

"You what?" Johnny said.

There was shock in his face. Alice felt that in a minute he would say, "That's not cricket!" not because he disapproved of eavesdropping but because it was she, Alice, who had done it.

They don't think I'm human. They expect so much of me, all of them expect too much of me and always have.

"I eavesdropped," she repeated, finding a certain pleasure in the word now. "The police wouldn't tell me anything and I felt it was my right to know. They—just took her away—in a basket—and I had nothing to say about the funeral or the autopsy or inquest. They asked me questions and refused to answer any of mine."

"High-handed," Johnny said, "as usual."

"What can you expect?" Philip said. "Any one of us might have . . ." His voice faded, emerged again. "Why did she want to kill herself? Because I said I was going away? She *knew* I wouldn't go, she *knew* I couldn't leave her."

Alice took the glass Johnny gave her. It was easier to talk to Philip if she had a glass to stare into, somewhere to look so she wouldn't have to look at his face, so strangely formless now that he no longer had Kelsey to fight against or to live for.

"She tried to kill herself," Alice said, "for the same reason other people do. Life didn't suit her. She couldn't have been content with half-measures. She wouldn't even try." She kept her voice calm. "What are we going to do about—her dog?"

"Send him back," Johnny said. "It takes a long time to train them and it wouldn't be fair to keep him." He gulped his drink and his hands were shaking.

Alice stared into her glass. Queer, they could talk about Kelsey and Kelsey's blindness almost with detachment, but they couldn't mention the dog without weighting the air with tears. It was as if the dog was a symbol and the

symbol had become stronger and realer than what it stood
for.

"Better have a drink, Philip," she said without looking
at him.

"No. No, I don't want—but I'd like . . ."

"Go ahead and play something if you want to. It will
make you feel better."

"I'd—if you wouldn't mind . . ."

Don't let him cry now, Alice thought. *He's such a fool
already, don't let him cry and break down.*

"Something loud," she said. "There's too much softness
in this house, too much whispering, tiptoeing. . . ."

The policeman, sitting on a garden bench at the side of
the house, heard the music. Of course it was kind of
funny to hear music in a house of mourning, but if they
have it why not something snappy? He began to whistle
softly, "Don't Sit Under the Apple Tree."

Mr. Heath heard it and moved to the window to listen.
Philip was playing wildly tonight. Dashing brilliant in-
accuracy, that was Philip. He had never been as good as
Isobel thought he was—but why tell Isobel? And there was
no point in telling Philip, he knew it already. He had
never arranged a third concert.

He pictured Philip at the piano. How strange he looked
when he played, his eyes wild as a tiger's. You could
hardly believe it was Philip.

Mr. Heath smiled and said aloud, "Tiger, tiger, burning
bright. Little lamb, who made thee?"

CHAPTER 12

STEVIE stared down at the broken glass, poking a splinter
with the toe of his shoe.

"Cheap glass," he said in a flat voice.

"A dime," Sands said.

"All right, I owe you a dime. Anything else?"

"Some thanks. I could have taken you down to headquarters."

"But you brought me here instead, to soften me up with shock, you think."

"You're not tough," Sands said, "and I'm not tough. I thought we'd get along. Come on in and sit down."

"What if I don't want to sit down."

"Stand up then, if you want to be childish."

"What's to prevent me from walking out of here?" Stevie said.

Sands smiled briefly. "Not a thing, except your head."

"You haven't got a gun?"

"No gun," Sands said, "and I can't fight worth a damn."

Stevie took a step toward him. Sands looked at him steadily.

"On the other hand, I have my weapons. I created this situation. In a very small way I played the disillusioning role of God. I put you on the stage, arranged the properties, and waited for you to do exactly what you did."

"For Christ's . . ."

"I wasn't sure, that time. This time I am. If you watch enough grasshoppers you know which way they'll jump. You're sober enough to know what you're doing, and you've had enough experience tonight of being a fugitive. So you won't walk out. You'll come in and sit down. Think it over."

Sands turned his back and walked without haste into the next room. He looked tired and there was a thin line of white above his mouth. Suppose you hadn't watched enough grasshoppers . . .

For five minutes Stevie was alone in the kitchen. He didn't even have to face Sands again if he wanted to walk out: there was a back door right off the kitchen. All he had to do was go through it and down some steps and he'd be free.

Free. For all of ten minutes he'd be free. Then the patrol cars would start prowling, slick bored voices would reel off his description by radio. They'd get his picture, put it on handbills, even, if he lasted that long, if he didn't talk to strangers, if his money held out, if he could get out of town and find another job or a friend.

So he didn't jump.

He found Sands sitting in an easy chair rubbing his eyes.

"All right," Stevie said. "So here I am, you bastard."

"Calm down," Sands said wearily. "Nothing to lose your shirt about."

"Except assaulting a policeman."

"You hit Higgins?"

"I hit him."

"Higgins can be persuaded to forget it—if you can be persuaded to tell me why in hell you were sitting outside the Heath house in your car at approximately three-thirty this morning, while a murder was being committed."

There was a long silence.

"Well?" Sands said.

"You wouldn't believe me. I hardly believe myself, that's how crazy it is."

"Try me."

"I wanted to see the house, Johnny Heath's house."

"Why?"

"For Christ's sake, I told you you wouldn't believe me."

"There's a reason for everything."

"All right," Stevie said. "The reason is, I hate his guts."

"That makes sense," Sands said gravely. "People go past houses for love, why not hate? You missed one of your cues, Jordan. You forgot to say, 'A murder! What murder?' You knew about it?"

"Marcie told me."

"Marcie?"

"Heath told her, she told me. Her name's Marcella Moore."

"So you knew there was a murder. That's why you hit Higgins?"

Another silence.

"No," Stevie said finally.

"You weren't afraid you'd be arrested for the murder?"

"No."

"But you hit him and tried to get away. Why?"

Stevie leaned forward in his chair. *"Because I don't want to be murdered, you bastard!"*

"Neither do I," Sands said dryly. "But my methods of avoiding it are less complex than yours. Who wants to murder you?"

"Nobody. Yet."

"Yet?"

"Yet," Stevie repeated grimly.

"But somebody will?"

"Yeah, after you get through with me. All this soft-lights-and-sweet-music atmosphere isn't fooling me a bit. This is just the test bout. The real bout will come later at the station and it'll be me against half a dozen ham-handed cops with rubber hoses . . ."

"It has happened," Sands said. "But not in my cases."

". . . and lights and no water and no sleep until I talk. You wouldn't do it to the Heaths but you'd do it to me. Well, I'll save you the trouble. I'll take a chance on being murdered. I've got a use for my face and I don't want it banged up, see?"

"So?"

"So I know who killed the girl."

He took out a handkerchief and rubbed it over the palms of his hands. His movements were careful, his voice careful.

"Sure. I'm a remarkable guy. I know two murderers now. And I don't think you'll get either of them. Especially the first guy you won't get. He's very smooth. What's in that bottle?"

"Scotch. Have some?"

"Yeah."

He drank it straight.

"We won't even talk about the first guy," he said. "He's so good he deserves to get away with it. The second guy is no good at all. You should have seen him running down the street, right out of the driveway, right past my car. I never saw anybody run so fast!"

He let out a hoarse laugh. "Jesus! His face was green. He's got the guts of a worm, same like me. I haven't any guts. I want to rent a furnished cell in the Dom jail until you catch up with him. Then I'll begin life all over again with a new rule: never make friends with murderers. Don't even speak to them. Shun 'em like rattlesnakes."

"Let's have it," Sands said quietly.

"Murillo. Tony Murillo, a gentleman handy with a knife, a wop with the sex life of a fruit fly. And don't ask me if I'm sure. Sure I'm sure. Sure enough to sock a cop and try and get out of town. Because there's a chance he saw me too. Maybe he's just as sure as I am. But I didn't begin to get scared until I found out it was murder. The second murder comes easy."

He paused to draw in his breath. "You're supposed to be looking surprised, Mr. Sands."

"I am surprised," Sands said. "But not very much."

"All right," Stevie said bleakly. "It's your spotlight. Take it away."

"By tonight I was pretty sure that the murder was an outside job with inside help. All the evidence pointed to the combination. The front door was left open. The lock on Miss Heath's jewel box had been picked, though nothing was missing. We found the marks of a pigskin glove on the box. On the rug, hidden by the nap, were some shreds of tobacco. But it wasn't tobacco exactly. It was marihuana."

"Murillo's brand."

"Yes. The stuff was stale as if it had been loose in a pocket and had come out accidentally when something like a handkerchief was pulled out of the pocket. I wouldn't have thought of Murillo if I hadn't had him in mind about another case. But the two cases are strangely similar: they are both unsuccessful robberies."

"What was the other one?"

"More about that later. Murillo couldn't have done the Heath job himself. He had to have someone leave that door open for him, he had to know the girl was blind, that it was safe for him to turn on the light. He had to have someone guide him to her room and tell him where her jewel box was."

"So why didn't he pick up the jewel box and get out of the house again? He wouldn't have had the guts to stand there and pick the lock on it even if the girl was deaf and dumb as well as blind. He's yellow and he's a nervous wreck."

"He might have had the nerve," Sands said, "if he was hopped up. Or he might have lost his judgment to such an extent that he didn't even think of picking up the jewel box and escaping. It was probably while he was standing at the bureau picking the lock that Kelsey Heath woke up. If she screamed no one heard her. He couldn't have done any thinking at all at that point. The girl was awake, there was the knife beside her bed, so he killed her. He didn't stop to figure that she was blind and couldn't identify him or that he could keep her quiet by hitting her. From start to finish he was consistently illogical."

"That part's all right," Stevie said. "It's the robbery itself that's a phony. He would never have attempted a house robbery except one of these soft jobs in a house vacant

122

for the night with windows and doors unlocked. Not even if he was hopped up. Marihuana's not like cocaine."

"How well do you know him?"

"Me? Not well at all by your standards, maybe. I've only seen him a few times. I had to kick him out of the club once, and he drew a knife on me. I've seen him a couple of times skulling around the alley waiting for Mamie. Those are the only times I've seen him, but I know him as well as I know the back of my hand."

"Intuition?" Sands said dryly.

"Mamie," Stevie said, smiling. "Murillo is Mamie's sole topic of conversation. I know what Murillo eats, what he wears, what he says, what he thinks. I know how many bowel movements he has in a week and what tie he was wearing on June the tenth two years ago. I've listened to the saga of Tony and Mamie for years, and Mamie has a very loose tongue. Mamie's loose tongue occasionally gets her a black eye. Oh, yes, Murillo has guts—with women and men under four feet and blind girls."

Sands took out a folded paper from his pocket and handed it to Stevie. It was a police picture of a man, front and side views.

Antonio Sebastian Murillo
Eyes: brown
Hair: black, curly
Complexion: medium
Height: 5′ 7″
Weight: 121
Born: 1914, Feb. 8, Chicago, Ill.
No fixed address
Identifying marks: none visible. Strawberry birthmark
    left hip
Charged: peddling marihuana
Convicted: same
Sentenced: two years less one day, Guelph Reformatory,
    June, 1932. Served full term
Remarks: carries knife, marihuana addict. Potentially
    dangerous.

The picture was that of a young man, handsome, insolent, thin almost to emaciation.

"So that's our boy," Stevie said, "as a boy. He's not so pretty now."

"The picture's ten years old. He'd have changed in ten years. How much?"

Stevie peered at the picture again. "Christ, you're sure it *is* Murillo? I'd never recognize him."

"That's too bad," Sands said, "because it's the only one we have and I doubt if Mamie Rosen will give us another. So we'll try something else. Excuse me while I phone."

He looked for a number in the phone book and dialed a number. The number rang fifteen times before it was answered by a sleepy male voice.

"Klausen?" Sands said.

"Yes."

"Are you still running the art college? Sands speaking."

"I'm not running it at one o'clock in the morning," Klausen said bitterly.

"This can't wait. Have you still got that little man Smithson around?"

"Yes. Now what?"

"I want him to do a job on a picture. Same thing he did to Galvison's picture last year: add thirty or forty pounds, ten years, draw in some disguises, you know the kind of thing."

"That's a good week's work and Smithson is busy."

"This man's a murderer. I want to get Smithson started right away if it's going to take that long. What's his number?"

"I thought after that Galvison mess that the police would go to a little trouble and renew their photo files, keep them up to date. Why haven't you hauled in this man and taken his picture again?"

"Can't be done without charging him," Sands said dryly. "He may have reformed and we'd hate like hell to persecute a reformed man since it's against the law. What's Smithson's number?"

Klausen told him, added a few remarks about the law and hung up.

It required thirteen rings to rouse Smithson, but there was no difficulty persuading him. He announced in a high tenor that he would be simply thrilled to help the police again, that he just adored reconstructing pictures, it was the most divine fun.

"I'll have them sent over immediately," Sands said. "What's the address?"

Sands rang off and wrote the address on the cover of the phone book.

Stevie said, grimacing, "I bet he lives in a frightfully ducky apartment in the Village."

"Right. Gerrard Street."

"What can he do?"

"Miracles," Sands said. "He used to travel around from city to city doing chalk portraits in poolrooms and restaurants and the like, until Klausen saw some of his work."

He called headquarters and asked for a patrol car. Then he wrote his instructions on a piece of paper, aided by Stevie's description of Murillo as he looked now.

"Add about forty pounds," Stevie said.

"Forty pounds," Sands wrote. "Height?"

"He's about as tall as I am, five eleven."

"Hair?"

"I never saw it," Stevie said. "He always kept his hat on. But I like to think he's getting bald."

"Tell me everything you know about his personal habits."

"I thought I had. What's that got to do with it?"

"In Galvison's case it was one of the determining factors that he had a habit of picking up gonorrhea. So when Smithson did his picture he treated Galvison to g.c. eyes, the sort of thing you can't easily get rid of or disguise. As a matter of fact Galvison turned up at the venereal clinic at the Royal Vic in Montreal and was picked up at the door."

In half an hour the instructions were ready. A patrolman took the paper and pictures, stiffly refused a drink, turned smartly on his heel, tripped over the rug and vanished.

"I hope," Stevie said dryly, "that Mr. Smithson does his job very, very well."

"Still scared?"

"I don't like knives."

"Another drink?"

"Don't mind if I do."

"Help yourself."

Over the rim of the glass Stevie looked thoughtful. "So why didn't Murillo take the jewel box?"

"Funk. It's pretty likely that he heard Mr. Heath come in and all Murillo wanted to do was get out. He must have been pretty nervy by that time because he'd already bungled once. He tried to hold up a beer dive."

"My God," Stevie said.

"He sat around the place first, drinking and leaving his fingerprints all over the table, glasses and bottles. Not our brightest light of crime, Murillo."

"Did he get away?"

"Of course he got away," Sands said, smiling. "Empty-handed, as later."

"This is beginning to smell." Stevie put the glass back on the table. He made his voice casual. "Know anyone who'd *pay* Murillo to do just what he did? It has been done, hasn't it? You pay a man to murder. Maybe you even pay him to make a murder look like an outside job and not to do the murdering."

"Maybe you do," Sands said.

"But I don't think *he* would."

"Who would?"

"He. My first murderer, the smooth one. He wouldn't pay anyone to do it, he'd do it himself. He'd make it look like an accident. He's good at that. You didn't catch on to him the first time."

"So I missed a murder?" Sands said quietly.

"Sure. You must miss lots of them."

"Probably."

"When you're not on the lookout for them."

"I'm still agreeing. I'd like to hear about it."

Stevie glanced at him sharply. "Do you think I'm crazy?"

"No. At least, no more than the rest of us."

"Thanks," Stevie said with a dry laugh. "Well, I've talked to a couple of people about this and they gave me the razzberry, so I didn't go to the police. The police now come to me and I'm going to go on record as saying that two years ago Johnny Heath murdered a girl called Geraldine Smith. . . ."

Sands said nothing.

"A perfect murder," Stevie added softly, "and it was perfect because it was perfectly timed and the stage was all set.

"You are sitting in a rumbleseat with a girl. It's a fine night and you have the girl's head on your shoulder. Her hair is blowing in your face. If it was some other girl's hair you'd think it was fine. But you've tired of this girl. She's not in your class and she's lived with another guy, at least one other, and she wants to marry you. So the hair makes you sick.

126

"'My arm is tired,' you say, and you push her away, maybe.

"'Johnny, what's the matter?' she says.

"Then later on you hit something and the girl with the hair goes flying out of the rumbleseat. The two people in the front are hurt. The man is bleeding, the girl, your sister is unconscious. You're shaken up a little but you're big, you're tough, you feel well enough to go over and cut Geraldine's throat. This is the only chance you'll ever get. Take it. You cut her throat with a piece of glass, you mess her up. Geraldine Smith has now been killed in an automobile accident. But you forgot something. Six months later another guy is going to remember, but you don't know that.

"You stagger around and get a cop. The cop doesn't ask many questions. Just another accident. There's an inquest but nobody does anything to you, they've got nothing on you, you weren't even driving the car. Perfect set-up, perfect timing, perfect murder.

"That's what you think. Six months later the other guy remembers something. . . .

"So I went down to a pawnshop," Stevie said, "and bought a magnifying glass. Tie that for a laugh, me with a magnifying glass playing Sherlock Holmes. I got out a copy of the Globe and Mail I'd saved, and I looked at pictures with my magnifying glass. The pictures weren't very clearly printed in the newspaper."

"We keep a file of accident pictures," Sands said, "if you want to look at them any time."

"Any time such as now?"

"That's right."

Stevie laughed. "Sorry, I haven't my magnifying glass with me. And maybe I dreamed up the whole thing, eh?"

"I don't think so. I think I know what you were looking for, and didn't see. You want to come now?"

"No, thanks," Stevie said. "Maybe after you've squared Higgins and Murillo is caught . . ."

". . . and Jordan quits shaking in his shoes. You're straddling a fence, Jordan. Jump on our side, or jump on theirs. You may think you're playing safe but where you're sitting you're a good target." He got up and picked up his hat from the table. "Can I drop you anywhere?"

"Don't bother," Stevie said. "I'll just flush myself down the toilet."

"I'm sorry you're acting childish," Sands said, walking to the door. "You're not cute enough to get away with it."

"Maybe not." Stevie followed him to the door, yawning. "I used to be cute as hell, though. In my prime I recited Kipling at Sunday School and rumor has it that I laid them in the pews."

Sands locked the door and led the way down the steps.

His car was parked in front of the apartment house, and he held the door open and motioned Stevie to get in.

"You want to hear about the rest of my life? After all, Kipling was only a phase, a mere facet of my many facets."

Sands let in the clutch and the car shot ahead in swift jerks.

"After Kipling and the Sunday School I was ready, come what may. And here's what came. My old man, having become justifiably sick of my old lady, jumped out of an airplane—without benefit of parachute. I personally think he showed good common sense."

"Must you talk?" Sands said dryly.

"That's my business. Or it used to be my business. I have an idea that Joey no longer loves me."

"You phoned him from the hotel?"

"That's right. He told me to go to hell."

"We'll go back now and square it," Sands said.

"No, thank you," Stevie said. "You think I want any of my friends to see me pally with a policeman? I'll square it myself, if you'll drop me there."

"Still don't want to look at pictures?"

"No."

"Mind if I do?"

"Go ahead. Won't do you any good. There's no chance of proving anything against Johnny Heath."

They drove in silence until Sands pulled the car up to the curb in front of Joey's. The doorman stifled a yawn and came over. When he saw who was in the car he said, "For Christ's sake. Where have you been?"

"Riding," Stevie said. "With my great and good friend Mr. Sands. Good night, Mr. Sands. See you at the morgue."

Sands sat and watched the two of them walk under the marquee up to the door of the club, Stevie slight and elegant in evening clothes, the doorman broad and tall in a green and gold coat to match the marquee. Their voices floated back to him, but the words were indistinguishable.

The car jerked ahead as it always did when Sands was tired and irritable. The dashboard clock said two. Joey's would be closed in fifteen minutes or so. Time to detail a man to follow Jordan if he hurried and Jordan didn't.

He stepped on the gas and was at headquarters in ten minutes.

There were three police men lolling at the main desk. When they saw Sands they tried to look busy by changing their expressions and hiding the deck of cards.

"Don't bother, boys," Sands said grimly. "Crime does not pay."

"There is no crime," Sergeant Havergal announced. "Tonight nobody is even beating his wife. There are no dogs howling and no suspicious characters loitering and not one spinster has heard strange noises downstairs."

"In that case," Sands said, "you can look up the photo file on an accident two years ago. Involved two Heaths, Geraldine Smith and Philip James. Smith was killed. Make it snappy."

Havergal sped out of the room.

To the men in plain clothes Sands said, "You know the Club Joey, Stern?"

"Officially, no," Stern replied, grinning. "But in my off hours I have been forced to attend."

"You know Jordan, the master of ceremonies so-called?"

"I've seen him."

"Okay. Take a car. He's at the Club now. Keep him in sight. I want to know where he spends the night."

"When do I report?"

"Phone me at home as soon as he goes to roost."

"Yes, sir."

When he had gone out, Sands said to the remaining policeman, "Any report from Higgins for me?"

"Yes, sir. Inspector Higgins telephoned in two hours ago and detailed a man to watch one hundred and ten Charles Street. The man is there now. Inspector Higgins is at home and wants you to phone him."

"All right. Get him for me."

Sands listened to Higgins talk for five minutes, said, "Good work," and hung up.

Havergal came back carrying some pictures, clipped together.

Sands passed up the first two, showing the wrecked car from two angles. The third was the body of a girl lying on

129

its back. The girl's clothes were torn and the blood on her face and neck showed clearly on the print. She had been badly cut by glass. But there was no glass.

Sands looked at it again, swearing softly to himself.

"Who took these pictures, Havergal?"

"Sergeant Breton. Bill Haines was on his holiday at the time."

"In the morning tell Bill to make two more prints of this one and enlarge them."

"Anything the matter?" Havergal asked curiously.

"Look at it."

Havergal looked for some time. "I can't see anything."

"No. Neither did anyone else. I'm going home."

CHAPTER 13

JOEY's customers were leaving. Half of them were drunk and the other half were pretending to be drunk. They jostled at each other and pushed their way to the checkroom. A fat woman without a brassiere spied Stevie at the door and flung herself toward him, crying shrilly. "Stevie! Darling! I missed you! Honestly, I came here just to see you, Stevie!"

Stevie grinned at her and hoped that Joey was within hearing distance and the lady's husband wasn't.

But the lady's husband was. He strode after her, a fat man who looked as if he'd be hairy under his clothes.

"Lilian," he said. "Stop acting like a whore."

"Who's a whore?" Lilian said. "You son of a bitch hairy ape."

"You're drunk. You're a drunken whore."

"Who's a whore?"

"You are."

Lilian stared at him, blinking her eyes slowly. "Who did you say was a whore?"

Stevie disentangled his coat sleeve from her hand and

slipped away past the checkroom in to Joey's office. The office was empty and he sat down in the swivel chair to wait for Joey.

He felt funny, almost dazed. Too many things had happened, that queer man Sands—and mixing beer and scotch —and thinking about Geraldine again. He couldn't have looked at that picture with Geraldine's face dead and covered with blood.

Someone knocked softly at the door.

Stevie said, "Come in," and the door opened slowly and Mamie came through it.

When she saw it was Stevie her eyes widened and she looked scared.

"You," she said uncertainly. "What are you doing here?"

"Waiting for the marster," Stevie said.

"But I . . ."

"But you what?" Stevie said in a hard voice. "Thought I was in jail maybe? You've been drooling maybe?"

She jerked her head in a defiant gesture and pulled her coat around her. It was the coat Tony had given her, she'd worn it tonight specially. There weren't many nice things to remember and the coat was one, with its real silver fox collar.

"I had to tell them what I knew," Mamie said in a whine. "That goddamn policeman . . ."

"What did you tell him?"

"Just what happened, what you did and what you said. Because after all you *said* it."

"You slobbering bitch."

"I—don't you dare to . . ."

"Wanted to pin a murder charge on me, did you? You thought I'd be the goat for Murillo. You knew Murillo had done it, didn't you?" He got up and walked round the desk toward her. "Didn't you?"

"You're crazy," she said in a strangled whisper. "Don't come any closer or I'll . . ."

"You'll scream," Stevie said with a laugh. But he stayed where he was. "I told you last night that I knew where Tony was. You thought I was kidding. I knew where he was because I *saw* him. Get that, Mamie, I *saw* him. He was running like hell."

"You're lying."

"And I bet you've got no idea how that guy can run— after committing a murder."

She half turned as if the suggestion of running was too powerful to resist. But when she had opened the door she didn't run. There were too many people, and no place to run to, and no reason for running.

She turned back. "Did you tell anybody?"

"Not a soul," Stevie said pleasantly. "I'm only telling you so you can get used to the idea of being a rope-widow. After all, Mamie, we're pals, aren't we? Maybe you *did* try to frame me for a murder, but I can let by-gones be by-gones—if it doesn't happen again."

"He—he did it? He really did it, honest to God?"

Stevie nodded. "The girl was knifed and Tony was running. Use your head."

"I can't believe it!"

"Yes," Stevie said sadly, "how hard it is to believe! Our Tony doing a thing like that, staining his honor, falling from the paths of virtue."

"Shut up!"

She was staring at him, her eyes bright with hate. She had her teeth clenched and her breath hissed in and out like a snake's.

Stevie took out a package of cigarettes. By the time he had one lit Mamie was gone, and he wasn't sorry.

I must have been crazy, he thought, wiping the sweat off his forehead.

The noises outside the door were becoming softer, less confused. You could distinguish individual footsteps and voices, hear the cars driving away from the front of the Club; the rattle of coathangers and small change had stopped, the orchestra was gone. A few minutes later all the noises ceased and the Club sank into its grave for the night.

Stevie lit another cigarette and looked around the desk drawers in the faint hope of finding a drink. He didn't find one but the act of looking reminded him again of Sands.

Sands was a little crazy, he thought. You couldn't be so sure of yourself if you weren't. Planning that whole thing tonight, taking the matches and killing the engine in the car and waiting at the other end of the alley.

So that makes me a grasshopper. And I jumped, but not all the way. He's a cop, I can't trust him. If I'd told him the works he'd have thought it was too pat and I was making it up to get even.

132

Let him look at the pictures of the accident first, let him see I'm not lying about that and then I'll tell him the rest.

He closed his eyes and leaned back in Joey's chair, smiling.

I'm going to blow Johnny Heath sky-high.

Sands sat on the edge of his bed and smoked a final cigarette. He was shivering. The apartment house had had its first spurt of heat for the season but that had already disappeared and the radiators had stopped clanging and hissing and were cold and quiet in a little death. Though there were no windows open, small winds formed near the ceiling and swooped down at him, slithering through his pajamas and whirling the smoke away from his head.

He did not get up to put on his bathrobe. The coldness had become important to him, it was a premonition, coming at him like the winds from the ceiling, effectual yet without source.

Something's going to happen tonight, he thought. Perhaps it was Murillo, perhaps Murillo was going to come out from his hiding place and blubber his confession. That's what Murillo's kind did when they got in over their heads and tried something too much for them. Murillo belonged to the substratum of criminals, the petty thieves and pickpockets, the pimps and hopheads and peddlers of dirty pictures. Nothing big-time about Murillo.

Yet he had committed a murder, a completely unnecessary and stupidly bungled murder. He had left behind the print of his glove and the shreds from his cigarette, and the jewels he had come to take. He had run madly out of the house—these were the footsteps that Mr. Heath had heard—and he had been seen plainly by Stevie Jordan.

Strange that Murillo, apparently content until now to live on this woman, should have returned to the field of crime by planning two robberies in one night, both of them failures. Not so strange that the first had failed. Murillo, unarmed, had demanded the night's receipts from the proprietor of the tavern and when he didn't get them simply ran away.

But the second robbery—easy enough to pick up a jewel box and escape. There was no need to pick the lock there on the spot, to wake the girl up, to kill her.

How had he known about the Heaths in the first place?

133

Through one of the servants, or through Johnny Heath. Johnny's current girl friend worked at Joey's with Murillo's girl friend. Probably they exchanged confidences: "Johnny says . . ." "Tony says . . ." "So I said . . ." Mamie fitted that picture, but Marcella Moore did not.

One of the servants. He thought of Ida and smiled. The golden girl, Ida. Unassailable virtue so frequently went hand in hand with acne and petty malice. It would be simple for a man like Murillo, well used to the ways of women, to persuade Ida to leave the front door open.

And it was Ida who had brought Kelsey Heath the morphine. No charge could ever be proved there, of course. Ida could have been told to fetch a box or phial of tablets and not have known what the tablets were. Whether she had known or not could never be proved. The whole business of the poisoning had better be laid aside. Loring had violated his professional code but his motive was understandable. No good would come of reporting him.

Yes, that part of the poisoning could be forgotten, but what of the girl's motive for killing herself?

Kelsey Heath was the common factor in both murders and the poisoning. She had been driving the car when Geraldine Smith was murdered. She had taken the morphine. She was murdered.

A lapse of two years between the first murder and the poisoning, a lapse of only a few hours between the poisoning and Kelsey Heath's murder.

Would she have lived, blind, for two years and then decided to kill herself because of her blindness, only a few hours before someone else killed her for another reason? Or did the attempted suicide *suggest* the murder?

In that case how did Murillo come into it? Had the robbery been planned before Kelsey Heath poisoned herself and was it then too late to change the plan, too late for Murillo's inside help to let him know?

Sands stubbed out his cigarette in an ashtray. He was no longer cold.

Murillo would turn up sooner or later. He'd confess, he'd tell who had helped him or who had hired him. There was no use worrying over confusing side issues now. Murillo had killed the girl, that fact was clear.

Sands looked at his watch. Three o'clock. He felt a vague excitement, a desire to talk to somebody.

He went into the sitting room and poured himself a

drink. He was very warm now, and cheerful. Might be a good idea to telephone and let Alice Heath know that Murillo had killed her sister. She probably wouldn't be sleeping anyway and she'd want to know that an outsider had done it.

He picked up the phone and dialed, and while he waited he kept smiling to himself: imagine ever suspecting Alice Heath of committing a murder—poor bloodless frigid constipated Alice.

So the first of the three telephone calls which were to solve the case took place at three o'clock.

A sleepy voice said, "The Heath residence."

"Is that Maurice?"

"Yes, sir."

"Inspector Sands speaking."

"Yes, sir." Maurice was politely irritable. "The family is in bed, sir. May I take a message?"

"It's not urgent. I thought Miss Heath, if she was still awake, would like to know that we have identified the murderer. We have a witness who saw him running away from the house."

"Oh." Maurice paused. "That's very good news, sir."

Sands thought he sounded surprised and rather disappointed.

"Yes, sir, very good news," Maurice repeated. "I shall see if anyone is awake."

"Tell them to relax," Sands said, thinking, he'll spread it around all right and maybe someone will relax too far.

"Thank you, sir."

"Good night."

"Good night, sir."

The second call was twenty minutes later. Stevie was still waiting in Joey's office for Joey to appear and count up the night's receipts. Joey never left this job until morning. He had a supernatural respect for money, and nickels might grow legs and walk off.

The phone rang. Stevie took his feet off the desk and picked up the receiver.

"Yes?" he said. That was how Joey answered, with polite suspicion.

"Joey?" The voice was a whisper. The man who owned it was either scared or unable to talk any louder because there were people around.

"Yeah, this is Joey," Stevie said. He put his hand in his pocket and jingled some loose change to complete the illusion. "Who's that?"

A silence, a faint cough, then the whisper again, "You all closed up?"

"Yeah. Must be the weather," Stevie said. "Who's speaking?"

"I want to talk to Mamie Rosen. Is she there?"

"Why, yes," Stevie said. "Why, of course, Mr. Murillo. Your friend is here. She says all is forgiven, come home to momma."

The whisper grew into a voice. "So it's you, Jordan, you wise little bastard."

"You come over here and say that," Stevie said, "and leave your knife at home. We'll talk this over like little gentlemen."

The dial tone began to buzz. Stevie hung up slowly. His hand was shaking and crazy little sentences teetered back and forth in his head: Trace that call. Herman the patrol car. Get Murillo. Calling car three six. Is there a policeman in the house?

"Hell," he said. "Holy hell."

So Mr. Murillo was alive and well and in town and mad. Some day he'd come slinking out of an alley with his black fedora pulled down over his eyes, and his mouth thin and sharp as a blade.

He wiped the sweat off his forehead. I'd better tell Sands, he thought. I'd better get it all off my chest and tell him about the other time too, when I saw Murillo coming out of Child's. With Johnny Heath beside him. Murillo looked quite respectable that day. You'd never have thought the two of them had been planning and working it all out.

"Yes?" Sands said into the phone.

"Mr. Sands."

"Mr. Jordan," Sands said dryly.

"Yes," Stevie said. He liked Sands very much then, he liked the way he'd said "Mr. Jordan," without surprise or interest. Silly to think you couldn't trust Sands. You could trust him because he didn't give a damn. "I'm in Joey's office. I just had a phone call from Murillo. Thought you'd like to know."

"Thanks. What did he want?"

"Mamie Rosen. And listen . . ."

136

There was a pause. Sands could hear the squeak of a chair before Stevie put his hand over the mouthpiece of the phone. He didn't hold his hand tight enough and Sands heard him say something in a muffled whisper.

The hand was removed then, and Stevie said, "Excuse me, Mr. Sands. I thought I'd better tell you I saw Murillo. . . ."

"Who's in that office with you?" Sands said urgently. "Jordan . . ."

"Who . . . ?" Stevie said.

Someone whispered, "Stevie," and the chair squeaked again just once before the shot. There was a sigh and a thud, then a crash as the telephone fell from the desk.

Sands said, "Jordan!"

For ten seconds there was no answer. Then he heard the faint sound of footsteps. The telephone must have fallen so that the mouthpiece was against the floor and picked up the footsteps.

Sands counted. Five footsteps. And then nothing.

"Jesus Christ!" Joey said.

He stood in the doorway and watched Stevie bleeding all over his desk, and thought how hard it was going to be to wash the blood off. Maybe he'd have to buy a new desk.

"Slaughter me for a pig," he said. "Move off there, you souse. What's the matter with you?" He edged closer to the desk and then he saw that Jordan was unable to answer, having a bullet in his stomach.

He moved back to the doorway and began to bellow names and obscenities, strangely mixed.

"Jesus Christ! Come here! Hey, Jim, Jesus Christ, police police, Jim!"

The doorman and Sergeant Stern arrived together. They had both heard the shot and had come into the club, leaving the front door unwatched.

Stern went over to the desk. He didn't recognize Stevie because Stevie's head was down on the desk, as if he'd gotten tired and decided to sleep there.

"Who is he?"

"Jordan," Joey said. "He works for me. Jesus Christ."

"Call an ambulance," Stern said. *"Not that phone!* Use another. Make it snappy."

Joey bounced out of the room, still swearing but feeling better now because an ambulance meant Jordan wasn't dead. He wouldn't want Jordan to die, for a number of reasons.

The doorman simply stood, dazed, and looked at Stevie, and shifted his weight from one foot to another. His mouth moved slightly as if he were practising an after-dinner speech.

He found a voice finally, and said, "A good guy, Stevie," but the voice wasn't his. It was too high and small and he discarded it hastily like a man who'd been given the wrong hat from a checkroom.

"What'd you say?" Stern asked.

The doorman coughed. "Nothing."

"You said he was a good guy."

"Well, he was."

"Well, why'd you say you said nothing?" Stern said, angry at himself, and the doorman and Stevie and even Sands. He thought of the razzing he'd have to take when the rest of them found out that the man he was supposed to follow got himself shot about fifty yards away.

The ambulance clanged up the street and shrieked to a stop.

"The ambulance," said the doorman.

"Yeah," said Sergeant Stern.

They parted forever on this note.

Joey's phone call to the hospital had been so vivid that the ambulance was equipped with an experienced doctor in addition to the usual interne and orderlies. They came prepared to give a transfusion, and they did it there, right in Joey's office. While Joey stood outside the door wringing his hands and swearing and wondering if he'd have to buy a new desk.

Sands himself arrived just after the ambulance clanged back to the hospital. He found Joey and Sergeant Stern glaring at each other across the bloody desk.

"Dead?" he said sharply to Stern.

"No, sir," Stern said. "This guy wants to wash off the desk and I said he couldn't."

Sands said to Joey, "That's right, you can't."

"Well, for Christ's sake," Joey said, sounding as if he wanted to cry. "He's still living, isn't he? It's not a murder, is it?"

Sands didn't answer. He was walking slowly around the room, not touching anything. It was a very small room. He stood in front of the desk, then turned and walked to the door, stealthily. Three steps, possibly four, if you tip-toed. But there had been five.

"You try it," he said to Joey.

"Try what?"

"Go to the desk and then walk to the door."

Joey made it in four steps, Sergeant Stern three.

"The gun wasn't very big," Stern volunteered. "Maybe a .32. I heard the shot."

"So did I," Sands said softly. "I was talking to him on the telephone."

"Talking to him?" Joey said, and began to swear again, almost absently.

"Powder burns?" Sands said to Stern.

"Yes sir."

"Fix up the telephone before an operator starts buzzing," Sands said. "Where's another phone?"

"Checkroom," Joey said.

"I'll find it. Stay here."

In the checkroom he dialed a number. It was a full minute before a man's voice, sleepy and angry, said "Hello."

"Miss Mamie Rosen live there?"

"Who wants to know?" the man said. "What's the idea waking people up in the . . . ?"

"Police-Inspector Sands speaking," Sands said. "Call Miss Rosen to the phone please."

The man said, "All right, keep your shirt on," and went away. Sands could hear his slippers flapping along the floor.

"She ain't come in yet."

"All right, thanks."

He went back to the office.

"Stay here, Stern, until the boys arrive. No need for you to stay, Mr. Hanson."

"Hell, no," Joey said bitterly. I should just leave and let your hoodlums tear up the office by the roots. *I stay.*"

"You stay," Sands said. "Who cares? Good night."

Once out of their sight Sands ran along the hall and out to his car. He was on Charles Street within ten minutes. Most of the house lights were out. The houses were built alike, a row of them, dark and blank and mysterious.

One hundred and ten in tin letters nailed on a muddy-red pillar. A hall light was burning. Sands got out of the car and walked up to the front of the house and looked in. But he did not press the bell because a light had gone on suddenly in the front left room and a woman came to the window and pulled down the blind.

Sands rapped at the door, very quietly, so that only the woman could hear him. She came out immediately into the hall as if she'd been expecting someone. She was smiling when she opened the door.

The smile fled from her eyes though her mouth remained as it was, with the corners turned up.

"What do you want?" she said.

A man came sauntering up the street, and both Sands and the woman turned to look at him. Sands recognized him as the policeman assigned to watch the house.

"Miss Rosen?" Sands said. "My name is Sands."

"Well?"

"I want to talk to you."

"So do a lot of other guys," Mamie said. "But I don't like their language. Beat it."

"I would like to borrow some of Mr. Murillo's clothes," Sands said. "Shall I wait here or come inside?"

She stared at him and her eyes were big brown glass marbles ready to fall out and roll down the steps.

"Police," Sands said.

"What do you want?"

"What I said. Some of Murillo's clothes."

"Why?"

Sands smiled. "Oh, say for sentimental reasons. Shall I come in?"

"No, don't you dare! Don't you dare!"

She leaned against the wall, breathing so hard that her breasts shook. She rubbed her left foot up and down her right leg, like a child seeking comfort. Sands noticed that her shoes were too tight. There was a puff of fat where the shoes stopped.

"Do your feet hurt?" Sands said.

"My—my *feet?*" The question frightened her more than the others. She didn't understand that he simply wanted to know, had always wanted to know if it was true that women would suffer to make their feet appear half an inch smaller. This seemed the right time to find out.

"What about my feet?" she said huskily. "You must be crazy. What about my feet? *What about them?*

"Did you walk home from the club?"

"Yes."

"In those shoes?"

140

"What's the matter with these shoes? You beat it. I don't believe you're a policeman. Get the hell out of here."

"I want some of Murillo's clothes. Hat, shoes, coat and a shirt, unlaundered if possible." He stepped inside the hall and she made no move to stop him. She was still leaning against the wall as if she was exhausted.

"Do I go in alone?" Sands said. "Or are you coming?"

She blinked at him. "I'm coming. But don't you touch me!"

"Why should I touch you?"

"Why in hell shouldn't you?" she said angrily. "Who do you think you are? Think you're too good for me?"

He had hit her professional pride for the second time and he knew she was dangerous without her pride. He let her walk in ahead of him, still watching her feet. She walked with small mincing steps, her body bent forward, adjusting itself to the high heels.

He looked around the room. The best room of the house undoubtedly, which was not saying a great deal. The bed had a chenille spread, there was a studio couch, a fireplace with a litter of unburned cigarette ends and waste paper, an easy chair, and a wardrobe standing along one wall.

He pulled open the wardrobe. Mamie's clothes and Murillo's hung together on the rack in conjugal bliss.

"Help yourself," Mamie said bitterly. "I can't stop you. Steal anything you want to."

"Borrow is a better word," Sands said.

He took a hat, a black fedora, from the top shelf, a coat, a dirty shirt from a pile of clothing on the floor, and a pair of shoes.

"What, no *pants*?" Mamie said.

He shut the wardrobe carefully. With the clothes piled over one arm and the pair of shoes in his hand he looked like a junk man who had just closed a bargain.

"Any rags, any bones, any bottles?" Mamie said, "Now get out and leave me in peace." Her mouth was shaking and she covered it with the back of her hand.

"Nerves?" Sands said. "I shouldn't wonder. What did you do with the gun?"

"G-gun? What gun?"

"The gun you used on Jordan."

She began to sob. "Oh, you're crazy, you're just crazy. You keeping saying these things to me and I can't stop you and I don't know what you're meaning. *And I just don't know. . . . "*

"Then I'll tell you. Jordan was shot in the stomach tonight in Joey's office. It's a very nasty place to shoot anyone. They don't die fast, they just bleed away. It's the place a woman usually aims for. Women like big targets."

"I don't know," Mamie sobbed. "I just don't know."

"That's why I'm telling you. Jordan isn't dead. They gave him a transfusion and took him to a hospital. The odd part of it is that he was talking to me when he was shot. I heard someone say 'Stevie' so it was someone he knew pretty well, don't you think? Not Murillo. If Murillo had come into the office Jordan would have yelled. And besides, Murillo doesn't use a gun. After the shot I heard footsteps, five of them. We tried it out later when Jordan was taken away. A man wouldn't need to take five steps to reach the door. A woman would, especially if she wore shoes that were too small and had high heels."

She stopped sobbing and cried, "And I'm the only woman in town who does?"

"Rather cool night," Sands said. "What did you wear on your walk home?"

"A coat."

"Gloves?"

"What about it?"

"Where are the gloves?"

"None of your business!" she yelled.

He began to walk toward her, slowly. "Everything you do is my business," he said softly, "because I'm out to get Murillo. I'm going to get Murillo. I'm going to get Murillo."

She fell forward on her knees, screaming.

" . . . in co-operation with the police department, the makers of Crispcrunch, the ideal new breakfast food that is teeming with vitamins and good flavor, are broadcasting this description of a dangerous criminal. Wanted for murder: Antonio Murillo. Eyes, brown. Complexion, medium. Hair, curly black. Height, five foot eleven. Weight 160 pounds. Age 28. Watch for this man, all you good people who are breakfasting on Crispcrunch. He is a dangerous criminal, and perhaps he is a dangerous criminal because he hadn't the advantage of a perfect diet with a balanced supply of minerals, vitamins and calories. And a perfect diet spells *Crispcrunch!* The time is fourteen and one-half minutes past eight o'clock, and your Crispcrunch announcer is Al Animal."

"Turn it off, John," Alice said irritably. "Your bacon is getting cold."

The thin stream of sunlight from the window caught her face and pinched it into angles as sharp as her voice. It was as if Alice, having given herself away last night, had turned up a new path, and the controlled gentleness by which they had come to recognize her had vanished never to return.

"John," she said, as a blare of music hit the room.

Johnny turned the knob and came back to the table. "Murillo," he said. "That must be the one."

"What one?" Philip asked, and then, "Oh. You didn't tell Alice?"

"Tell me what?" Alice said.

Philip reached over and put his hand over hers. It was all she ever got from Philip, a pat on the hand, or a friendly arm around her shoulder. It was all she ever would get. She looked at him with dry cold eyes and said, "Why the affection? More bad news?"

143

He drew his hand away. "No. Good news, I suppose you'd call it. This man Murillo—Inspector Sands telephoned last night and said they had proof that Murillo killed—killed Kelsey."

Her mouth opened in surprise. "Incredible!"

"Why incredible?" Johnny said.

She gestured with her fork. "I mean, how could a man, a man we've never even heard of, how could he change our whole lives like this? It's fantastic."

"Meaning it doesn't fit in with your orderly philosophy," Johnny said. "That can't be helped. I wonder what this Crispcrunch tastes like. I don't think I'm getting enough vitamins." Though he spoke lightly, he was perfectly serious and Alice knew it.

She said coldly, "Don't be moronic. What else did the Inspector say?"

"Just that," Johnny said. "Maurice answered the phone. Phil and I were having a cigarette in my room and he saw the light under the door and came in and told us. What's moronic about wanting more vitamins?"

"We have a whole cupboard full of vitamins," Alice said, "that you've been persuaded to buy by radio announcers. Get rid of those first."

Philip said wanly, "Let's not have a fight about anything."

"Who's fighting?" Johnny said. "All I want is a balanced diet."

Alice rang the little bell in front of her plate and Maurice came in with the coffee.

He set the coffee in front of Alice and gave her a small prissy smile and said, "Good morning." Alice knew from the smile and the voice that Maurice had some kind of bad news and was determined to relay it. Usually the news was impersonal: he had heard on the kitchen radio or read in the morning paper of a bad fire or an accident or a murder or a robbery. If there was nothing like this on hand he would quote verbatim from a fireside chat or mention the name of some Russian village where so many Nazis had been captured or killed. It was necessary to Maurice to bring tidings, to have all eyes turned up at him, Maurice, the kingly messenger: "Yes, miss, burned right to the ground, two children burned to death." "Fifty thousand corpses strewn on the ground."

"Well?" Alice said sharply.

144

Maurice said, "Inspector Sands has arrived."

Philip said, "But I thought—didn't he say he had proof that . . . ?"

"Yes, sir. *Nevertheless.*"

"Does he want me?" Alice said.

"No, Miss Alice." Maurice, kingly messenger, would not be hurried. He arranged his face and his voice carefully, while all eyes turned up at him. "He's talking to *Ida.*"

"Ida?" Alice repeated.

"I thought you'd like to know, miss."

"Yes. Thanks."

Maurice went out again. He had had his moment.

"Be kind of funny to meet this Murillo on the street," Johnny said. "Mind if I see if any other station is featuring him?"

"I do mind, yes," Alice said.

"That's too damn bad."

He got up and turned the radio on again. Alice had given herself away, she had lost her mystery, and with it her power. She had no hold over these two men, Johnny fumbling with the radio, Philip eating his bacon politely and without appetite.

We've all changed, Alice thought, and this man, Murillo, whom we don't know and never will know, has used the knife on us all. Kelsey is dead, and Philip is like a man who's had a tumor removed and the pain is gone but the knife has left him weak. And Johnny—Johnny has simply had the years cut from him. He is the Johnny who came home for holidays and filled the house with noise and music and bulky sweaters and coon coats with human legs and heads which turned out to be other Johnnys.

And then one day he brought another young man who was not a Johnny and who had no coon coat, a serious, pale, hungry-looking young man whom Johnny had picked up in a movie, casually, the way he picked up girls or stray dogs and cats. The young man played the piano for his dinner while Johnny sat back beaming proudly at his discovery. Those were the days when Isobel still came down to dinner. When the young man had played Isobel said, "Good. Excellent," in the firm way she had, though she knew nothing about music.

But it was good, perhaps even excellent. The young man was embarrassed and pleased and promised to come back.

He didn't come, though, for a long time. He tried everything in the meantime, then one evening he came to the door again. Johnny was out, so Alice and Kelsey and Mrs. Heath had him all to themselves. To Isobel he was everything that Johnny wasn't, and to the two girls he was a new young man, not one of Johnny's friends older than they and inclined to patronize the kid sisters. They sat on each side of him as he played and he couldn't reach the keys properly. He was humiliated at his own failure and deeply embarrassed at the easy manners of the two girls who were used to Johnny's friends. He wanted to go away and never come back, but the house was warm, the girls were friendly, and Mrs. Heath told him he had a remarkable talent. You could tell from Mrs. Heath's face that she was rarely pleased with anything. You could also tell—he felt this even that second night—that she was planning something. Behind the graciousness of the smile her eyes were narrowed: "Would this work out? Would it be to any advantage? Would this boy influence Johnny or Johnny influence him?"

She asked him to stay.

"Criminal to waste such a talent. . . . It would mean nothing to us financially, you understand. . . . Lessons and set hours of practice. . . . A friend for John too—John is so irresponsible. . . . "

He didn't want to stay. He had never wanted to. It wasn't his life and the people who came to the house weren't his people, and the drawing room was never really his to use. He had always to apologize for practising. Isobel hadn't realized that you practiced scales and arpeggios and Pischna. She thought you practiced on Debussy and Bach and Mozart, simply by playing them over and over.

He stayed away a year the first time. But the movies weren't using pianists any longer and he missed tea at four and clean bathrooms and good linen and servants.

When he came back he used his small store of money to rent a room to practice in. His life began to improve. He gave a concert in a church, he fell in love with Kelsey, he gave another concert in a larger church. He was away from the house a great deal and could appreciate it when he got back.

He had even done what Isobel had wanted him to do, influenced Johnny. Johnny had a job and he didn't drink

146

so much because Philip didn't drink at all. There remained the question of Johnny's women, but Isobel didn't know such a question existed. She was pleased with herself, as patroness of the arts and guider of destinies, and gratified at the engagement between Kelsey and Philip.

She had arranged everything. In spite of the pain that twisted and writhed inside her like a snake, she had had enough control to arrange everything before she retired to her room. She never came down again. She died hard, fighting her pain, fighting even the morphine that numbed the pain. She was too tired to feel the full force of Kelsey's accident and her blindness. She only realized vaguely that Kelsey was now a cripple and that cripples must have power as she, Isobel, had power.

To clear her mind she went without morphine for a day and the next afternoon her lawyer came. She made a new will.

She never thought of *me*, Alice thought bitterly. I was always to remain here, managing and controlling but never living. I was the older, I had more right to the money, more right to Philip.

"Excuse me," she said and rose abruptly from the table and went out into the hall. She could feel Philip's eyes following her, and she knew if she turned around that he would be looking puzzled but not really interested. She closed the door quickly so she wouldn't look back.

Other women fell in love and were loved. They might lose their men to death, to other women, but they had had something more than this patient, puzzled stare, this hand patting, this brotherly touch of shoulders. *I have all this love and no one to give it to, no one wants it. I'm a farm girl who's come to market with baskets of produce and can't sell it, can't even give it away. Take it home to rot or give it to the pigs or dump it out on the road. Get rid of it some way, it's beginning to smell.*

It's my *mind.* I'm worse than Ida. I don't want physical love, I want simply to know I am loved.

She passed a mirror and stopped to smile wryly at herself.

"Passionate by post," she said in the cold reasonable voice she used even to herself. "That's my limit. My idea of a bedroom scene is lots and lots of lovely conversation."

Perhaps if I were to be loved I'd become different, I'd learn all the tricks, I'd be *seductive.*

147

The Idas, and the girls that Johnny knew, were brought up to have all the tricks, they knew these things instinctively and had never been thwarted. They lived in homes where the man was master, the man breadwinner and boss, having to be coaxed, cajoled and flattered. The man, the important figure.

If you had a father who was important in the home, Alice thought, perhaps all males were important to you all of your life.

Mr. Heath had been never more than a guest in his house, and his wife and children were never more than polite to him. He had no part in their lives, made no plans or decisions, or contributions to their income. If he was kind his kindness was unnoticed and unnecessary. If he cut any figure at all it was a comic one, a huge helpless ghost moving around the house.

Perhaps my parents aren't to blame, Alice thought.

A brief picture of Dr. Loring flashed into her mind. He was wearing his white coat and was smiling in his half-gentle, half-exasperated way.

Ahead of her the door to the kitchen was closed, but Ida's tearful whine crept through the cracks.

"A good girl I am! The nerve of . . . A good girl!"

Smiling dryly to herself, Alice moved quietly up the stairs.

"Take it easy," Sands said. "Have you a handkerchief?"

It appeared that when you wore an apron a handkerchief was excess baggage. Ida snuffled into starched broadcloth.

"Wait'll I tell my mother," Ida said. "I'll tell her what you . . . "

"I'm asking you once more about the doors. Once more. Maurice tells me the self-lock is kept on all the time. When Maurice and the nurse came in that night after twelve the self-lock was on. So was the light in your room. The nurse saw it."

"Her!" Ida said. "And my light was on because I had a toothache!"

"Some time later in the night the lock was slipped back. We know that because when Mr. Heath came into the house the door was unlocked."

"Why didn't he lock it then?" Ida said sulkily.

"He did, but it was too late. The man was already inside."

"Man! Always this man! You don't have to go looking around for someone to throw it on, not if you got eyes in your head. They all wanted her dead excepting me. Her own sister making calf-eyes at . . ."

"There *was* a man," Sands said, "and the door was left open for him by someone in this house."

"Well, why don't you pick on the rest of them? Old high-and-mighty pussyfoot could have done it the same as me. The old goat sniffing around that nurse!"

Sands smiled, pleased with this picture of Maurice with a cloven hoof.

Ida did not return the smile. To Ida smiles and jokes were always personal. If you and somebody else smiled, that was all right, the joke was on a third person. But if someone smiled *at* you . . .

Her mouth shook with rage. "Ask them all! Ask them about money! Ask them why my only friend in this house tried to kill herself!"

"With your help," Sands said quietly.

She stared at him with her mouth open. Then she bounded toward the door and hurled herself against it.

"Wait," Sands said. "No one is going to bring any action against you."

"I didn't know!" Ida screamed. "I didn't know what she was asking me to do! She said a box on the top of the bathroom cupboard. She said to make her sleep. She said, sit there, Ida, with me, while I go to sleep. I'm tired, she said, and I'm scared, alone here in the dark. So I sat there and told her things, about my mother who is a seventh daughter of a seventh daughter and the sparks fly from her in the dark and she talks with people not of this world. And pretty soon she is quiet and I think, she is dead. I think, I'll ask my mother to get in touch with her spirit."

"And why did she want to die?"

"She was scared. There was these eyes on her watching her. She said, someone is waiting for me to die; someone is watching me and waiting, someone hates me."

"And you didn't think it might be her imagination?"

"You can feel hate," Ida said simply. "It's like she said, it's like eyes on you. And when you got no eyes yourself and people are wishing you dead and you're scared of what comes after you're dead . . . Me, I'm not scared because I know if I'm a good girl . . ."

"You'll go to heaven. All right," Sands said. Ida, enchanted angel, purged of sin and acne and provided with a handkerchief. Ida, ectoplasmic wraith, writing on slates and rapping on tables: this is Ida, I am well and happy here. Green pastures and streets of gold, smelling faintly of sweat and cabbage, hair and Ben Hur perfume. This is Ida, come to heaven. Hello, momma.

"Sarcasm don't hurt me," Ida said. "Sticks and stones may break my bones but names will never hurt me."

"Irrelevant, surely," Sands murmured, but he moved to let her out of the door. He had reached the saturation point with Ida and he was convinced that she had not unlocked the door for Murillo. His conviction came from nothing she said, but the impression she gave to him and would have given to Murillo. He felt strongly that Murillo would never have bothered with her under any circumstances. Murillo, vain and dapper in black fedora, mauve silk shirt and pointed shoes, would never have stooped to Ida.

Joe Lee would have the clothes by now, would be finding out from the hat what color Murillo's hair was now and how much there was of it and if he had dandruff. The coat would give the weight, the shoes the height. Joe had Mamie's black kid gloves. The case would soon be closed. They'd have Murillo within a week or two and the loose ends would be caught up or snipped off. Yet Sands felt uneasy.

He phoned the hospital and talked to Pearson, Stevie Jordan's doctor. Pearson inclined to the dark view: Mr. Jordan was still unconscious and would probably remain unconscious for a long time, if not forever. The bullet had been removed and sent to the police lab.

"I beg pardon, sir."

Sands swung around and said, "Don't sneak up on me, Maurice."

"No, sir. I didn't intend to, sir. I merely wondered if you were through with the kitchen. I am going to prepare Mr. Heath's breakfast. Mr. Heath doesn't come down to breakfast."

"Why not?"

Maurice coughed. "Well, sir, he's not what you might call a—a sociable man."

"I found him sociable."

"You did, sir?"

"I found him delightful, as a matter of fact."

150

Maurice swallowed hard and turned away.

"He's hardly old enough to be senile, is he? Let's see. About your age, Maurice?"

"Yes. sir." Maurice said tightly.

"Fond of him?"

"I have been with him for nineteen years."

"It doesn't follow, Maurice. Suppose you are fond of him, why not quit treating him like an imbecile? Get him down to meals, get him talking."

Maurice flushed a deep red. "One would think to hear you that the family was mistreating him."

"Perhaps they are," Sands said, wishing he had never started the conversation. "From ignorance, not malice. Perhaps this family doesn't understand human values. When the girl Kelsey was dying and afraid to die alone, she asked a kitchenmaid to sit with her."

Maurice said stiffly, "She suffered from delusions, sir."

"What, *another one?*"

"There is such a thing as heredity. Miss Kelsey imagined the eyes upon her and because Ida had come to the house after she first imagined the eyes she trusted Ida. It's very simple. I must make Mr. Heath's breakfast now."

"Go ahead. I'll watch."

"I prefer . . . " Maurice began, but Sands was already arranging himself at the kitchen table.

"Why doesn't the cook make Mr. Heath's breakfast?"

"She has a migraine." Maurice placed two slices of bread in a toaster with such careful attention to detail that the act seemed very difficult, one to be attempted only by an expert like Maurice.

"All sorts of nervous disorders in this house," Sands said, "from delusions of persecution through senility to neurosis. Or has the cook an allergy?"

"I don't know," Maurice said grimly.

"The toast is burning."

"The toaster is automatic and can't burn the bread."

"You think," Sands said, watching a plume of smoke rise to the ceiling. "Maybe the toaster has a complex."

Maurice folded his lips and removed the charred bread and flung it on the table. One of the pieces slid across to Sands. He caught it neatly.

"Good for retreads," he said. "I'll keep it."

"Why are you here annoying me?" Maurice said savagely.

151

"I don't know," Sands said, and he didn't know. He was aware only that he wanted to annoy someone because he was tired and uneasy and the refined stupidities of the Heath family irritated him.

Yet the reason was more basic than this. He was a reformer who despaired of reform. He wanted to sting them all into awareness, and change; but he had merely the sting of a bee, not the fangs of a snake. He couldn't change any of these people. Let Maurice keep his prissy ceremonials, let Alice freeze over and Mr. Heath sink deeper into his bog and Ida wiggle her way to heaven.

He pushed back his chair and there was the high wail of wood on wax.

"Go to hell," he said, and left Maurice brooding over the toaster like an alchemist over a crucible, intense and important.

"Watch it, Maurice, you never know what might come out of a toaster, might even be toast."

CHAPTER **15**

JOHNNY HEATH, at thirty, should still have been at college. It was the life he liked, the life that suited him: people to talk to and drink with, girls who didn't expect him to propose after two dates, careless comfortable clothes, men to look down on (those who got A's) and to sympathize with (those who shared his own C's). No woman to boss him, except by post and long-distance telephone. Fun and games, horseplay and rugby.

He had even thought, once or twice, of going back to take a post-grad course. But it wouldn't be the same, and besides they wouldn't let him into grad work since he had required five years to finish a three-year course.

But still. Nice to think about. Nice to have everything planned for you again, to have a goal post set up. All you had to do then was get there, any way at all, gain yards inch by inch or make a spectacular touchdown. And after the goal, what? Another goal post further away and hazy, with blurred lettering: Success. Make something of yourself.

Get a job. Be at the office at nine. Sell bonds. Sell five hundred thousand dollars' worth of bonds and then look up and see if the goal post is any nearer, or if you've reached it. It isn't and you haven't.

Somebody's moved the damn thing further back, the lettering is no clearer. Or maybe your eyes aren't so good, you're older, your uniform's wearing out, somebody's got a grip on your ankle and your face is on the ground and the umpire went home to lunch. Get up. Another day, another nine o'clock, another bond.

He snapped the radio off and yawned.

"You're late," Philip said.

"I hope so," Johnny said. "I hope to God so."

"I thought they gave you a week off."

"They did," Johnny said. "One week off. But I'm too noble to take it. I go down today, stricken though I am. Then I break down. Then the boss says, 'Heath's a fine fellow, let's give him two weeks off.' You begin to perceive?"

"Yes," Philip said shortly, "and I don't like it."

"You'll live." Johnny waved his hand and went out into the hall.

Inspector Sands was standing at the front door with his coat over his arm.

"Good morning," Johnny said. "Going or coming?" I'm going."

"I want to talk to you," Sands said.

"Sure, but I'm late."

"I'll drive you down."

"I always take my own car."

"Always except this morning," Sands said. "Get your coat and hat."

Johnny whistled. "Tough. Very, very tough this fine fall day." He went to get his coat.

" I am investigating the death of Geraldine Smith."

"Geraldine . . . ?" Johnny turned around, his eyes blank. Sands knew the blankness was real, that Johnny had forgotten the girl.

"Smith," he said.

"Oh."

"Died, apparently, in an accident while riding in your car. Remember?"

"Of course I remember," Johnny said irritably. "That was settled years ago."

"Your mistake. I'm just settling it now."

"I don't understand. Why rake that up?"

"Get your coat and hat."

"I'm not going," Johnny said. "If you want to talk, talk here."

"As you like." Sands put his coat on the hall table and followed Johnny down the hall into a small room furnished with sun, wickerwork and yellow chintz. Johnny filled one-half of the room nicely which, Sands thought, made the whole thing far cosier than was necessary.

Johnny dangled one leg over the arm of a wicker chair and smiled at Sands.

"Why be cute?" Sands said. "Or can't you help it?"

The smile faded. "Why be tough for that matter?"

"I just wanted to make it clear that no matter how charming your smile or glistening your teeth or open your countenance, you leave me cold. Save yourself trouble and just answer questions. How long had you known Geraldine Smith before she died?"

"A month or so, maybe. I met her at the club and took her out a couple of times. She was their singer then."

"Nice girl?"

"Average. Rumor had it that she raped easily, but I wouldn't know about that. I didn't try it. She always acted very prim. Anyway, she had a boy friend at the time."

"Who?"

"She never told me and I didn't give a damn. I wasn't trying to get her away from him. She was just a girl."

"What happened the night of the accident?"

"It's a long time ago. . . ."

"Go ahead."

"Well, Kelsey and Philip and I had gone to a football game at the stadium. Alice stayed home with my mother. After the game we felt the way you feel, you know, sort of festive, as if we should be doing something interesting. We went downtown and had dinner and after dinner Kelsey wanted to go dancing somewhere and told me to get another girl. I rang up Geraldine from the restaurant and she said she'd come if we could have her at the club at nine-thirty. Then I went back to the table and told the others that I'd gotten a girl and we piled in the car and went to pick up Geraldine. That was about eight o'clock."

"Dark?"

"Yes. Kelsey drove. She'd had a couple of drinks and Philip objected, but Kelsey always got her own way. So they waited in the car while I went in to get Geraldine. She was ready, waiting. I took her out and introduced her to the others and we got in the rumbleseat. We decided to go out to the Golden Slipper for a while. But we didn't get there. That's all I can tell you."

"I hope not," Sands said dryly. "How did the accident happen?"

"I was in the rumbleseat and can't swear to it. But Kelsey said she asked Philip for a cigarette and while Philip was lighting it the car skidded. Philip grabbed the wheel but we crashed anyway. That's all I remember."

"You were unconscious?"

"We all were."

"Go on."

"When I came to there was a motorcycle cop and an ambulance and a lot of other people around. They took the other three away in the ambulance. I wasn't cut and didn't seem to be broken anywhere so I stayed and told the cop all I could and then one of the people drove me home. Later on I went to the hospital and found out Geraldine had been killed. She'd been cut by flying glass."

"Where did you come to?"

"Where? In the rumbleseat, naturally."

"Not naturally."

Johnny stared. "Why not? That's where I'd been sitting."

"The girl's body was found some distance from the car. She'd been flung out by the impact. You were sitting beside her."

"You mean, why wasn't I flung out too?"

"No. I mean you were and came back and parked yourself in the rumbleseat again."

"While I was unconscious?"

"No, while you were conscious."

"What in hell would I do that for?" Johnny said violently.

"Because you wanted to be found as far from Geraldine's body as possible, having just cut her throat."

155

There was a silence. Sands reached in his coat pocket and brought out an envelope.

"See," he said. "Here's Geraldine when she was found. Here, take it."

"No," Johnny whispered. "No, I don't want it!"

"Go on, look at it. It's only a picture taken a long time ago of a girl who doesn't look like that now."

He took the picture out of the envelope and held it in front of Johnny's eyes.

"See. This is Geraldine."

Johnny raised his eyes slowly and looked at the picture. "Well?" he said hoarsely. "That's her. What about it?"

"Dead as a doornail, isn't she? Yet the rest of you got off pretty lightly. It was a freak that your sister was blinded, she wasn't badly hurt and Mr. James was merely cut. You were simply knocked out. Geraldine was killed."

"Well, hasn't that happened before in accidents?"

"Often," Sands said. "But look again. Where is the glass? Where is all the glass that cut Geraldine's throat?"

"I don't know!"

He lunged out of his chair nearly knocking Sands across the room. "I can prove I was unconscious. I can prove I didn't do anything to her. Wait here. *I'll prove it!*"

He ran out, shouting, "Phil! Phil!"

A couple of minutes later he came back thrusting Philip ahead of him into the room.

"Tell him," he shouted. "And you, you smart bastard, you listen." He pushed Philip into a chair and towered over him. "Go on, tell him."

Philip looked wanly up at him. "What am I to tell him? I don't even know what you were talking about."

"Tell me about the accident," Sands said.

"Accident? What accident?" Philip said. "If you wouldn't make so much noise, Johnny—I don't know what I'm supposed to say."

"He thinks I killed Geraldine," Johnny cried. "He says I cut her throat, murdered her." He swung back to face Sands. "Why in hell would I murder her? Have you thought of that?"

"Stevie Jordan thought of it," Sands said quietly. "He was the boy friend whose name you didn't know."

"Jordan?"

"Geraldine moved out of his place. She expected to marry you and I gather you didn't want her."

156

"So I killed her! I didn't just quit seeing her, I had to *kill* her!"

"You're making this stuff up," Philip said to Sands. "You know as well as I do that the girl wasn't murdered."

"She was murdered," Sands said. "Jordan's known for some time. Last night he told me—a couple of hours before he was shot in the stomach."

Johnny opened his mouth wide as if he were going to shout, but his voice was merely an echo of itself. "Jordan's dead?"

"Not quite. As good as dead for the time being, though. Somebody's safe. Jordan wanted to tell me something, about Murillo. I was talking to him on the phone when he was shot. By a friend of his. A friend of yours, too, Mr. Heath, a woman."

"What if it was done by a friend of Johnny's?" Philip said anxiously. "Why, Johnny has millions of friends, He's not responsible for what they . . . "

"Shut up," Johnny said. He stared at Sands, blinking his eyes slowly. "What's Jordan got to do with Geraldine dying? You think I asked one of my friends to shoot him? You think I can't do my own shooting?"

"Johnny," Philip cried. "Don't talk . . . "

"Shut up," Johnny said again, without looking at him.

"I won't shut up! I—you get so irresponsible. Don't say any more till you've cooled off." He looked at Sands. "Johnny couldn't have killed Geraldine. He was unconscious. I know, because I came to first and got out of the car to help Kelsey. When I saw I couldn't do anything for Kelsey I went around to the rumbleseat. Johnny was bent over, his head had cracked against the seat and he was unconscious. Then a motorcycle policeman came along. . . . "

"You didn't go over to help the girl?" Sands said.

"No. No, I'm sorry. I—I forgot she was with us. I'd never met her before and the shock . . . I just forgot her."

"You think I can't do my own shooting?" Johnny said. "You think I couldn't shoot up this whole goddamn bastard town and get away with it?"

"That's right," Sands said, "you couldn't. If I'm lucky you and your friend Murillo will hang together."

"I don't need my friends to help me!"

"You can't be serious," Philip cried, "either of you!

157

You're just talking! How could Johnny know a man like Murillo?"

"Ask Johnny," Sands said. "How much did you fork out, Heath?"

Johnny smiled coldly. 'Nothing. He did it free on account of we're pals, Murillo and I. We were talking one day and he said, 'Johnny, is there anyone you want murdered?' 'Yes,' I said, 'Geraldine Smith and my sister Kelsey and a guy called Jordan.' Now how about getting out of here before I lose my temper?"

"You won't lose your temper," Sands said mildly. "You can't afford to. Try to smile your way out of this one, charm boy."

Johnny walked to the door. "I'm cool," he said over his shoulder. "And now that I'm onto your methods I'm going to stay cool. I'm going for a walk. The hell with the office."

When the door slammed, Philip kept staring at it as if he were trying to convince himself that it *was* a door. At last he turned his eyes to Sands, almost pleadingly.

"You don't understand Johnny," he said. "He never means what he says. He's always boasting, talking big. He's never grown up, he's still a boy."

"You think such boys are harmless?"

"Johnny's harmless. Anybody knows that. He brags because his sisters and his mother have always tried to boss him. He doesn't know Murillo. He never even heard of him until this morning."

"Yes?"

"I'm sure of it. Johnny's harmless. He gets his small pleasures from trying to outwit people. Like this morning. He intended to appear at the office as a sign of good-will so they'd give him an extra week off. That's typical of him."

He spoke gravely and pedantically, and like a schoolmaster finishing a lecture he inclined his head slightly and left the room.

A dull young man, Sands decided, with a faint air of apology about him as if he didn't feel entitled to the air he breathed, the rarefied air of the Heath family. The type of man the Heath sisters would choose, to bully and to mother alternately.

Yet Sands could not dismiss the man from his mind with such a simple classification. Could there be irony in the naive blank smoothness of Philip's manner? Irony, Sands mused, there are a dozen kinds of irony. I'm an ironist myself: Socratic irony I suppose you'd call it—but when I say I know nothing it's often true. Johnny is a romantic ironist, defying fate, fighting his own mediocrity with a loud laugh and big muscles and his family's money. And Philip? If Philip was an ironist the division between the external falsity and the internal truth lay so deep in his nature that it could not be decried. Perhaps so deep that it lay in the center of his mind, so that when his right lobe said white and his left lobe said black he himself could not tell which was right and which was wrong, but only that both were ironic in relation to each other.

Then the truth would be in neither, Sands thought, the truth would be in the irony.

The sun was becoming stronger and warmed the back of his neck. It was pleasant to sit in this strange bright little room and consider the destinies of other people and not have one of your own. Alice and Philip would marry, and eventually Maurice and Letty, and Maurice, in the manner of men who marry too late, would show his affection by patting Letty's rear. The pats would be too hard to be playful, yet not hard enough to be anything else. They would undress, partly, in the dark, and Letty would close her eyes and think things. What did women think of at such a time? It had never been told or written. Women never gave themselves away completely.

CHAPTER **16**

THE section of the city was a bad one but the cottage itself was well kept and neat. A row of salvias still bloomed on either side of the veranda. Sands used the knocker, a brass lion's head with a piece of felt glued to it to dull the sound.

159

The woman who came to the door was a small timid scrawny woman in a house dress and hair curlers. She opened the door about six inches and peered hostilely through the crack.

"Mrs. Moore?" Sands said. "I've come to see your daughter Marcella. My name is Sands."

"My daughter's sleeping," Mrs. Moore said abruptly. "She works late and she's got to get her sleep no matter what your name is. You can come back later."

"No," Sands said politely, "I can't."

"Well then, I guess you won't see her."

She sounded firm enough but she didn't close the door. Sands guessed that Marcella had given her orders and that Mrs. Moore herself didn't care who came to the house.

"Detective-Inspector Sands," he said, giving her his card. "I want to see your daughter right now. It's important, about a murder."

"About—about a murder?" She looked shocked yet at the same time relieved that the decision had been taken from her hands. "Well, come in, I guess. I'll call her."

She flung open the door and stepped back quickly into the hall to let Sands come in. She put one hand up to her head as if to hide the curlers.

"I—I'll go and call her. In there's the parlor. You can sit down and I'll . . . "

"Yes. Thanks."

He left the door of the tiny parlor open. He heard Mrs. Moore go upstairs and call softly, "Marcie! Wake up, dear. There's a . . . "

"How many times have I told you not to wake me up before . . . "

"Hush, dear. You weren't sleeping, were you?"

"I *was* sleeping! Why do you think I wasn't sleeping?"

"Not so loud. You just sounded sort of awake. I'm— I'm sorry. There's a man downstairs. A policeman, he says he is."

"Tell him to wait." Marcie's voice was deliberately loud and clear. "I'll be down when I'm good and ready to come down."

There were more sounds of hushing and then Mrs. Moore came downstairs again. She did not come into the parlor but stood in the doorway looking down at her fingernails.

"She'll be down any minute," she said in a low voice. "She's kind of tired and . . . "

"Thanks," Sands said again.

"And if you'll excuse me, I'll just—I'll go and . . . "

"That's all right."

He waited for ten minutes. When Marcie appeared she gave him a curt nod. He saw that she had been making him wait deliberately, because she had not combed her hair or dressed or made up her face. Sands, tolerant of the larger sins, was always shocked by petty spite.

He said coldly, without rising, "Sit down, please."

She crossed the room and sat down with exaggerated care for the long skirt of her housecoat. She didn't look as young as she did under a spotlight, and not at all shy. She didn't have to pretend anything here in this house that she herself supported. Behind this door she didn't have to waste any of the shy fleeting glances she used on Stevie Jordan or Johnny Heath.

"Well?" she said.

He handed her his card. She took it, holding it by one corner.

"You don't have to be so smart," Sands said. "I'm not trying to get your fingerprints."

She let the card flutter to the floor. "I was just being careful. The police think up a lot of cute things, like the insurance agent that came yesterday. He didn't fool me. I can take care of myself."

"You didn't by any chance take care of Stevie Jordan too, did you?"

"Stevie? What are you talking about?"

"Jordan was shot last night in Joey Hanson's office. He's in the hospital and he probably won't get out of it except the hard way, feet first."

"Stevie," she said in a dazed voice. "Stevie. I don't believe it. No one would want to hurt Stevie. He was a very—he's a nice guy."

"Yes, I liked him," Sands said quietly. "He wasn't shot because he wasn't a nice guy. He was shot because he got mixed up in this quite accidentally. The same as you did, Miss Moore. And once he was mixed up in it he lost his head, the same as you might."

"I'm not mixed up in anything!" Marcie cried.

"Not actively, no," Sands said. "But you knew them all,

161

didn't you? Kelsey Heath, Geraldine Smith, John Heath, Stevie Jordan, Mamie Rosen, Tony Murillo . . . "

"Murillo? I don't know Murillo. I never even saw him." Sands stared at her.

"Well, I never did. I only know his name from listening to Mamie."

"Strange," Sands said.

"What's so strange about it? Do you think any dame in her right senses would bring her boy friend backstage and introduce him to that bunch of bitches?" She paused and repeated "bitches," because she liked the sound of the word coming from her own mouth. It was a word she often thought but never said. Bue here behind her own doors she didn't have to pretend, she could say what she wanted to.

"Murillo's been at the club," Sands said. "Jordan and Joey Hanson know him."

"Just out front though," Marcie said. "And not very often. Mamie told me Joey had warned her to keep Murillo away."

"Did Geraldine Smith know him?"

"I guess so," Marcie said. "She knew Mamie."

"You weren't working there when Geraldine was alive?"

"No. But I heard about her from Stevie and Mamie."

"I suppose you knew that Geraldine was John Heath's girl friend for a time?"

She leaned forward, looking at him levelly. "Get this clear, Mr. Sands. Johnny Heath and what he did or does or will do don't matter a damn to me. He's responsible for getting me into this mess. I didn't do anything to anyone. I made one lousy mistake and that was going out with Heath and putting up with that snotty sister of his and that stuffed shirt of a James. Well, they got their money's worth of laughs out of me. Now I don't want to hear any more about the Heath family. I'm sick of the name. Any woman's a fool to have anything to do with men unless she has to, to get by. Well, I don't have to. I can *dance,* and some day I'm going to prove it and the custo-mers won't be all drunk either."

She leaned back in the chair again and closed her eyes. She had never talked like that before to anyone and never would again. It was tiring to tell the truth, pretending was easier. She must remember how much easier pretending was the next time she felt like giving herself away. It got you nothing to give yourself away and it took too much out of you. She'd go back to the club and pretend she was shy, she'd be aloof from the other girls and careful of her language, *and some day* . . .

Sands left her sitting in the chair, her eyes hard with dreams.

Her mother fluttered back into the parlor, making subdued clucking noises with her tongue.

"It's all right," Marcie said irritably. "Don't make a fuss."

"But—but he said a murder!"

"Nothing to do with me. A boy at the club was shot."

"Oh, you should never have to work in such a place," Mrs. Moore said plaintively. "I don't know, I think it would be almost better to have a job in an office where you get decent people."

"We won't go into that." Marcie turned her head away and gazed blankly out of the window. "It was Mr. Jordan who was shot."

"Mr. Jordan! Isn't he the nice one, the one you said you liked."

"I never said I *liked* him. I said he was better than the rest of them. That's not so hard."

"Well, I thought you—well, all right, dear. You going to stay up now? I'll go up and make your bed."

"All right."

She waited until her mother had gone upstairs, then she slipped into the hall and picked up the phone.

A woman's voice said, "General Hospital."

"Mr. Jordan, please," Marcie whispered.

"Jordan? First name?"

"Steven."

"Room number?"

"I don't know. I just want to know how he's getting along."

"One moment, please." There was a rustle of paper and the drone of distant voices. "Mr. Jordan is not allowed visitors. I'm sorry."

"But how is he? I mean, he's not—not dead?"

"Heavens, no," the woman said with an efficient laugh. "If he were dead his name would be crossed off my list."

"Thank you," Marcie said, and hung up and leaned against the wall, giggling, and crying a little.

The nurse was young and ugly. When she smiled the long scar on her cheek merged with the smile.

"Hello, Kitty," Sands said.

She turned her face so he'd see only the good side of it. "Hello, Inspector."

"They making you at home here?"

"Oh, sure. Most of the time I'm just sitting beside his bed. His temperature's down a little."

"May I see him?"

Kitty smiled again and said, "You don't have to. I did what you said. I got it written out. Wait here a minute."

She disappeared into Jordan's room. When she came back she handed Sands a notebook.

He did not open it. He said, "How's the cheek?"

"Fine." She touched it quickly. "It's nice to be back at work again, though I'd rather be on something more exciting." She rubbed her cheek, smiling, and thinking of how dull her police job had been before she investigated the case of juvenile delinquency that had given her the scar. The juvenile had thrown a bottle.

"They've taken Billy to the epileptic hospital at Woodstock," Sands said, guessing her thoughts.

"Better for him," Kitty said. "He wasn't responsible."

"No."

"Though in a way it makes it worse, having no one to blame, really. Next time I'll duck."

"Good idea," Sands said and opened the notebook. The report was headed, "Steven Jordan—9 A. M.," and was carefully detailed from the moment that Jordan had asked for a drink of water at 9:03 and relapsed into semiconsciousness.

When Sands had finished, Kitty said anxiously, "Of course it's not much, but you can see pretty clearly what was on his mind and from the way he spoke I knew it was urgent. He seemed *frantic*."

"Yes," Sands said.

"He must have seen these two together some place, this Heath and Murillo. Does that make sense?"

"Yes," Sands said gravely. "That makes a lot of sense. Thanks, Kitty."

"Do I read about it in the newspapers some day?"

"Some day, perhaps."

"Well, good luck."

"Good luck," he echoed. He found his way to the

elevator and for the six floors down he stared unseeingly at a woman whose figure was a probability curve. The woman went home and cried bitterly in front of a mirror. Sands went home and lay down on the bed with his clothes on.

Perhaps if he got some sleep he could work it out. If he started at the beginning with the accident, and pictured it all clearly—Kelsey Heath driving, Johnny in the rumble-seat with the girl, the football game and the dinner and the phone call, the date and the girl who was to die ready in her best clothes waiting . . .

She knew it was only a matter of time now. They hadn't found the gun, but the policeman had taken her gloves and there was some test they gave to prove you had fired a gun. Tony had told her about the test. He'd said, "They don't have a test for knives though," and laughed in that crazy shrill way he laughed when he was bragging.

Only a matter of time. She wondered what they'd do to her. Put her in prison, if Stevie lived. For years she'd be in prison, getting older, not even waiting or hoping to get out because there wouldn't be any reason to get out, nothing and no one to come back to.

Or maybe Stevie would die and they'd hang her.

Well, so what? Other people were dying all the time and hanging was quick, quicker than cancer or things like that, and there was no hell and no heaven. What could you lose? You'd lived your life. You asked for it, you got it, you took it. That was the only hell there was. And the only heaven.

But she didn't want to think about love, not just now. Hers wasn't the kind you thought about to make yourself feel good. No moonlight and roses, no love whispers. He'd never told her he loved her. Maybe he would now, if he knew what she'd done for him. If she could tell him, if she had the nerve . . .

She lifted her head from the pillow and looked at the clock. It was only ten. She hadn't wakened so early for years. Maybe that was an omen, to tell her that it was her last day. Last day. Make it long. Make it a good last day. Make the phone ring.

But he wouldn't phone, she knew that. And if she phoned him . . .

Think of the surprise he'd have, imagining he was so well

165

hidden! Think of the fear (that would pay him back a little), and maybe some pleasure too (and then she'd be sorry for having thought of paying him back). Because there was nothing to pay back. She needn't have stayed or let him stay.

If she phoned she'd hear his voice. She didn't even have to ask for him. She'd keep on phoning until he answered it himself. All the other times she'd just hang up without saying anything. She could try it just once. Maybe he'd answer the first time, if she was lucky. And last days should be lucky days to make up for all the other days that had everything in them but luck.

No, she couldn't phone.

She gave a little groan and rolled over on her face and one of the feathers worked through the pillow and pricked her cheek. She propped herself on her elbows and pulled the feather out and looked at it. She began to giggle suddenly, because the feather reminded her of a song Tony had sung once, about a pig who flew past with a feather stuck in him to see which way the wind blew.

"And the wind blew north," Mamie hummed, "and the wind blew south, and the wind blew the feather . . ."

Imagine. Here it was her last day and she was giggling and humming as if nothing was going to happen to her.

Maybe I really *want* something to happen to me. Maybe I don't give a damn as long as it's a change, any change. I think I'd be ready for anything if . . .

No, don't think about phoning him. How do you know the cops wouldn't be listening in? Maybe they tapped your telephone wires. But they wouldn't do that, I'm not important enough, and besides they think I don't know where Tony is.

She sat up straight on the bed and pulled down the sheets. She wasn't conscious of any of her usual morning pains and irritations—the sunken feeling in her eyes, as if they had fallen into her head from their own weight, the sight of herself in the mirror, the pale puffy face and mottled white legs. She went past the mirror without even looking at herself and opened the door into the hall. No one was using the telephone, and Mrs. Malley was upstairs making beds and swearing at her husband to get him up.

She slipped down the hall quietly in her bare feet. She waited until Mrs. Malley had started a new theme, then picked up the phone and dialed the number. She knew it by heart.

It rang three times, then a girl's voice said, "Hello," and Mamie hung up without speaking.

Well, you couldn't count on luck, could you? The luck all went to the wrong people, the kind with brains and looks and money, who didn't need luck. The kind like Tony and her didn't get anything except what they snatched from each other. You had to grab something from somebody else before somebody else grabbed it from you. That was how you had to live. Mamie knew that. She knew that when Tony hit her he wasn't hitting her at all, he was just hitting out at the first thing that was handy, he was hitting out at *Life*. Nothing personal in it. Funny how all these things became clear if you only had a little time left. If people could always think that, that they had only a little time, they'd be nicer, they wouldn't always have to be thinking so far ahead of their own future.

Shivering as her feet struck the bare cold floor she went back into her room and sat in the chair by the window and looked out at Charles Street.

She thought, Stevie was right, it would be kind of gruesome to see the sun rise on Charles Street. Or even the moon. Charles Street was made for darkness.

She wondered if Stevie was dead. And now that things were clearer she even wondered why she shot him. It was late, she was tired, the gun was there in her bag, Stevie had been nasty and he was the only one who'd seen Tony running out of the house. When she shot him she thought she was doing it just for Tony, but this morning she knew that the other reasons counted too. She knew she wouldn't have even thought of shooting him if the gun hadn't been right there in her bag. She had been carrying the gun because she thought if she met Tony she'd give it to him. He might need it, and he'd forgotten to take it along.

It was very funny to think that Tony had murdered someone. He'd always talked about killing—"I'd like to kill that . . . " or "She needs a knife between the ribs," or "I'd like to strangle you."

Just words. He thought he was tough. And then it turned out he was. That was what was funny.

Just like me, Mamie thought. I'm always talking about

killing myself and if I really did that would be funny too. I wouldn't shoot myself because maybe I wouldn't die.

She thought of the pills she had hidden in a drawer. You took the whole dozen of them and then you went to sleep. Then everything was settled for you. You didn't have to worry about jail or Tony or getting old or holding a job or having headaches or washing your stockings. . . .

She went back into the hall. The door into the kitchen had been closed, so that meant that the Malleys were in there and Mr. Malley was eating and Mrs. Malley was watching him, grudging the very grains of sugar he used.

She dialed again, slowly this time, putting off the moment when the girl's voice would say, "Hello," again and she'd have to go back to her room without hearing his voice. But it wasn't the girl.

"Hello," Tony said.

She hung onto the mouthpiece hard to keep from falling. He had only to speak one word and everything began to move inside her, churned up by hope, every kind of hope. *This wasn't the last day, it was just a day. And she wouldn't go to prison because the cops were dumb. They'd never catch Tony. Joey wouldn't fire her. Stevie would get better.*

"Hello," he said again, impatiently.

"Hello," she whispered huskily. "Tony?"

He didn't answer. She knew what he was doing in that silence. He was looking around quickly and furtively, he was frowning, he was trying to control his voice.

"Tony?"

"How did you . . . " He was so scared he could hardly speak.

"I knew," Mamie said.

"What do you want?"

"I've got to see you, Tony."

"See me? You must be crazy!"

"Sure," Mamie said with a weak giggle. "Sure, I'm crazy. We could meet some place. Listen, Tony . . . "

"You shot Jordan?"

"Yes. For you. I did it for you. Honest, I did it for . . ."

"Not so loud, you fool!"

"I want to see you. Just once. He knows I did it. The policeman knows. I haven't got much time left, Tony. I want to see you."

"You must . . . "

168

"He took your clothes, to measure. And he knows I did it, and I haven't got much . . ."

"Shut up, you fool."

"I'll kill myself. I will! I got those pills."

"Go ahead. It'll save me trouble. Only you won't. Listen, what did you tell the cops?"

She was crying now and shivering and none of the words would come out of her mouth. He said something she couldn't hear, and then the receiver was banged down.

She cried with her face up against the wall as if it could comfort her, pressing her forehead against the limp and faded daisies of the wallpaper.

"Please," she said once, not to Tony or to God, but to the limp daisies and the telephone and the hard wall.

She heard Mrs. Malley moving in the kitchen and she left the wall and went back to her own room.

When she could see well enough she poured out two glasses of water from the pitcher; one was her glass and one was Tony's glass. She used Tony's glass for the first six pills and her own glass for the other six.

Then she went over to the mirror and combed her hair, twisting each curl carefully around her finger. She powdered her nose and put on some lipstick and straightened out her nightgown and the bedclothes. Then she lay down precisely in the middle of the bed and closed her eyes.

CHAPTER 17

THE country road, the blonde girl behind the wheel, the crash, the splintering of glass . . .

When Sands opened his eyes, he knew the answer. An impossible answer. He smiled and shook his head at the ceiling and said, "Nonsense." It sounded like nonsense at first. It was like looking in the back of an algebra book and finding an answer that seemed impossible; and because it was so impossible you began to work over the equation and gradually everything came together and the answer was right.

He rolled off the bed, gave his suit a few ineffectual swipes with a clothes brush, and pushed his hat on his head. He moved briskly, like a man who is sure what all his actions for the day are going to be, or who is pretending to himself that he is sure.

He was pretending. As soon as he went out small things began to go wrong for him and hold him up. The ignition key wouldn't fit the lock and when it did the engine wouldn't turn over.

Delay. He drove a whole block with the emergency brake on. He stopped at green lights thinking that at any moment they might turn red. He let other cars pass him and didn't pass anything himself except a popcorn man pushing his cart. The popcorn looked very buttery. You didn't often get really buttery popcorn any more. He stopped the car and waited for the man to catch up.

When he drove on again he had two bags of popcorn on the seat beside him. At the next traffic light he glanced over at the two bags. He knew then that he was stalling himself and he began to swear softly.

"For Christ's sake maybe I should get out and buy a couple of ties or do my Christmas shopping, or go for a swim at the Y."

A blare of horns behind him. He let in the clutch and drove on, but he still didn't hurry. He had no idea of what he was going to do. Talk, probably. Stall a little more. Give them all half an hour or more in their little world and then blow it up, sky high.

The beginning and the end. The first sight of the corpse and the last sight of the murderer. These were the moments to hold back.

But you couldn't hold them back forever. He was on St. Clair already. When he stopped in front of the Heaths' one of the bags of popcorn fell on the floor. He picked it up and thrust it savagely back on the seat, and got out of the car. Another car was pulling up behind his and he recognized Dr. Loring at the wheel.

Loring came up. He smiled from force of habit but the smile was brief and it fled, never touching the eyes.

"Well?" he said, clearing his throat.

Sands nodded. "Going in here? Social or professional?"

They looked at each other with cold hostility, yet the hostility was not personal, it was directed against their own situations and against the Heath family who were responsible for the situations.

"Social," Loring said, "or both." A falling leaf grazed his face and he brushed at it impatiently. "I'm a little worried and I don't like to leave cases up in the air like this."

"Your patient is dead," Sands said, "not up in the air."

He turned and began to walk up the driveway. After a moment Loring followed him and caught up.

He said, "Have you reported me?"

Sands shook his head. "Nothing to report, as far as I'm concerned."

"Because bigger, more important things have happened? If they hadn't happened, I suppose you'd report me?" He sounded bitter. "Don't bother answering that. I should be grateful. I *am* grateful. Just look at me, how grateful!"

"Why are you a psychiatrist?" Sands said.

"Why? My father was one."

"Personally, I don't think you're a very good one, are you? You upset easily."

"Thanks. I'm grateful again, for the encouragement this time."

"You should be," Sands said mildly. "Probably no one else will ever tell you. I seem to have been divinely chosen to tell people things. Oh, skip it."

"I don't like being a psychiatrist," Loring said, after a time. They had paused at the bottom of the steps of the veranda. "It's so *indefinite*. You have to guess a lot and I'm no good at guessing because I'm afraid I'll be wrong."

"Aren't we all?" Sands said, and went up the steps and put his finger on the doorbell.

While they waited Loring kept rubbing his foot absently on the doormat.

"Damn it," he said finally. "I'm too old to start over. Why couldn't you have kept it quiet?"

"Thirty-two, perhaps?"

"Thirty-three."

"Ancient of days," Sands said.

"I'd like to—well, I was pretty good at pediatrics."

"Kids, you mean?"

"Yes. I sort of—I do, in fact, *like* them."

"Extraordinary," Sands said dryly.

"If I were a psychiatrist explaining it I'd say I had an inferiority complex and that the reason I prefer to deal with children and like them is that they do not challenge my superiority."

"This is where I get out," Sands said.

Alice opened the door. When she saw Loring she flushed slightly.

"Well," she said. "Two of you this time. Come in."

Loring coughed and said, "I—I just dropped in to see how things are going."

"Oh, things are going beautifully," Alice said, with a cold glance at Sands. "Mr. Sands here is trying to hang my brother and has driven Philip into heroic hysterics and Ida into a fit. Ida is praying, Johnny is drinking, Philip is girding his loins to go out and prove Johnny is innocent. And I—" she smiled bitterly "—am the keeper."

"Sorry," Loring mumbled. "I'll wait, if you want to talk to the Inspector."

"I do," Alice said grimly. "But what I have to say to him is no secret."

She turned to Sands. "And that's not all, Mr. Sands. Maurice has given notice. He is up in his room taking a *sunbath* because you made him *nervous!* Of all the preposterous, ridiculous . . ."

She paused and beat her fists together. "I thought you were polite and quiet and very nice for a policeman. And yet here I am, the only sane one in the house now, thanks to you! I have to answer the phone and the doorbell and cook lunch and serve it and get people to eat it. . . ." Her voice broke and she looked like a child about to cry.

"Oh, come now," Sands said. "The exercise will do you good."

She might have cried then from sheer rage but she was too conscious of Loring's presence, aware that he was watching her, analyzing her.

She said to him quietly, "No, I'm not going to have hysterics. You won't be called upon to . . ."

"Alice!"

Philip came lunging down the stairs, shouting, "Alice! I forbid you to have anything to—I forbid you to say anything more to that policeman!"

Alice turned, watching him come closer, her eyes narrowed. He had his topcoat on and was knotting a scarf

172

around his neck. His hat was on the back on his head and a strand of hair hung over his forehead.

She thought, *what a fool he looks, why must he, every time? I must protect him against looking foolish.*

She went to meet him. She put her arm through his. He was too astonished to move, and stood silently with his mouth open, staring at her.

She knew that Sands and Loring were watching and that Philip had no dignity, no defense.

"Philip," she said, smiling, and pressed his arm.

The surprise went out of his eyes and he began to smile too, gently, as if they were alone in the hall. He leaned down and brushed her forehead with his mouth, still smiling.

"Going out, Mr. James?" Sands said dryly.

Philip turned around, all the belligerent uncertainty coming back into his face. Alice quietly took her hand from his arm and walked toward Loring.

"You wanted to talk to me?" she said gravely. "Come in here."

She didn't look back at Philip. Loring followed her into the drawing room, frowning faintly at her back as if she had done something he couldn't explain and didn't like.

When the door had closed again, Sands repeated, "Going out?"

"Yes, I was," Philip said. "I was going to see you."

"Why?"

"I wanted to find Murillo and prove that Johnny never had anything to do with him." He didn't sound like a hero, or look like one.

Champagne to stale beer, Sands thought and wondered if Alice Heath had planned this change in him. Incalculable woman, you couldn't tell about her. "And how would you go about finding Murillo, Mr. James?"

"The girl," Philip said. "His girl, the one you said shot Mr. Jordan."

"Mamie Rosen," Sands said.

"Mamie Rosen," Philip repeated eagerly. "Yes. If she was his girl, she'd know. You have only to insist, really *insist* on her telling."

"You think so?"

"If I could talk to her and tell her just what it means to people like Alice and Johnny, nice people who've never

173

done any harm, I'm sure she'd see—see *reason,* and tell where this man is hiding."

"There are all degrees of reason," Sands said. "She might just say to hell with nice people like Alice and Johnny. In fact she did." He took a step closer to Philip so that their eyes were only two feet apart. "No. See, she loves this man Murillo. It doesn't matter what you call him, murderer, thief, anything, he's the *one.* Love. For Mamie it may come down to something quite simple like Murillo being better in bed than any man she knows."

"Not so loud," Philip said, frowning. "Alice might hear you."

"Some day," Sands said, "Alice will have to be told where babies come from, but you better put off telling her until she's thirty-five."

"I . . ." The hero in him wanted to object but was far too feeble.

"Go ahead," Sands said. "You go and tell Mamie Rosen all about Alice and Johnny. Tell her about the house they live in, tell her about Maurice tiptoeing around in a monkey suit and taking sunbaths. She won't know what a sunbath is but tell her anyway. Tell her that Alice put her hands in dishwater today for the first time in her life and broke down. Tell her about that little room down the hall where Alice sits and makes her powerful decisions, like whether to add mushrooms to the chicken patties."

One corner of his mouth turned up in a half-smile. "Yes. Mamie will break down. You'll have her weeping. She'll tell you where Murillo is, if you really want to know. She lives at one hundred and ten Charles Street."

For a time Philip's face loosened, the jaws were slack, the eyes undetermined. But he had the mulishness of an insecure man who feels he's being pushed and the pushing gave him something definite to fight against.

"I'm going," he said at last.

"Of course you are," Sands said.

"You mean—you're letting me?" he said, sounding almost indignant.

"Sure. It's your funeral."

"Funeral? You mean she's dangerous?"

"Want me to come with you?"

"No! No, of course not! I'm—perfectly capable of—of managing her. Well. You say one hundred and ten Charles Street?"

"I say one hundred and ten Charles Street," Sands said. "Happy Landing."

Philip took a couple of steps toward the door, then he swung around to find Sands smiling, an idiotic smile like a well-fed happy baby.

"I—" Philip said.

"Yes?" Sands said softly. "Go on, Mr. James. You want to save Alice and Johnny, and your own soft berth here, don't you? Go on."

The door opened and banged shut again. With the banging of the door the smile disappeared from Sands' face.

"I'm so smart," he said. "I'm so goddamn smart I have to go messing around."

He looked out of the little square windows at the top of the door and saw Philip disappearing around a bend in the driveway.

Loring saw him too, from the windows of the drawing room. He hadn't spoken since he entered the room, but had stood watching the leaves falling from the trees, almost hypnotized by the constant motion. One leaf, a second leaf, a million leaves.

And one of them's me, he thought, and it doesn't matter a damn what I do. My time's half up, I've fluttered half-way down. The rest is up to me, and if I like kids, there's no reason . . .

"Mr. James has gone out," he said.

He didn't turn around, but he heard her move, sigh.

"Has he?" she said after a time, and he knew from her voice that she had been crying noiselessly since they'd come into the room.

"I guess I haven't anything to talk about after all," he said abruptly. "I don't know why I came except . . . "
Except to see you, he finished silently.

"Except to see how things were going?" Alice said. "That was nice of you."

He turned from the windows and looked at her to see if she was being ironic. But her face told him nothing. It was expressionless, and the eyes beneath the pink lids were dead.

If any man loved her, Loring thought, she'd kill him, gradually, day by day she'd kill him as her mother killed her father.

Frozen-face. I want to get out of here.

"Won't you sit down?" Alice said.

"No. No, thanks," he said violently. "I have a few calls."

"Could I offer you a drink?"

Don't offer me anything, stay away from me, sit there in that chair while I run away from you. "No, thanks, nothing." He walked quickly toward the door.

She stirred in her chair but did not rise. "Shall we see you again?"

"See me again?" he said hoarsely. "No, no, I'm leaving town. I'm thinking of starting over again—pediatrics."

She blinked slowly when the door slammed and thought, how peculiar. But an instant later she had forgotten him. It was not Loring who had left, but Alice herself. She had slipped back into the past, skipping lightly like a child over the well-known paths. Her fingers lay tense, stretched out along the arms of the chair as if they were ready to grasp some half-forgotten word or thought or gesture and fondle it.

The past was dead and dear, it couldn't change, it didn't threaten. Comfortable and pleasant, like a closet full of old clothes. You could wear some of them when you were alone, but you didn't have to bother with the rest, even to look at them.

Some of the clothes were ugly with sagging seams, and evil stains, tattered, too loose or too tight. Leave these in the closet. Bring out the yellow linen dress and slip it over your head. See how thick the cloth was and how well it fitted. It made you twenty again.

Twenty. You were sitting on a piano bench with a young man beside you. . . .

She put her hand up to her forehead and moved her fingers gently over it. Yellow linen. Ah, that was a dress, with Philip sewn into every seam and the pockets full of music and the cloth soft as a baby next to your skin.

She opened her eyes suddenly and they were wild and anguished.

"Where is it?" she whispered. "Where is it now? Where is my yellow dress?"

Given to the poor or used as dusters or burned or decayed into nothing or grayed with mildew in an attic.

Behind her she heard the door opening, and turned her head slowly. Loring was standing in the doorway holding her yellow dress over his arm.

He's brought it back to me, she thought. He has found it and brought it back. I'll never lose it again now.

Then she saw that it was only a trench coat that he was carrying and she began to shiver violently and twist her hands.

"Alice," he said gently. "Alice, you're frightened. You're cold."

"Yes."

"I'll put my coat over you, Alice."

"Yes, I'm cold."

He put the coat around her shoulders. It felt strange and rough against her skin, but she drew it closer.

Philip took Johnny's car. He had no car of his own and they had never offered him one. When Isobel Heath was alive she would send him down to the Conservatory in her own car with her chauffeur at the wheel. Philip would sit in the back seat with his music across his knee, never at ease because any moment the chauffeur might glance in the mirror and catch him off guard looking awed and excited, not belonging at all to the car or the life it implied. And the chauffeur's eyes would be mildly contemptuous, or else frankly disrespectful: *Come up here, buddy, where you belong.*

But when he could forget the chauffeur the car gave him a pleasant feeling. He could look out of the window and pretend to people that he was very bored by the whole thing. It was very hard to look bored. It almost seemed as if you had to be very rich, or very tough, you couldn't let yourself be excited by little things, like taking Alice to the opera. She had only gone with him once because she didn't like opera. When he was sitting in the box beside her he kept glancing at her out of the corner of his eye and thinking that she looked like a princess, and he tried to look bored and accustomed to princesses.

"You're like a fish out of water," Alice had said. "Can't you sit still?"

Princess voice, soft and lazy. Oh, yes, whatever else you could say about Alice you liked being seen with her. It was funny to think that if she had run in her stocking or if her slip showed, her whole pose might disintegrate. She might blush, or look furtive or try to hurry, she might become a shopgirl quite suddenly. It showed how important it was, not just money but the air that money could give you.

He turned south on Yonge Street. At the first stoplight

he looked around and saw people staring at the yellow roadster. For a second he was ashamed and sick that he didn't look like Johnny, that he didn't fit this car any more than he had fitted Isobel's car. But the feeling passed. In his way he probably looked better than Johnny because he had more brains. The people who stared at the car would surely recognize this: *Intelligent young fellow, not one of those idle rich.*

A girl walked in front of the car. Philip watched her hips swinging under the cheap skirt. She turned her head and her glance stabbed his eyes and went right through out the back of his head as if his skull was made of paper.

He flushed and thought, slut, little slut. But when he drove on his hand on the wheel was unsteady and his eyes were hot and uneasy. He had been tried and found wanting by a girl in a cheap skirt. He wanted to turn the car around and follow the girl, to reason with her, convince her: *You have no right not to see me. I am Philip James. I play the piano. I gave a concert.*

He jerked at the gearshift and it made a grinding noise and people turned their heads toward him. He got away from them, he drove fast to escape their eyes, though here too he wanted to go back and explain that he was really a good driver, that he was nervous, he didn't often grind the gears, he was nervous.

Every time he stopped the car he had new wounds to lick. A policeman shouted at him because he went through on a yellow light. A child, crossing, thumped his fist on the fender of the car and grinned. An old lady with an armful of parcels looked bitterly at him and her mouth moved over something ugly. And with every wound his eyes darted quickly, wildly, from one side to the other, seeking other wounds.

When he got to Charles Street he was scraped and lacerated, torn by his own teeth. But Charles Street soothed him. The houses were so old and shabby and the yellow car so new and he was driving the yellow car. He began to look bored again and the wounds began to close, one after another. The people who had hurt him were no longer static in his mind, they went on with their business and faded. The girl in the cheap skirt went on walking, the grinning boy crossed the street, the policeman shouted at someone else, the old woman carried her parcls home.

He stopped the car and got out and began to walk along

the street, peering at the numbers of the house, saying them aloud: "Eighty-eight. Tourists. Running Water. Special Rates by Week or Month."

His voice reassured him. He didn't want to think about Mamie Rosen just yet, and if he could keep talking even to himself he wouldn't have to think about her.

"Ninety-four. Board and Room."

He pulled his hat down over his eyes. He didn't want anyone to see him, recognize him. He even put his hands into his pockets as if to hide everything of himself that he could.

"Ninety-eight. One hundred and two. Tea Cups Read. Have your Fortune told."

He went past that one fast, almost afraid that his fortune might come at him out of a window if he didn't hurry, a grimy fortune floating out of a grimy window, floating faster than he could walk.

"One hundred and six." That was better. A row of shrubs and a pram on the veranda. He didn't want children himself but he liked to think of other people having them. It gave him a sense of security, of continuance and respectability. He called them kiddies, and if they hadn't dirty noses he sometimes said, "Hello, there!" If they had dirty noses he hurried past, feeling surreptitiously in his pocket for his own handkerchief. A little later he would have to blow his nose, he would blow it hard and hurry on, and once he had thrown the handkerchief away into the road.

A man was standing on the curb ahead of him reading a newspaper. Philip pulled down his hat brim again and hunched inside his coat. He looked around once, then walked quickly past the man, his head bent forward like a goat about to charge.

One hundred and ten.

The man with the newspaper raised his eyes then and looked at Philip's back.

Now that's a hell of a funny way to walk, he thought. If it was winter now and he was cold you could figure he was trying to keep warm.

He didn't pretend to read the paper any more. It just fell out of his hand. He thought, *he's got a gun in his pocket. Well, that's all right, so have I.*

He said, "Hey!"

Philip was nearly at the door. He made a quick half-turn.

179

"Hey!" the man said. "Come here!"

For a second neither of them moved. Then Philip's hands came out of his pockets and he used them to swing his body around, to help him run, propel him along the street. His movements were mad and violent as if every muscle was straining to help him get away. His breath rasped, his arms flailed, his feet hit the sidewalk, heavy and powerful. He was running, escaping from the man with the newspaper, the girl with the skirt, the grinning boy, the policeman. He was escaping from Alice and Johnny, from Isobel in her urn and Kelsey on her table in the morgue and Geraldine and Sands and Mamie.

He began to shout, "Eeeee! Eeeee!" swept by a surge of ferocious joy in running, getting away, escaping them, never to see any of them again, never, never. . . .

He was running bent almost in two and when the bullet pierced his back he fell on his face and his nose squashed against the sidewalk like a splash of rotten fruit.

He had a moment left, a moment to hear someone shout, "Murillo!" to move his mouth in protest, to taste his own blood, and to feel in the last part of the last moment that he was glad to die like this on a velvet rug with some warm soothing liquid pouring over his face.

"I got him. Shoot to kill, they said. Is he dead?"

"Jesus, is he! Turn him over. What's that in his pocket?"

"A letter. Here, you take it."

" 'Philip James!' Philip James! Jesus, this ain't Murillo!"

"It's got to be Murillo. I shot him. It's got to be. Shoot to kill, they said. Sure, it's Murillo. It's got to be! It's got to be! He was carrying a gun. He had his hands in his pockets ready to shoot first."

"No gun."

"Must be a gun!"

"No gun."

"Oh, Jesus, Jesus Christ!"

CHAPTER 18

"I'M SORRY," Sands said. "I'm sorry."

"Sorry," Alice said dully. "A stupid word to say."

"Yes."

They sat in the twilight and the room was hushed like a museum and except for their moving mouths they were wax figures in a timeless world. At any moment a group of school children might come in with their teacher. "That was how they dressed in nineteen hundred and forty-two," and some of the children would giggle and others would make notes.

"That first night," Alice said, pausing to give herself time to go into the closet and take out the yellow dress and slip it over her head again, feel it, smell it.

"That first night when he came with Johnny—I remember his eyes. They were unhappy, seeking eyes and they never changed. I never knew what he was seeking, what he was trying to find in this world!"

"Security," Sands said, but her head moved a little. She didn't want Philip to have been seeking security. Too easy and simple, Sands thought. She would like to think he was chasing a rainbow, something unattainable and worth dying for, not security which she had and which meant nothing to her.

"Restless," she said. "You could tell it when he played, brilliant, savage, like a lion in a cage."

This was the cage, Sands thought, but she won't want to know that. Let her walk around in a fog for a while until she bumps into something.

"I think he was proud That was why he didn't stay from the beginning when mother asked him to. He had to go away twice before he came to stay. And even then he'd be away a lot, he'd stay in the room he rented to practice in."

"He didn't rent the room . . ."

181

"Stop it," she said, without anger. "Let me dream a little. He went to concerts, even to New York. Mother gave him an allowance, and when she died Kelsey kept it up."

"He had to go to her for the money?" Sands said.

"Yes. We all did. He didn't mind. He was always very pleasant. He never went out with Johnny, to parties or nightclubs or anything, he didn't like that kind of good time, he didn't require it. When he wasn't practicing he stayed at home and we talked."

They *talked*, Sands repeated silently, with bitterness. They talked a hundred billion words, they taught him how to talk and what to think without giving him any foundations. They taught him a whole foreign language without telling him what the words meant or giving him a dictionary or a grammar book.

"I thought he was happy here," Alice said. "I didn't think he needed to blow off steam, or if he did need it I thought he could do it by playing, you see." She half-closed her eyes as if the lids were mirrors to reflect herself and her family. "We are cramped people here in this house, cramped and cramping. If we had been different he would never have become . . ."

"No," Sands said quietly. "No, don't fool yourself. He didn't *become* anything, he stayed as he was. He was never Philip James, not for an instant. He began to look a little like a man called Philip James might look. He got fatter and began losing his hair. He lost that cocky defiant look you can see on his pictures, his police pictures, and he didn't get anything to replace that look so his face was formless, soft. I didn't recognize him from the pictures. You don't recognize a man by his skin color or his eyes but by his expression and his bones. And the expression had changed and the bones were padded with fat living."

"No," Alice said. "I don't want to hear . . ."

"He was never Philip James," Sands said again. "Maybe he got the name from a movie while he watched and played the piano. The name must have meant something to him. It's a book name not a real one, it sounds like upper-class English or Scotch, and he was an Italian."

"No. No, he wasn't . . ."

"A wop," Sands said. "A wop with some talent and no money. Twenty years of that, you see, twenty years of being a poor wop and then Johnny Heath brought him home. He had the name ready, probably. Perhaps it was the name he intended to use when he got rich peddling marihuana or picking pockets. Even the petty criminals have dreams and Murillo's dream must have crystallized when he came into this room and saw you and Kelsey and the piano. His feet must have felt funny on this soft rug, that was why he went away and came back again. Here was the dream but he must have been smart enough to see that it had cracks in it. But he came back anyway and tried to live it out and be Philip James. He couldn't do it. When he came back the second time he had it figured out. He could live in the dream but he could still be Murillo some of the time until he got used to being James. Then he could make the break completely. He didn't intend to go on being Murillo all of his life. But he met this girl."

"Don't tell me about the girl," Alice said.

"She had been around a lot with other men before she knew Murillo," Sands said. "That's probably how he met her. And they must have come together the way two people like that would, right away without any thinking or shunting back and forth or planning. I don't suppose they even talked about love, they just started to live together and she was his woman. He'd come down to Charles Street to her room every time your mother packed him off to a concert out of town. Every chance he got he went back to his other life, his woman, his doped cigarettes, his clothes that he kept there in her room, the black fedora and the bright silk shirts and pointed yellow shoes. I think the clothes were important to him, not because they were different and emphasized his other life, but because they were the kind of clothes he *liked* to wear. He was still a wop. He never felt at ease in those baggy tweeds and English brogues that he wore here.

"As soon as he left this house he must have started to change, gradually, block by block, crossing from one world into another, like a man flying from here to the moon, knowing there was a point where the earth's gravity stopped and the moon's hadn't begun, a vast sinking and falling into nowhere. Perhaps he had a special street which was this point and after he'd passed it he could have something under his feet again. Once he was there he was all right, he was Murillo, there was no need for pretense. Every humiliation he had suffered in this house he could take out on Mamie."

"Mamie," Alice said. "Mamie."

"And everything he learned in this house he could teach to Mamie. He must have taught her some things because when Joey's opened she got a job in the chorus and later on she became the singer. He didn't go to Joey's much except to call for Mamie a few times. He was scared he might meet Johnny there or one of Johnny's friends, so he stayed in the background. Only one or two of the people at Joey's knew him by sight: Stevie Jordan, Joey himself, and a girl called Geraldine Smith who was Mamie's friend.

"He didn't let his two lives merge. The only way they touched each other was that as Murillo he worked off the repressions he suffered as James. It was as if he set up a rigid set of rules for himself so that the two men he was were as different as possible. Mr. James was pleasant, earnest, did not drink, and paid no great attention to women."

"Except Kelsey," Alice said bitterly. "My sister. My *sister* and a prostitute called Mamie."

"How he became engaged to Kelsey I don't know," Sands said.

"She was used to him, and she felt sorry for him."

"And she loved him."

"No, no, never!"

"Yes, I think she did," Sands said. "I think you both did."

She hung onto the arms of the chair. "*I! I* love a man with a woman like that, a murderer, a thief!"

"You didn't know he was a murderer and a thief. Mamie did, and she loved him. I think that sometimes it must have pleased him to have Kelsey here and Mamie waiting for him down there. Yes, there'd be a lot of satisfaction in that. Probably it was his happiest period, when he was engaged to Kelsey before the accident. He didn't even have to choose, you see, he could have both his women and both his lives, his tweeds and his pointed yellow shoes, his music and his dope."

"A dope fiend!"

"Not a dope fiend. A lot of musicians use marihuana and some need it all the time, but Murillo didn't. As Philip James, marihuana was even distasteful to him, incongruous, like using the sheets from Mamie's bed on the bed he had here. Yes, I think for a time he was almost happy, until one night Johnny made a date from a restaurant downtown.

184

Kelsey and Philip waited in the car and when Johnny came out of the house with the girl he had phoned, the girl was Geraldine Smith.

"He had only a little time to work things out. He knew that Geraldine would have to die and die soon before she could say anything. The road was slippery and the car skidded a little. He was Murillo then, gambling on his life. He took the wheel and the car ran off the road and crashed. It was his only chance. James would have muffed it, but Murillo didn't. The girl, Geraldine, had been flung from the car. Johnny was still in the rumbleseat, Kelsey was unconscious on the road. He dragged Geraldine away from the road in case a passing car should come along. He was bleeding badly where the glass from the windshield had struck his chest. That may have given him the idea.

"He took a piece of glass and cut her throat and face and threw the glass away and came back to the car."

"He did it," Alice said dully. "You thought it was Johnny and *he* did it."

"Yes, I thought it was Johnny. He was the only one who knew the girl, and I didn't consider that the accident was planned. Very few men would have the almost insane irresponsibility and guts to drive a car deliberately into a ditch unless their lives depended on it. Yet, in a sense, his life did depend on it. With Geraldine dead he could keep going, and for another two years he did keep going.

"They were bad years. Kelsey was blind and he was tied to a blind girl. Geraldine was dead and he had her murder on his conscience."

"Conscience!" Alice said bitterly.

"Yes, he had one, as all sensitive men have, but it was a subjective conscience. He had no standards except his own personal welfare, and so he wasn't sorry he had killed the girl, he was merely sorry that he had been forced to kill her. Kelsey, too, had changed in other ways besides her blindness. Her mind had sharpened and splintered and the splinters were like antennae which could pick up and relay to her waves that the rest of you missed. I think that for two years she relived that accident, every detail of it, and I think that at the end she *knew*."

"She dreamed of it," Alice said, "of the girl. She'd scream out in her sleep."

"For two years," Sands said, "she kept postponing her marriage, she gave away her ring to a maid, not because

185

she loved him and didn't want him to be tied to a blind girl, not because she wasn't sure about the accident. It must have seemed incredible to her at first, or perhaps it came so gradually that it was no shock."

"She tried to kill herself."

"Not from shock, from uncertainty. She had all that time to think, to feel it all out, the wheel under her hands, the skidding, the sudden swerve of the car as Philip jerked the wheel, the crash. She thought of it for two years and at the end of two years she wasn't sure, she knew she could never be sure that it was Philip who had swung the car off the road and killed the girl and blinded her, Kelsey. Even apart from her blindness this uncertainty was enough to twist her mind. And there was no solution to her doubt, she could never bring herself to ask him outright. If he denied it she wouldn't have believed him. Perhaps she was actually frightened that he'd admit it, and kept trying him out, subtly."

"The last day," Alice said, "she said, 'I can't trust anyone, can I, Philip?' He told her, no, she couldn't."

"So she asked Ida to bring her the morphine."

"Why didn't she confide in me?" Alice said bleakly. "She never hinted . . ."

"Would you have believed her? Even as it was, didn't you go to a psychiatrist about her? Only one of you would have believed her, Philip himself. He knew what she was thinking, he saw her reliving the accident day by day. He must have wanted to escape from her, to leave this house and never come back, but he couldn't go. If he went Kelsey might talk. If he left her he knew she'd realize the truth and be *sure* of it. So he had to stay and watch her. He couldn't stop watching her, and she must have felt his eyes. His were the eyes that stared at her, that meant hate and danger, a wall of eyes that must gradually have closed in on her. She had only one way of escape, Mamie's way.

"While the doctors were working over her you sent Philip out for a walk. It was then that he went to the tavern and sat drinking at the table leaving his fingerprints on the glasses. He didn't go to Mamie this time, he just sat there in the tavern, falling and sinking into that big hole that always waited for him—caught between two worlds.

"He must have known why Kelsey had tried to kill herself and known too that she wouldn't die. And if she didn't die, you'd all be after her asking *why?* And she'd tell you.

186

He was desperate, he wanted to do something, to fight something. So he got up from the table and tried to get the bartender to hand over the night's receipts. Crazy, isn't it? That feeble gesture, that frail little sock at fate, as if by robbing a till he could become the doer and not the done-by.

"The bartender told him to go to hell. He ran then, and a couple of men chased him for a block or so and gave up. After all, nothing had been lost by them. The loss was Murillo's. He had tried and failed, and failure was to him a living pain through his whole body. He came back to the house. The hall light was on. He went upstairs into Kelsey's room and switched on the light. He must have been insane with hate standing there and seeing that she was breathing and hadn't died. Perhaps she woke up and knew who had come to her room and why he had come. Or perhaps he killed her right away, as soon as he saw the knife on the table beside her bed. After he killed her he was calmer, his mind was working again. He took his pocketknife out of his coat—that was when some shreds of marihuana scattered on the rug—and picked the lock on the jewel box. He was going to take some of the jewels to make the murder look like robbery. But Mr. Heath came home then. He went past the door, very slowly, while Philip stood inside the room, knowing that the light was shining under the door, knowing that Mr. Heath might come in and find him there with Kelsey dead.

"The shock of Mr. Heath's footsteps going past the door stunned him. He didn't notice he hadn't taken the jewels, he didn't notice the shreds that had fallen from his pocket, he didn't think of turning Kelsey's light off. His only wish was to escape. As soon as he got out of the door he began to run.

"He was always escaping from something, he ran out of the tavern and out of the house, he was running when he was killed. It's dark in here. Shall I turn on the lights?"

"No." Alice said. "Not just yet."

"They'll have to be turned on sometime."

"Yes. A little later."

Their voices throbbed in the hushed room and the walls threw back echoes of implication.

"You're as good a runner as he was, in your way," Sands said. "You sit in the dark, you shut your eyes. The present

187

is a burden to you and the future is a danger. You have only the past, not all happy, but *healed*."

"Go on with your story," she said hoarsely.

Story, Sands thought, it's a story to her. He's already unreal and remote because he had Mamie and the yellow shoes.

"He ran down the driveway past the car where Stevie Jordan was sitting and Jordan recognized him. I don't think he saw Jordan but he must have seen the car, must have realized that he was running and would attract attention, that he'd have to come back to the house and face it out. He did come back and he was calm enough this time to slip back the lock on the door which Mr. Heath had set when he came home and found it unlocked.

"So he left the door unlocked. He had no idea that as James he was building up a case against Murillo. He couldn't anticipate that irony or the final one, that as James he should die for Murillo."

"You sent him down there," Alice said.

"He wanted to go."

"You knew he was Murillo when you sent him."

"He wanted to go," Sands said again. "He had to get down there somehow, to kill her, not knowing she was already dead."

"Not to kill her," Alice said.

"Perhaps not. I think so, but perhaps he only wanted to see her again. Anyway, she was dead. She had fixed herself up before she died almost as if she knew he'd be coming to see her and she wanted to look nice for him.

"She had shot Jordan to save Murillo. Jordan is a brittle man in some ways, and I think that when she came into the office after the club was closed and she taunted her by telling her about seeing Murillo, and she shot him without thinking or planning. It was the way she did everything, all her thinking was done below the neck. She cried and laughed easily like a child and had a child's strange loyalty."

"She knew who he was?" Alice said. "She knew he lived here?"

"Yes, I'm sure she did. She was jealous of him, she wanted to know where he went when he wasn't with her. It took her a long time to find out, I suppose, because Murillo was shrewd and he didn't trust her. He never went directly from here to there, he used the room he rented to practice in as a half-way house, and she must have followed him there and asked questions of the landlady. Well, she found out some way."

"That telephone call," Alice said. "I answered the telephone this morning and there was someone who hung up as soon as I answered."

"She was waiting for Murillo to answer it himself," Sands said. "I think she did get him finally, and that's why he went down to kill her. She was the only one who knew, he thought."

"You knew."

"Yes. His first murder was the best, he got away with it for two years, yet in the end it was Geraldine who gave him away. There were only the three of them who were in the car who could have killed Geraldine. Kelsey was out because she did not know the girl and she was blinded in the accident. Johnny could have killed the girl but you had to scrape the bottom for a motive for him and the motive didn't suit Johnny's type. He wouldn't kill to avoid marrying a girl."

"No," Alice said. "He'd walk away. He'd leave it to settle itself, or he'd leave it to *me* to settle. He's already forgotten this dancer and in a week he'll have forgotten Philip."

"That left Philip James," Sands said. "It seemed improbable at first but it led me up Mr. James' alley in the search for Murillo. And little things began to fit—James had had chest cuts from the accident, Murillo had been knifed in the chest by Chinaman, Mamie said. It explained the unlocked door, Murillo's knowledge of the house and of Kelsey's blindness, the similarity between the two murders and the motives for both. And it explained, chiefly, why Jordan had seen Johnny and Murillo together. Jordan didn't know the other side of Murillo's life, he thought it meant that Johnny had hired Murillo to kill Kelsey."

"You let him go down there," Alice said. "You wanted him to be shot."

"Yes."

"You—you may even have told them he was coming, ordered them to be ready to shoot him."

"Maybe I did," Sands said.

"You did. I know you did." She was not accusing him, she sounded eager to believe it, slyly happy as if they shared a secret triumph. "Thank you."

"Don't thank me for something I may not have done,"

189

Sands said irritably. "Or if I have, not for you or your family."

"I could have killed him myself," she said. "I wish *I* had killed him."

He did not answer. He was thinking how wondrous a mixture were the women of Alice's class. Combining barbarism and decadence in equal parts they passed as civilized and were eager to thrust their philosophies on the weak and unwary, to teach others how to live as Alice had tried to teach Murillo. Doomed and damned. Too weak for this world, and too hard for heaven.

"I wish," he said, "that I could feel when I walk out of here today that you had learned something in this past week, that you were more *humane.*"

"Humane?" She sounded surprised and a little contemptuous. "You think it makes you more humane to have your sister murdered and your—your . . ."

"It could," Sands said in a tired voice, "but it won't."

He got up from the chair. She could see him as a shadow moving, see the outlines of the hat in his hand.

She rose too, reluctant to have him leave, to be abandoned here in the darkness. After he was gone the dark would come alive with ghosts that crawled and slithered and bit with their little teeth, a cellar full of rats. Humane!

"Don't go," she said.

"Turn on the lights," he said.

She switched on a lamp, quickly, as if by instant obedience she could coax him to stay, to take back what he'd said about her.

"I thought I was humane," she said.

"Did you? Well, maybe you are," he said over his shoulder, and she knew from his voice that he meant: *You aren't, but I'm too tired to argue.*

She clenched her hands together. What does he know about it? *Conceited little—a policeman—just an ordinary policeman—I've always done my duty.*

Sands shut the door. The hall was brilliantly lighted and he squinted his eyes against the glare. Then he saw that Mr. Heath was standing in the hall waiting for him. He looked as if he'd been waiting a long time.

They smiled at each other and Mr. Heath said, "Well," in a tone of sad satisfaction.

"Listening?" Sands said.

"Oh, a little."

190

Sands squinted again. "You don't find it a tragedy."

"No." Mr. Heath said. "No. He's dead and the girl's dead and Kelsey, they have nothing to fear."

Decadence, Sands though, they all have it, they have none of them a will to live.

"I heard you phoning," Mr. Heath said, "telling them that Murillo was on his way. You have a lot of courage, and wisdom."

"Oh, sure," Sands said. "Oh, hell, yes." He wanted to get home, back to his familiar loneliness and anonymity, submerge like a submarine for a time.

"Guess I'll be going," he said, twisting his hat.

"I—we hope you'll come back," Mr. Heath said.

"Oh, I'll come back," Sands said.

"This man, Jordan . . . ?"

"He's getting along fine." He could no longer keep the impatience out of his voice. "Everything's fine."

Oh, hell, yes. Everything is hunky-dory in this hunky-doriest of all possible worlds.

"Don't be too hard on Alice," Mr. Heath said. "She hasn't had enough affection, I'm afraid, enough love. Dr. Loring wants to take her away from here. And when she's gone I intend to assume control."

"Do you? That's fine."

"You think it's a good idea?"

"Oh, yes. Well, good-bye."

"I didn't thank you."

"No, you'd better not," Sands said.

Thanks. He was going to thank me for standing around watching everything work out like an astronomer watching the stars—just about the same control over them.

Thank you kindly, Mr. Galileo.

Oh, that's all right, I'm sure you're welcome to move about in the universe.

The door slammed.

Willie Morris

BLOCKBUSTER   BESTSELLER

The Last of the Southern Girls

18614 $1.50

In all the glitter of Washington's elite, she shines the brightest . . . she's Carol Hollywell, Washington's Golden Girl. The President's favorite dancing partner, the Senator's confidante . . . the rising young Congressman's lover. And in a town used to dirty politics, she brings another kind of scandal.

OVER 350,000 COPIES IN PRINT!